Rose's Thorn

A Joe Erickson Mystery

ROSE'S THORN

A Joe Erickson Mystery

By Lynn-Steven Johanson

LEVEL
BEST BOOKS

First published by Level Best Books March 17, 2020

Copyright © March 17, 2020 by Lynn-Steven Johanson

This novel is entirely a work of fiction. The names, characters and incidents portrayed in it are the work of the author's imagination. Any resemblance to actual persons, living or dead, events or localities is entirely coincidental.

Lynn-Steven Johanson asserts the moral right to be identified as the author of this work.

First edition

ISBN: 978-1-947915-25-1

This book was professionally typeset on Reedsy.
Find out more at reedsy.com

for my mother and father

Praise for the Joe Erickson Mysteries

"A twisty tale of a parent's worst nightmare, Rose's Thorn reminds us of the cost of our past actions and that small towns aren't as safe as they seem." – Liz Milliron, author of The Laurel Highland Mysteries

"A detective still reeling from the after-effects of capturing a serial killer finds himself on the trail of a new criminal, and only by uncovering a dark secret can he stop the murders. This is a fast-paced, terrific debut novel by Lynn-Steven Johanson." — Peter W. J. Hayes, author of the Detective Vic Lenoski series

Chapter One

B lack Fast's "The Coming Swarm" rocked through the car's eight speakers, and she was in a groove enjoying the lightning-fast guitar solo. Suddenly her eyes caught it and her heart nearly leaped in her throat as the headlights revealed a deer standing on the shoulder of the road. Her foot hit the brake pedal, and she instinctively veered left. A lot of animals were active at night, but especially deer, and her father always emphasized the need to watch out for them while driving. Their behavior was always unpredictable, and she feared one would jump out into the path of her car and she would hit it, not only killing the deer, but also doing considerable damage to the front of her car. Fortunately, the deer chose the ditch over death. Once past, she sped up again.

Jenny Callaghan tossed back her blonde hair and drove on toward home. She had a great future planned, and she was looking forward to the fall when she would be moving out of her parents' home for the first time in her life and living on her own in another city. Freedom! It wasn't that her parents were tyrants or had ever mistreated her in any way. On the contrary, her mother and father were better than most. They never had to set many rules because she was a responsible girl. An honor student, she had always achieved good grades and applied herself to whatever endeavor she chose to pursue. But she was eighteen years old, and she had outgrown the nest. It was time for her to spread her wings, fly away, and begin building a nest of her own. It had been her dream to attend the University of Iowa and major in communication disorders, and this fall it would become a reality. She had registered for classes, received her residence hall assignment, and been

1

awarded her financial aid. A new chapter in her life was about to be written.

On this particular Saturday evening, she attended a party where she drank several beers with friends. She didn't like beer all that much but she drank just to be sociable. Most of the time she walked around holding an empty can. She knew there would not be many more opportunities to see her friends again as each of them would be going their separate ways soon: off to college, joining the military, or entering the workforce. She remembered her mother's words: "After high school, you may never see some of them again. Cherish the time you have left." She had no idea mother's words would prove prophetic.

Normally, she would have been in a good mood after such an outing, but on this particular night, she was feeling a little put out. A cute guy named Jess was supposed to meet her at a softball game and come to the party. He promised her that he would be there, but he never showed. The more she thought about being stood up, the more it pissed her off. Not even so much as a text saying he couldn't make it. How rude! She'd been looking forward to meeting him for days, and his absence cast a shadow over what should have been a fun-filled evening.

What a dick, she thought. *Why is it good-looking guys are always so full of themselves? They couldn't care less how they treat girls. We're only objects to them. All they seem to want do is to get in your pants. And if you let them, they just want to use you or they don't want to see you again.* She knew that from past experience, and she wasn't about to become another jerk's conquest. Her thoughts flashed back to her ex-boyfriend, Tom Cowan, during the summer between her sophomore and junior years. He was a hot guy, too, and she'd been captivated by his good looks, smooth talk, and self-confidence. He was going into his senior year, and she thought he was such a dreamy guy, a real stud. A top athlete scouted by numerous colleges and universities, he was quite full of himself. He said all the right things to make her feel so special, and she would eventually give in to his advances. But it turned out he only wanted her as long as she would be his own personal sex machine, and she had the good sense to drop him like a hot rock. She remembered how bruised poor Tommy's ego had been when she actually had the nerve to dump him. Him, of all people! The memory caused her to snort a laugh. Then her mind snapped back to this evening and she let out a sigh. Oh, well. Live and learn. This guy was probably no different than Tom and all the other sex-crazed jocks she'd been going to school with. She couldn't wait for the chance to meet some mature guys at the U of I.

Midnight in the Iowa countryside can be deadly still, the only sound an occasional wisp of wind rustling the green leaves of corn growing in the fields. A cloudless sky revealed a sea of stars while the full moon illuminated the land, and the field of freshly cut alfalfa filled the air with a most pleasant scent.

Jenny's car zoomed past the old settler's' cemetery that occupied a small corner of ground surrounded on three sides by a farmer's soybean field. It existed as a kind of landmark for her because she knew when she passed the old graves she had only seven miles to go before she would be home. Thoughts of her mother came to mind. She would undoubtedly be waiting up for Jenny as she always did. It wasn't that she didn't trust her daughter. Rather, she was a self-proclaimed "worry-wart" by nature, and she never felt at ease until her daughter walked through the door, safe and sound. Jenny wondered how her mom would ever cope when she moved out of the house and began living in Iowa City, some four hours away. Maybe she would have to transfer all that angst to her younger sister, Ellen. Now, that kid will end up giving her mother a nervous breakdown! She laughed out loud at the thought of it.

Jenny checked her rearview mirror and saw headlights in the distance. She drove on another quarter of a mile and checked again. The lights were much closer now. *Looks like someone's in a hurry,* she thought. In no time at all, the headlights had closed in on her rear bumper, and at that point she became concerned. *What the hell? Why would someone be following so closely behind?* She thought the car was going to pull out to pass, but that was not the case. It remained close behind her for about half a mile, and she was beginning to get annoyed about it. "Get off my ass, will ya?" she said out loud as she looked into her mirror. She sped up, trying to put some distance between her and the car behind her but it matched her speed.

"What do you think you're doing?" she muttered as she glanced in the rearview mirror again. Could it be one of her friends messing around with her? "Not funny, Mark or whoever you are! It's going to be payback time when I see you again, mister!"

Then it happened. It was both sudden and unexpected. The blue and red emergency lights of a police cruiser began flashing behind her. The shock of seeing the lights and their implication of wrongdoing frightened her at first, and she froze for a few seconds. But it didn't take long for her to regain her composure.

"Oh, great!" she said. "What does he want?"

She'd never been pulled over by a law enforcement officer before, but she knew what to do. Bringing her car to a gradual stop, she pushed the shifter into park and reached in her purse for her driver's license. Her hands were shaking, but she managed to retrieve it from her wallet along with the registration and proof of insurance card from the glove compartment.

The black police cruiser had stopped behind her, and after what seemed like an interminable amount of time, an officer got out and sauntered up to her car, flashlight in hand. She could see him approaching in her side mirror so she pressed the electric window switch. When the officer stepped to her door, he shined his flashlight in her face, causing her to wince. The intensity of the light partially blinded her so rather than seeing him clearly, she could only make out his silhouette and hear his voice.

"Driver's license, please," the officer stated.

"Did I do something wrong, Officer?

With no emotion in his voice, he repeated, "Driver's license, please."

"Here."

She handed him her license, still trying to think what may have given him cause to stop her. She knew she hadn't been speeding. Maybe she had a taillight out or some other issue she wasn't aware of.

As he was checking her license, she could see another car approaching in the opposite lane. Its headlights came closer and closer, and finally it slowed to a crawl, its two occupants mere silhouettes inside the car. Marv and Lorraine Koehler, a couple in the early sixties, were returning home from visiting Marv's recently widowed brother. They both looked intently at the stopped car as their vehicle approached.

"Has there been an accident?" asked Lorraine.

"No," scoffed Marv. "This late at night, it's probably some drunk."

Getting a glimpse of Jenny's face, Lorraine remarked, "Look! It's a girl."

"They can get drunk, too, you know," commented Marv.

"These young kids, nowadays. I'll tell ya," grumbled Lorraine.

The officer had turned his back to them as they approached, seeming to shield himself from the glare of their headlights. He waved them on, and as they drove past, he turned his back to them again and focused on Jenny, the light still shining in her face. He continued.

"You're Jennifer Callaghan?" he asked.

"Jenny. Yes," she replied.

He handed her license back, holding it by the edges between his thumb and forefinger. She thought the way he held it was a bit odd, but she took it from him. Before she could return it to her wallet, he spoke.

"Would you step out of the car, please?"

"I beg your pardon?"

He repeated, "Would you step out of the car, please? Now."

She sighed a big sigh. This was getting annoying. What did he want, anyway?

I'll bet he thinks I've been drinking, she thought. "All right," she said.

Opening the door, she got out, the officer's flashlight continuing to shine in her eyes, obscuring her view of his face. She put up her hand to shade her eyes from the flashlight's beam.

"Put your hand down, please," ordered the officer.

She complied and then asserted, "I don't think I was doing anything wrong, Officer. I was just—"

A shot of pepper spray hit her square in the face, sending her to the asphalt gagging and coughing. Her driver's license dropped from her hand onto the surface of the road, and she struggled to catch her breath. She couldn't open her eyes and her face burned like hell. *Oh, my god! What the hell?* she thought as she felt the officer pulling her arms behind her back and slapping handcuffs on her wrists. She was in a panic. This can't be happening! She tried to scream but she couldn't make a sound. Before she realized what he was doing, he had placed ankle restraints on her. She tried to kick but it was useless. She managed to roll over on her back and thought, *What's going on? I don't get it. What did I do to deserve this?*

Subdued now, she was his. He looked her over as she lay in front of him. *Pretty girl,* he thought after giving her a once-over. *Nice face.* As she lay there, he began to fantasize what he would be doing to her later, but realized he could not afford to waste time. He had to get going. Picking her up, he carried her to the police cruiser, and pushed her into the back seat. Finally, she managed to cry out.

"Why are you doing this to me? What did I do?"

"Shut up!" he growled as he closed the door. The cry of a hawk circling above distracted him for a moment, causing him to look up. Only stars. He scoffed at how ridiculous it was looking for a bird in a dark sky at night. *Dumb ass,* he thought to himself. *Get moving!* He reached for the driver's door and pulled it open. Sliding into the driver's seat, he turned off the emergency lights, and proceeded to drive away into the night.

Despite her burning eyes and tears running down her cheeks, thoughts of escape ran through her mind. But with the interior door and window handles removed, and a wire partition cage installed to separate the front passenger area from the rear, she was a virtual prisoner. She thought of kicking out one of the rear door windows, but the chain running between her handcuffs and ankle restraints did not allow her range of motion. He had thought of everything.

***

When Jenny had not come home by one a.m., her mother became frantic. Carla tried calling Jenny's cell phone, but there was no answer and her call got rolled over to voicemail. After several attempts to call her failed, she finally left a message. When she had not heard anything by two, she woke up her husband, Jack. It was too late to make any phone calls to Jenny's friends, but after explaining everything to Jack, he suggested they go out looking for her, thinking that she may have lost her cell phone, experienced car trouble, or had an accident on the way home. They knew she was going to meet friends in Spencer, so they began retracing the route she would have taken. They drove along looking in the ditches and on the side roads for the silver Camry. Then, five miles down the road, Jack pointed and exclaimed, "There!" He had spotted her car in the distance. It was sitting on the opposite side of the road, and he parked in front of it. They both got out and looked around but Jenny was not there. Where could she be?

They called out for her but there was no answer. They searched the ditches for a quarter mile in each direction but she was nowhere to be found. Jack drove on to see if she may have been walking to get help while Carla remained with the car. But when he returned, Carla informed him that Jenny's purse and cell phone were inside the car. If she'd had car trouble, she would have used her phone to call home. She wouldn't just leave like this with the car door ajar. At that point, they began to fear the worst.

"You didn't touch anything, did you?" asked Jack.

"No. Why?" asked Carla.

"Make sure you don't touch anything."

"Why? What are you...?"

"I hate to say it, but...this could be a crime scene."

"You mean like..." Carla said as fear choked off her words.

"No! I don't want to go there. It may turn out to be nothing but..."

"Oh, my god, Jack," she began sobbing. "Not Jenny, too."

Jack pulled out his cell phone and called nine-one-one. Within a matter of minutes an Iowa State patrolman and a Buena Vista County deputy sheriff arrived on the scene. They had responded quickly, and with good reason.

Chapter Two

At six a.m., the cool morning air felt invigorating as Joe Erickson left the house and began jogging, something he'd done religiously for more than a year. Sleep eluded him for much of the night before, his slumber interrupted by a gruesome, recurring nightmare that jolted him awake a few minutes after midnight. Afterwards, insomnia prevented sleep.

At forty, he could best be described as ruggedly handsome with intense dark brown eyes and dark hair with a few silver hairs beginning to show in his sideburns and temples. Not a big man, although he stood right at six feet tall, he had an average-sized frame but his body was lean, like that of a swimmer or distance runner. His most striking feature was his face, for it reflected a weariness that came from years of experiencing the absolute worst humanity had to offer. Joe was a cop, a homicide detective with the Chicago Police Department.

As he ran through the streets of Marathon, he passed houses, familiar from many years ago. Not knowing who lived in them now, he noted them by their former occupants' names: the Anderson house, the Simmons house, and the Peterson house. He'd grown up in this community and knew it well. Marathon was a small, northwest Iowa town founded in 1883 at a place where the tracks of the Chicago and Northwestern Railroads crossed. And it was here where his father had grown up and served as the local postmaster and where his mother had worked as a teller at the local bank. Some of the old timers remembered him as Carl and Eleanor Erickson's son, but they were getting on in years, and they were few and far between these days. All of his former classmates had moved away years ago. And if he wanted to visit their parents, he would have to take a stroll through the cemetery.

Turning the corner next to the old feed mill, Joe began jogging west. Glancing to his left, he spotted the rusted-out hulk of a 1957 Chevy sedan next to a dilapidated shed. It was a far cry from the pristine '57 Bel Air two-door hardtop his father had proudly owned. His interest in classic and high-performance cars derived from his father's obsession. Turning wrenches and getting grease under his fingernails was one of the ways he bonded with his father during his formative years, and it was an interest they would continue to share.

He passed the house once owned by Mr. Murphy, his history teacher, who once pulled him aside after school and lectured him about failing to live up to his potential. Acceptable grades were never a problem, and he never had to study hard. It was much easier to float and concentrate on other things like cars and girls. Not until he went to college and discovered a passion did he decide to buckle down and apply himself. A course in criminal justice sparked his interest in crime and police work, and that led him to pursue a degree in law enforcement from a state university in Illinois where he graduated magna cum laude. Following graduation, he moved to Chicago where, with help from his department chair, he was accepted into the police academy and became one of Chicago's finest.

Curiosity, insight, and attention to detail soon made him a real asset when it came to investigating crimes, and eventually these skills along with his tenacity and hard work brought him to the attention of his superiors. Ten years ago, he became a detective and swiftly rose, moving from vice to the homicide unit where he maintained one of the highest closure rates in the unit.

As he was passing an alley he abruptly stopped. Something about it tripped a wire in his brain, reminding him of the night he apprehended the serial killer David Eugene Burton. It became his most celebrated case, and it was also his undoing. He paused for what he thought was a few moments. Then, looking down at his watch, he saw that five minutes had passed. *Christ! Get moving!* Shaking it off, Joe continued his run.

Joe had witnessed David Eugene Burton's handiwork on multiple occasions, the mutilated bodies of young women, their pubic areas scalped and taken as trophies. When Burton killed and mutilated Anita, a passing acquaintance of Joe's, her death had a profound effect on him. He became obsessed with apprehending her killer and had driven himself without mercy, channeling his rage into working night and day to find the animal responsible for at least twenty grisly murders that had taken place over a two-year period.

Finally, Joe caught a break when someone spotted a car leaving the scene of a minor fender-bender that occurred three blocks away on the night of one of the murders. No one else thought much about the hit-and-run incident. A man reportedly drove away from the scene without stopping to attach a note to the windshield of the car he'd bumped into. A few hundred dollars. What the hell, it happens. The murder was what took precedence. No one put together the possible link between the two. But a passerby witnessed the incident, and she was a good citizen. She wrote down the license number. When Joe heard about the report of the hit-and-run, he didn't ignore it like his colleagues chose to do. Instead, it got him thinking.

David Eugene Burton was eventually issued a citation for leaving the scene of an accident, but Joe decided to pursue it further. Who was this guy? And what made him decide to drive away when the damage to the other vehicle was minimal? Did he have something to hide or was he just an inconsiderate asshole? Joe needed to find out. Maybe it was nothing at all or maybe...So, he chose to start watching Burton. For two months he kept him under surveillance, following him at night, observing his habits and his haunts. Burton was clever and meticulous. Women were attracted to him. Not only was he good-looking, but he also had considerable charm and was comfortable talking to the opposite sex. Joe observed him in bars, restaurants, stores, almost always going out of his way to interact with women.

Joe was getting very little sleep, and what sleep he did get was not restful. One night his surveillance paid off when he saw Burton pick up a young prostitute standing by herself next to a stoop. She'd made the mistake of soliciting alone rather than being in the presence of other working girls who could have afforded her some degree of protection. Joe observed them as they walked down the street together and then turn into an alley. This would not be the first time one of the victims was found lying in an alley so it sent up all sorts of red flags.

Joe paused, and then moved quickly to the opening of the alley, and peeked around the corner. No one. He drew his gun and listened. Nothing. Then he entered the alley and slowly crept down the narrow, dark passage, looking, listening, each step carefully planted to make as little noise as possible....He heard a muffled scream and took a few hurried steps toward the sound. When he flipped on his flashlight, the beam revealed Burton kneeling near a dumpster, leaning over the body of the girl. Holding a bloody knife in one hand and pulling down her underwear with the other. About to take another trophy. Caught red-handed! Looking down the barrel of his Glock, Joe commanded Burton to "Freeze!" And Burton did. Their eyes locked, and Joe almost hoped he'd try to do something. Make an aggressive move or try to attack him so he could shoot the bastard for what he did to yet another girl. But he didn't. He calmly complied with every command: dropping the knife, raising his arms, getting down on his knees, placing his hands behind his head. With trembling hands, Joe cuffed him, and pushed him to the ground. As he lay there, Burton looked up at Joe and had the nerve to crack a smile. An arrogant, perverted smile. That was a mistake. A hard kick in the face followed. *You son-of-a-bitch! That's for Anita!* Kneeling down to Burton, who was no longer smiling, Joe read him his rights. Then, pulling a cell phone from his pocket, he called it in.

It was hard for him to believe he finally nailed the guy. He should have felt satisfaction for the arrest. Instead he felt regret for failing to save the girl. If he'd only gone into the alley a few moments sooner, she might still be alive. Why had he hesitated? That question nagged at him as he shone his flashlight on her face and studied her features. She looked to be about sixteen, seventeen maybe. Just a kid. Yeah, she was plying a dangerous trade but she didn't look neglected or undernourished like a street kid. She was someone's daughter, someone's sister, someone's little girl. Chances were she was loved, and now she was dead. He could have prevented it if...if only he'd ...Her death would always haunt him.

Evidence found in Burton's apartment sickened investigators and sent a twenty-year veteran of the force running outside to puke his guts out. All the papers covered the arrest and it was broadcast by news agencies nationwide. Burton pled guilty to the murder of seventeen-year-old Jamie Chambers from the downstate town of Mendota, the victim he'd killed in the alley. He was now serving a sentence of life without parole in the Statesville Correctional Center, a maximum-security facility in Crest Hill, Illinois. The Cook County district attorney had filed additional murder charges when DNA samples from more victims were matched to the trophies found in Burton's apartment.

Because Joe was responsible for the investigation as well as the arrest, he received praise from his superiors and a nervous breakdown as his reward. The aftermath was stressful and, mentally, he could not let go. One day at work he'd had a meltdown and wound up in the hospital. Recovering now, and on medical leave from the Chicago PD, he returned to Marathon to bury his father and to take care of all the legal aspects that death brings with it. The death was not unexpected. His father had been failing for months, and one day his heart gave out. Not a bad way to go when you think about it. His mother had died seven years earlier from dementia-related pneumonia. Watching her slowly drift away had taken a lot out of his father. With his death, Joe became the last in the Erickson family line. The only son of an only son, he was the last remaining descendant from an undaunted family of Swedes who emigrated from Småland in 1903. No matter. As far as he was concerned, continuation of the family line simply was never meant to be.

Almost finished now, Joe jogged past the tavern on the south corner of the town's main street. Oddly enough, it was just such a place that provided the catalyst for his jogging regimen. When he became a cop, he fell into the habit of hitting the bar with his brothers in blue. An easy thing to do since it's part of the camaraderie that exists among fellow officers. But after a while, he found that drinking was not only detrimental to his health, but also to his work. It dulled his edge, and he knew he needed to make a change. So, the bar became an occasional thing. He joined a health club, hired a physical trainer, began eating right, and got himself back into shape. And that was when he began his jogging each morning. It wasn't that it kept him in good physical shape. It did. Without a doubt it improved his strength and endurance. But what he found most helpful was early morning provided an opportunity to think about his work, to reflect and get those creative juices flowing. That did wonders preparing him to solve some of those tricky puzzles known as homicides. And now it was helping him make a comeback from his nervous breakdown. He felt it was contributing to the progress he was making, each day another step toward getting off medical leave and back on full-time duty.

Joe finished his run by the Lutheran Church and began his usual cool-down walk toward his father's house three blocks away. He was looking forward to a shower followed by a breakfast of Eggs Benedict and a couple cups of his favorite Jamaica blue mountain coffee. The morning newspaper was lying on the step, and he picked it up, opened the door, and went inside. Tossing the paper onto the kitchen table, it fell open. A news article on the front page caught his eye: "No Leads in Murder of Linn Grove Girl." *Linn Grove. Only about fifteen miles away.* Curiosity got the best of him so he sat down to read the article.

Chapter Three

The gold letters on the large plate-glass window read, "Law Office, Foster Simmons, Attorney at Law." The old dark brown brick building had been built in 1901, and it had served the location of the Simmons law office since Foster Simmons's grandfather returned from World War I and became a partner in the law office of Robertson & Simmons in the bustling town of Marathon, Iowa, population 560.

The smell of ancient history wafted through the office, not an unpleasant sensation, mind you. It was the odor of an interior that had remained virtually untouched for a hundred years. The gray and white marble floors and the dark oak-paneled walls had been maintained with pride by three generations of attorneys who never felt the need for any major renovations. There were some updates of course: electrical, heating and air conditioning and the addition of computers and contemporary office equipment. But the basic structure and lighting fixtures resembled some kind of historic preservation, even down to the framed sepia-tone print of Woodrow Wilson on one wall.

In the conference room, Joe sat across the table from Foster Simmons, a gentleman seventy-five-years young. His once silver hair had gone white but his mind was still as sharp as a razor. In front of him was a dossier with a number of legal documents. He pulled a pair of half-round reading glasses from a case in his shirt pocket and slipped them on.

Peering over his glasses, he asked, "Can I get you anything? Coffee or...?"

"No thanks. I'm fine," Joe replied.

Slipping off his glasses, Foster paused a moment and said, "Wonderful people, your folks. Jane and I considered it an honor to have been their friends. Carl and Eleanor were real assets to the community. So were your grandparents for that matter."

"Thanks. I don't wish to be rude, but uh…could we just cut to the chase?" Joe asked. He knew Foster could go off on tangents for long periods of time, so he figured it would be best to be direct so he would stay on task. He didn't want to be there all morning listening to his stories, and Foster had many recollections tucked away in his memory banks.

Taken aback by this unexpected abruptness, Foster said, "All right," and handed Joe a document. "Here is a copy of your father's will." Slipping on his glasses once again, he looked down at his notes and said, "He left everything to you except for a ten-thousand-dollar memorial donation to be evenly divided between the Lutheran Church and the Community Center. I assume that's acceptable?" he asked seeking Joe's' confirmation.

Joe nodded in agreement and managed an "Mm-hm" as he read through the will.

"As you know, his funeral expenses were pre-paid. So, in addition to the house and his possessions, he had life insurance and savings amounting to sixty-three thousand dollars." Foster scrutinized Joe for a reaction but there was none.

"I see," replied Joe without emotion.

"Since your home is in Chicago, do you think you'll be wanting to sell the house?"

"Mm," Joe nodded. "I have no use for it."

"Well, I can help you out with that if you like—the real estate listing and so on. And there's an auction company that will come in and take the contents of the house and auction them for you. After you take what you want, of course."

"Fine," said Joe.

"Houses don't bring much in this town, I'm sorry to say. Not like they do in Storm Lake and Spencer. You can buy a house here for a song these days. In the last forty years, these little towns have simply withered away. There are only two hundred and thirty-five people living in Marathon now, half of what it was in 1960. Nothing left but a post office, a bar, and a grain elevator." Foster sighed.

"And you, of course," kidded Joe as he put down the document.

Foster chuckled, apparently not expecting a quip from someone exhibiting such a serious demeanor. "Not for much longer, I'm afraid. Time for me to retire. I'm sure there are a few people around here who think I'm getting long in the tooth."

"I find that hard to believe."

"Well, you know how some people are."

"I do." There was an awkward pause that Joe filled. "So, are we done here?"

"Pretty much," replied Foster as he closed the dossier and rose from his seat. "I'll have some papers for you to sign in another day or so. I'll let you know."

Joe picked up his copy of the will, pushed his chair back, and stood. "I'll count on you to work out the details. I'm staying here for another week or two, and I'll be at the house if you need to get ahold of me. The phone is still connected and there's an answering machine."

"Certainly," Foster said as they walked together into the reception area. He extended his hand and Joe shook it. A good, firm handshake.

"I wish you the best, Joe. Your dad said you had a tough time there for a while. How have you been feeling?"

"Much better, thanks. Itching to get back to work."

"Good to hear. I can't imagine doing the kind of work you do. Dealing with depraved and violent people day after day. I'm grateful there are people like you willing to do that kind of thing, keeping criminals off the streets."

Before Joe could answer, Marge Jensen, Foster's blue-haired secretary, rose from her desk and moved toward them with a worried look on her face. Foster noticed her immediately.

"What is it, Marge?"

"I'm sorry to interrupt, but…" she hesitated. "Another girl has gone missing. Over by Sioux Rapids.

"Dear god," Foster lamented. "Not another one."

"Found her car abandoned in the country just like that other girl"

16

"You mean—?" Joe asked.

"A girl was kidnapped and murdered two weeks ago, over by Linn Grove," Marge interrupted him.

"I read about it in the paper. Are you saying this—"

Again Marge interrupted, her nervous energy cutting him off mid-sentence.

"It was horrible! They found her body along the river. I don't know how someone could do something like that."

"Things like that normally don't take place around here, do they?" Joe asked.

"No. They don't," said Marge. "I've lived in this county all my life, and I can't recall anything like this ever happening. What's the world coming to, anyway?"

Joe had an opinion on that subject but wisely chose not to voice it.

Foster turned to him and stated, "It looks like we could use a little of your professional expertise around here, Joe."

Once his conversation concluded with Foster and Marge, Joe walked down to the Community Center, a building that used to be Marathon Consolidated School. Back in the 1970's when the school reorganized with Laurens, it was agreed the Marathon facility was to be used for the junior high program. But when it proved too costly to operate both facilities, the junior high was moved to Laurens and the Marathon facility was signed over to the Marathon community. It was eventually remodeled to hold offices for the mayor and town clerk. And later, with the help of a state grant, an addition was built to house the fire trucks, emergency vehicles, and the library. Joe's main reason for going there was to visit the library so he could access the Internet since his laptop had acquired a virus and was being de-bugged in a computer shop in Storm Lake. His curiosity was getting the best of him. He wanted to read up on news accounts of the kidnapping and murder that Marge had mentioned and the article he'd read in the newspaper.

He introduced himself to the librarian, Diane Richmond, whose husband, he discovered, was a year behind him in school. After chatting with her for a few minutes, he sat down at one of the library's computers. From there, he got online and read as many news articles about the murder of Tina Olson as he could find. So far, it appeared the authorities had made no arrests, and there were no reports of any leads in the case. He assumed he might be there for an hour or so. Instead, he was there the rest of the morning and came away with only a single page of notes. Not much to go on. Either the authorities weren't releasing any information or the investigation was going nowhere.

Chapter Four

The building was old but sturdy, built about a hundred years ago from wood of a quality no longer available today. Its wooden plank interior and concrete floor had been power washed, and then covered with black polyethylene sheeting that had been attached to the wall studs with duct tape and staples. Each of the windows was boarded shut from the inside as were all but one of the doors. The interior walls were also covered with the same black sheeting but the ceiling joists and rafters remained open and uncovered. Those boards had darkened with age and provided support for the pine roof sheathing that had acquired a golden-brown patina over the years.

Down the center of the building at evenly spaced intervals were four-by-four-inch wooden joist supports that formed a center aisle. Black, cloth-covered electrical cables connected porcelain light fixtures mounted onto the joists. The once white fixtures were speckled with tiny black dots thanks to the many flies that had left their marks, drawn there by the hundreds of animals that were born and raised for market over many decades. The fixtures closest to the door held incandescent bulbs that illuminated a small area of the interior. A slit in the plastic at one end allowed access to an exterior Dutch door. A few feet away, a rusty iron water hydrant rose out of the floor.

Toward the middle of the room sat an old iron bed. On top of it was a well-worn, blue striped mattress with brown stains and cotton stuffing protruding from several of its seams. Haphazardly thrown across the foot of the bed was an olive-green wool army blanket. No luxuries like a pillow or sheet. On the bed, Jenny Callaghan lay spread-eagle on the mattress, her hands cuffed to each post at the head of the bed. Shackles attached her ankles to the posts at the foot of the bed, and a blue bandana covered her eyes. She had fought so hard against the restraints, her wrists exhibited bruises and abrasions, and her voice had grown hoarse from her screaming for help. But the more she fought, the more she came to realize it was useless.

She prayed to God long and hard to come to her aid, to save her from her plight. She promised to do anything to atone for any sins she committed and to live a good life if he would only use his power to set her free. She read about miracles occurring, and now she desperately needed one. *Please, Oh Heavenly Father, help me. Please!* Her prayers continued until she succumbed to fatigue and dozed off.

The sound of the door latch and the click of the light switch jolted her awake. Footsteps. Walking toward her. Then he spoke. She recognized the voice of the man who stopped her car along the country road. The same man who shot her in the face with pepper spray, who cuffed her and threw her into the back of his car. The man who drove her to this location and shackled her to the bed. But his voice seemed different now. Soft and controlled. It was a mellow voice that could have belonged to a tenor in a church choir had it not had such depraved overtones.

"Did you sleep well?" he asked. "I hope so because you have a big day ahead of you."

"What?" she asked.

"You see, you have the privilege of being the second."

"The second? What do you mean 'the second'?"

"You'll find out soon enough."

Frustrated, she pulled hard against her restraints.

"You may as well save your energy because you're going to be here for a while," he said.

"How long is a while?" she asked with fear in her voice.

"Oh, a few days anyway."

He moved to a makeshift table he had improvised out of rough planks and two ancient sawhorses with drips and spatter from half-a-century of painting projects. From the table, he lifted a bottle of water, unscrewed the cap, and set it back down. Then he picked up an orange prescription container, shook a blue Viagra tablet into his hand, popped it in his mouth, and washed it down with a long drink.

"Ahhh," he breathed with a smirk. "Better living through chemistry!" The quotation was an old DuPont slogan, and he chuckled, amused by his own joke.

"What's so funny?" she asked.

"Oh, something I read somewhere. You're too young to remember. But you're going to understand very soon."

He placed the water bottle back on the table, picked up an orange-handled sewing scissors. Moving the blades quickly back and forth, he listened as if he enjoyed the snipping sounds.

"What are you doing?"

"You'll see."

Then he walked over to the bed and stood, lusting over Jenny's body.

"Why are you doing this to me? Who are you, anyway?" she cried.

"You can call me...'Jess.'"

"Oh my god!" she gasped as she realized she'd been duped by some online predator. "You're Jess?" she asked, her voice cracking.

"Are you surprised?" The question coupled with his condescending tone of voice revolted her.

"Sorry I missed the party last evening. I would have met you there but...well, I did eventually."

This set her off and her temper exploded. "You sick son-of-a-bitch!" she raged, pulling hard against her restraints. She wanted to rip his face off!

"You're a feisty one, aren't you? Oo, I like that."

He reached down and slowly slid his hand along her thigh. He smiled as he watched her writhe and protest even more.

"Don't! Don't touch me, you piece of shit!" she screamed.

"Now, that's not nice. What would your mother say if she could hear you?"

He watched intently as she gritted her teeth and pulled against the restraints. But it was to no avail. After a while her anger dissolved into tears and she lay motionless on the bed.

"That's better," he said. "I have to tell you that no one is ever going to hear you, so all that struggling is for naught. You need to save your energy for later."

"Why me?"

"I have my reasons. Now hold still. If you move, you could get hurt. I wouldn't want to cut you. These scissors are quite sharp."

And he slipped the scissors under the bottom of her top and began to slowly and methodically cut up to the neck.

"What are you doing?" she demanded.

"Just getting these things out of the way."

"What are you going to do?"

"Oh, you'll just have to be patient. It's going to be...fun!"

With precision, he cut through the rest of her top and pulled it away revealing her bra. He marveled at what good physical shape she was in. Nice firm abs and minimal belly fat. There were more protests as he snipped the straps of her bra.

"Hold still, now. There's nothing you can do to stop this, so it would be in your best interest to cooperate."

When he pulled off her bra, he paused, his curiosity now satisfied

Jenny began to cry and squirm, pulling against the restraints.

"Settle down," he said as he unconsciously wetted his lips with his tongue. "It won't help, you know."

Then he moved to the foot of the bed where he proceeded to cut through her jeans. Starting at the bottom of the leg and cutting up past the waist on both sides, he slid them off and proceeded to snip through the sides her panties. As he pulled them away, Jenny sobbed, resigned to the fact that he was going to rape her. Naked now, she was completely vulnerable and at his mercy. *This can't be happening,* she thought.

He held them up remnants of her clothes to his nose and breathed in their scent as he peered at her body. The combination of sight and smell excited him. Once he'd experienced enough, he tossed her clothing into a barrel next to the table. And with a perverse sense of tenderness, he covered her with a blanket in much the same way a mother would tuck in a child at night. "There you go. We wouldn't want you to catch cold now, would we?"

Jenny only responded with a thought: *"Go to hell."*

"I have to leave you for a little while now, but I'll be back soon," he said, "and then we'll have some fun together. I promise." Moving to the door, he unlatched it, switched off the lights, and stepped out into the morning light. He needed some time for the Viagra to be fully absorbed into his system. Then he would be back for some fun, some better living through chemistry.

Chapter Five

"Mom said I can catch all the fish I want, but she said I may as well throw them back cuz she won't be cooking anything that comes out of the river," said Kevin Larson as he and his twelve-year-old classmate, Bud Steiner, walked along a gravel road with fishing poles and tackle boxes. They were each decked out in casual, everyday summer clothing—T-shirts, jeans, and sneakers. Kevin wore a Cubs baseball cap sent to him by his uncle Johnny who lived in Chicago while Bud left his curly light brown hair exposed to the sun.

"Yeah. Because of all the chemicals and stuff, huh?" Bud replied. "Besides, it would most likely taste like the food we get at school. Hey! Maybe we could donate them to the cooks!"

"I'll bet they'd be better than the fish sticks we get," Kevin said.

"Yeah, they probably would."

Kevin and Bud had been friends since first grade, and since that time, they'd been practically inseparable. Both came from working class families that had lived in or around the Sioux Rapids area for many years. Each family scraped to get by, but their mothers saw that they adhered to certain rules, and they weren't allowed to run wild like some parents let their kids do.

Today, the two boys were going fishing in the Little Sioux River that snaked along the north side of Sioux Rapids. Fishing in the river was one of those activities that not only allowed Bud and Kevin to pursue catching one of the big channel catfish local sportsmen occasionally pulled from the muddy waters, but also to rebel against authority by smoking cigarettes.

"How about right here?" said Bud, pointing to a small space between trees.

"Looks good to me," agreed Kevin.

The Little Sioux River stretched from its beginnings near the Iowa-Minnesota border and flowed 258 miles to where it emptied into the Missouri River. It was a small river, but spring snow melts and heavy rains could turn it into a raging torrent. It had flooded numerous times in the past causing havoc in communities along its path. Volunteer trees of all types and sizes grew unchecked along its banks, and the low hanging branches formed jungle-like foliage so thick it obscured the sight of the river from the road. As the boys made their way through the trees and tall grasses, Bud pushed away a branch, and as he passed, it snapped back hitting Kevin in the face.

"Ouch! Watch it, will ya?" Kevin protested as he shoved the branch away.

"Sorry," Bud replied half-heartedly.

"You did that on purpose!"

"Did not!"

Bud pushed away another branch, and this time he made sure it snapped back on Kevin.

"Ow!" barked Kevin. Bud laughed.

"Asshole!"

"Wuss!"

"Hey! Do it again, and I won't let you have any of my old man's cigarettes!"

"Camel's," complained Bud. "Why can't your old man smoke cigarettes with filters?"

"It's not my fault you spit all over them. Besides, beggars can't be choosers, you know."

After walking about thirty yards along the shore, Bud spotted a large flat rock a few feet back from the river's edge that would provide a good place for sitting.

"How about right over there? On that rock."

"Okay."

As they moved toward the rock, Bud turned back to Kevin and said, "Did you bring any matches?"

"Matches?" asked Kevin.

"Yeah, you know…fire."

"No, I didn't bring any matches."

"What the hell good are cigarettes if you don't have matches?"

"Who needs matches…when you have a lighter?" teased Kevin, producing a disposable lighter from his pocket. "See," he said, enjoying his one-upsmanship.

"You peckerhead," replied Bud.

The two boys got to the rock and set down their tackle boxes and poles.

Bud looked at Kevin. "Give me one of those cigs, would ya?" Kevin handed him a tin of breath mints. "What's this?"

"Here, open it." Bud took the tin box, opened the lid, and inside he saw four unfiltered Camel cigarettes. "If I took the whole pack, he might notice," explained Kevin.

"Good thinking," complimented Bud. Then he turned and glanced past a dead tree and some tall grass on his left. What he saw stopped him dead in his tracks. In a small grassy area near the shore about twenty yards away, a girl was lying on her back, sunbathing in the nude.

Kevin had his lighter out offering it to Bud, but Bud just stood there, transfixed. "Hey, do you want to light it or not?" But he was oblivious to the question. Kevin gave him a push, and Bud turned toward him. Reading the strange look on his face, Kevin asked, "What?"

"Holy shit!" Bud said quietly.

"What?" demanded Kevin.

"Shut up," Bud whispered. "Look over there."

He pointed toward the girl. Kevin saw her and was equally taken aback. Both stared silently, focusing their eyes on body parts they'd only seen in photos on the Internet. After a few moments their immaturity began oozing to the surface and they started giggling quietly, poking each other and making a few typically adolescent remarks. But the more they watched, the more it became apparent something was wrong. There was no blanket, no personal items like suntan lotion, and she had not moved.

"Something's not right," said Bud.

"What do you mean?"

"Does she look kinda weird to you?"

"I don't know."

Finally, Bud decided to call out, "Hey!"

"What are you doing?" whispered Kevin.

"Shut up!" He called out again, and there was still no response. "What the hell…?"

Bud and Kevin exchanged concerned glances. Summoning up some courage, Bud decided to take the initiative. He stepped closer and urged a reluctant Kevin to follow him.

"Come on."

"What?" demanded Kevin incredulously.

"Come with me," urged Bud.

"What if she wakes up and sees us, and she starts screaming at us or something?"

"What if she does?"

The boys moved slowly and quietly toward the girl, unsure they were doing the right thing. As both of them drew closer, they could see a few insects buzzing around. And as they approached the body, they saw her open lifeless eyes. Even boys who'd never seen a corpse recognized death.

"She's…she's dead," said Kevin.

"Yeah. You think she might be Jenny Callaghan?" asked Bud. "You know, the girl that's been missing."

"I don't know," said Kevin. "Maybe. It kind of looks like her."

"Yeah."

"Come on, let's get outta here," pleaded Kevin.

"Okay."

Kevin and Bud turned around and made their way back to the flat rock where they picked up their fishing gear and climbed up the bank to the road.

Kevin asked nervously, "What are we gonna to do?"

Bud pulled a cheap cell phone out of his pants pocket, one that his mother gave to him in an effort to keep an eye on his whereabouts. He flipped it open and began pushing numbers.

"Who ya calling?"

"Nine-one-one, who else?"

Ten minutes after Bud's call, Bill Snyder, a county sheriff's deputy assigned to the Sioux Rapids area was on the scene. The youngest of the Buena Vista County deputies, he was just twenty-eight years old and had been a deputy for only three years. He was already acquainted with Bud's father, having arrested him for drunken driving the previous year. At first, he thought the call might be a prank and was prepared to read the boys the riot act, but when Bud and Kevin escorted him to the body, he knew they had discovered the remains of Jennifer Callaghan. He matched her face to a photo and a small rose tattoo on her ankle, something noted in the description provided by her mother. Immediately, he recognized how this was a replication of Tina Olson's crime scene two weeks earlier. After calling dispatch, he took down more information from Bud and Kevin, placed them in the backseat of his police cruiser, and awaited the arrival of additional law enforcement personnel.

The flashing red and blue lights of his car lit up the shady road as County Sheriff Vince Pollock and another deputy, Matt Wilson, pulled up, their lights also flashing. Wilson was one of the county's most experienced deputies, and he was an officer that Sheriff Pollock relied on the most when he had a crime scene. Both men got out of their cruisers and walked over to Deputy Snyder.

A thickset man of sixty-two, Sheriff Vince Pollock had been working as a law enforcement officer most of his life. A hard-talking guy from the old school, he was both respected and well-liked by his men and popular with the public. He'd served as Buena Vista County sheriff for twelve years, and deputy sheriff for eighteen years before that.

"The missing girl?" Wilson asked.

"Yeah. Photo's a match and she has a rose tattoo on her ankle," informed Snyder.

"Christ! That's two girls now," muttered Pollock. "What the hell is going on around here, anyway?" Snyder shook his head.

"Where's the body?" asked Wilson.

"Make your way down to the river through there," pointed Snyder. "When you get to the shore, turn to your left and it's about forty yards."

"Forty yards?" questioned Wilson. "Why not go forty yards up the road and drop straight down?"

"The trees are so thick, you can't get through. I tried. You need someone with a chainsaw to cut through it. And something else…and this is really spooky," he added.

"Spooky?" asked Pollock sarcastically.

"Yeah. The girl is laid out on the shore…It's almost an exact match to how Tina Olson was found."

"Are you shitting me?" said Pollock. "Just what I need. A year from retirement and now I got two dead girls, and it looks like they're connected."

"What's with these two?" Wilson asked Snyder, nodding toward Bud and Kevin.

"Couple of fishermen. They found the body."

Wilson leaned into the back window of Snyder's cruiser and asked, "You boys okay?"

Bud and Kevin muttered, "Yeah. Okay." By their reactions, it seemed they were feeling pretty numb right now, most likely experiencing a delayed emotional reaction to what they'd seen. But the trauma of an event like this could hit them later on. "We'll get you home before too long," he said in a reassuring voice.

"Matt, we're going to need to contact the Department of Criminal Investigation and get a forensics team up here, again," directed Pollock. They had to make the trip from Des Moines, and Pollock knew it would take a few hours for the team to arrive.

"Bill," Pollock said to Snyder, "get a couple of State Patrolmen over here. I want this road blocked off half a mile in each direction. "We don't need any god damned gawkers like we had two weeks ago."

"Got it," replied Snyder who stepped to his car to use the radio.

"Well, we better go down and take a look," Pollock said as he took a step toward the river.

"Vince," Wilson said, stopping him. "Are you thinking what I'm thinking?"

"Yeah, and I hope we're wrong."

***

Later that afternoon, yellow crime scene tape surrounded the area and ended at the water's edge. The county coroner, Dr. Milton Fredericks, a tall, wizened man of sixty-five, was working alongside the state medical examiner and several white-suited members of the forensics team from Des Moines. Two of the crime scene techs were in the process of bagging the body. They secured Jenny Callaghan's remains onto a gurney, preparing for the difficult trek up to the road.

Sheriff Pollock was talking with Deputy Snyder next to a car with an "Iowa Department of Criminal Investigation" logo on the side.

"You inform the girl's parents?" asked Snyder.

"Barnes is doing it," said Pollock. Snyder knew informing someone about the death of a family member was one of the worst parts of the job, especially a young person or a little kid. But on this occasion, he'd assigned the task to Phil Barnes, one of his deputies. He should have been the one to do it, but he felt his place was here. The family needed to be the first to hear the news rather than learn about it from the media. Barnes was the kind and empathetic type, with fifteen years of experience delivering bad news to next of kin.

With some difficulty, Dr. Fredericks made his way up the bank to the road.

Sheriff Pollock walked over to him. "What have you got, Milton?"

"She was killed around midnight, but not here," said Fredericks. "It's just like the other one in every detail—raped, strangled, and then neatly laid out. Bruising around the wrists and ankles indicate restraint devices."

"Great," muttered Pollock.

"I'd say we've got a serious problem on our hands, Vince."

Dr. Dale Henry, the state's forensic pathologist, moved to his car and began removing his white jumpsuit. He motioned the sheriff over."We've almost got things wrapped here. We're taking the body to Des Moines for autopsy."

"Doc filled me in on the details," Pollock said.

"Yeah. It's the same perp, little doubt about that. I'm going to recommend a profiler be brought in. You ever worked with one?" Henry asked.

"No. Never had the need," replied Pollock.

Henry tossed the remainder of his protective garb in a plastic box in his trunk and said, "If you have a serial killer on the loose, you're going to need all the help you can get."

Six reporters were already gathered at a roadblock half a mile down. A state patrolman was making sure no one made it past the barrier. Deputy Snyder pulled up in his cruiser and the patrolman let him through. He was returning from taking Bud and Kevin home. When he had parked, Sheriff Pollock walked over.

"You get the boys home all right?"

"Yeah," replied Snyder. "They called their parents, and I talked to them—told them they should leave work so they could come home and be with their boys. Not a good idea for them to be alone after witnessing something like this, you know."

"Good," replied Pollock. "Once the DCI guys leave, you can have the patrolmen open the road back up."

Pollock addressed Wilson, "Tomorrow morning I want to have a meeting with all deputies present. I want everyone to start checking out any new people that may be in the area. See if they have alibis for the times of the abductions and murders. And if you see any of the other deputies, tell them not to speak to any god damned reporters. I don't want anybody mentioning the words 'serial killer' and starting a panic."

As the coroner's vehicle containing Jenny Callaghan's body slowly drove past on its way to Des Moines, Pollock sighed. "Well, I guess I'd better go down and face those reporters. This is going to be a media wet dream."

Chapter Six

At 6:30 a.m. Joe Erickson left his father's home clad in a T-shirt and sweatpants.

He was out for his daily three-mile jog through the streets of Marathon, and if he felt like pushing it, he would run out to Poland Township Park two and a half miles farther. The park was once a pit where for many years the county extracted gravel for use on roads, leaving large depressions in the earth that filled with water. Popular with local young people who came out to swim, the community, motivated by a couple of local drowning tragedies, acquired the land and reclaimed it as a park. The W.P.A. assisted by building a stone shelter house with changing areas for swimmers and eventually the park became a popular destination for picnics and family reunions.

Pushing himself didn't just improve his cardiovascular fitness. As a cop he never knew when he might find himself in a chase with some twenty-year-old suspect, and he never wanted to be forced to give up a chase because he was out of breath, huffing and puffing like some of his fellow officers. This morning he was clearing out the mental cobwebs and enjoying himself in the process mainly due to his body's release of mood-enhancing hormones that contributed to his "runner's high."

He was thinking positively about his job and about when he might be able to rejoin the force. He was doing rather well, or so he thought, and was anxious to get back to Chicago once his business in Marathon was concluded. As he passed an alley, he glanced to his right and saw another runner pull onto the street and begin jogging near him. Her brunette ponytail swung rhythmically back and forth as she ran. She was clad in black and orange spandex workout gear that showed off her figure, a figure that he noticed had pretty damned nice proportions. She pulled up alongside him and looked over.

"You're new around here, aren't you?" she asked.

"Not really," Joe replied.

"Oh, yeah? Then why haven't I seen you before?"

She was beginning to amuse him with her questions so he decided to play along to see where it went. "Probably because you weren't born yet."

"Yeah?" she said.

He didn't respond right away, focusing on his pace, then said, "I grew up in this town, and then moved away."

"Really."

"Yeah. Back in the late Stone Age."

"You don't look that old." She smiled.

He shot her a glance.

"As a matter of fact, you look kind of hot for someone from the Stone Age"

Joe chuckled. "How old are you, anyway?"

"Eighteen."

"Eighteen going on thirty-five."

"I know which way the pickle squirts," she stated matter-of-factly.

"I'll bet you do," Joe said, shaking his head slightly in disbelief. *God, this kid is ballsy,* he thought. They jogged another block without talking, and finally she spoke up.

"So...what brings you back to town, if you don't mind me asking?"

"And if I mind?"

"Oh, come on."

"My father died, and I have some legal issues to take care of. I have to sell the house and get rid of a lot of his stuff. People have way too much stuff."

"Who was your father?"

"Carl Erickson."

"Carl was your dad?" she asked.

"Yeah. You knew him?"

"We live down the street four houses. I'm Melissa Kincaid. My father's the banker."

"I'm Joe," he said as they jogged on.

"Do you run every morning?"

"Have to if I'm gonna keep this body." Joe gave her a quick look.

"Not bad, huh?" she said.

"Not bad," Joe agreed. He didn't know if she was putting him on or if she was auditioning for jailbait. As they approached a stop sign at the corner of Athens and Agora Streets, Joe stopped running.

"Why are you stopping?"

"I've done my three miles. I need to start my cooldown."

Unseen by Joe or Melissa, Deputy Will Tucker was sitting in his cruiser, observing Melissa and Joe from an alley. The baby-faced deputy had never seen Joe before, and given the recent murders, a middle-aged guy interacting with a teenage girl grabbed his attention.

"Well, I've got longer to go," Melissa said. "Maybe I'll catch you some other day."

"Maybe so," said Joe, and they parted, with Melissa jogging east on Athens Street and Joe walking south on Agora.

Deputy Tucker drove out of the alley and pulled up beside Joe, signaling him to stop. Tucker eased his large, doughy frame out of his cruiser.

"Hold it right there." He slid his nightstick into his belt and stepped toward Joe. They made eye contact, sizing each other up.

"Don't think I've seen you around here before."

"It's been a while," Joe stated, both hands resting on his hips.

"I need to see some identification."

"Well, I don't have anything with me."

"That's a problem."

"Did I do something wrong?" Joe asked.

"I'm asking the questions here," said Tucker. "Where do you live?"

"303 South Agora. Carl Erickson's house."

"Really. He's dead."

"Yes, he is," said Joe, still eye to eye with Tucker.

"You related or something?"

"I'm his son."

"I'm still going to need some I.D."

"Look, I don't carry anything with me when I run. I have it at the house."

Tucker opened the rear door of his cruiser and said, "Okay, get in." Joe obliged, and they drove the two and a half blocks to Joe's father's house. Tucker pulled into the driveway and followed Joe through the side door of the house that opened into the kitchen.

"It's in the bedroom," Joe said.

"Lead the way," Tucker instructed.

Joe entered the bedroom and picked up his wallet from the dresser. At the same time, Tucker spotted Joe's service revolver on a small table next to the bed. Taking no chances, he slowly removed his gun from its holster and held it next to his leg.

When Joe turned to him with his Illinois driver's license and Chicago PD identification in hand, Tucker raised his gun and pointed at him, saying calmly, "Hold it right there. Do not move!" Joe realized what was happening and froze. "Maybe you'd like to explain that weapon on the table," Tucker said.

"Oh…that."

"Yeah…that."

Joe had forgotten about his Glock 17 sitting on the nightstand and was taken aback for a second. But he understood Tucker's reaction. Not wanting to escalate the situation, he remained calm.

"I can explain that."

"I hope so."

"I'm a cop. You'll see. I have identification."

"Fine. Toss it on the bed," Tucker instructed. Joe did as he was told, and Tucker picked it up and looked it over. He glared at Joe, and then back at the photo I.D. a couple of times. Finally satisfied, he lowered his gun and said, "Chicago, huh?" Joe nodded. "Detective," he continued.

"Yeah," Joe replied. "I didn't think about my piece sitting there. I wasn't expecting a visitor."

Tucker holstered his gun and handed the I.D.'s back. Joe let out a breath, thankful Tucker wasn't some kind of redneck cowboy who would just as soon shoot first and ask questions later.

"Sorry," Tucker apologized. "We're taking extra precautions given everything that's happened lately. When I saw you talking to that young girl, it set off alarm bells."

"Understandable. Look, Deputy, could—"

"Tucker," he interrupted. "Will Tucker."

"Okay, Tucker," said Joe. "You mind if we talked someplace other than the bedroom?"

"If you like."

They walked back to the kitchen where Joe poured himself a cup of coffee. "You want one?"

"Sure. I'll take one."

Joe filled a cup. "Take anything in it?"

"Black's fine."

He handed the cup to Tucker. Physically, he reminded Joe a little of the late actor, John Candy, that affable, good-hearted character seen in numerous films, but he showed none of that wacky sense of humor Candy was known for.

Tucker sipped his coffee and decided it was probably safe to confide in Joe. "I suppose you've heard about the two girls?"

"From what I've read in the newspapers."

"Uh…We're not supposed to say anything about this," said Tucker. "But I'm sure you know to keep this under your hat. The sheriff thinks we may have a serial killer on our hands. But I guess he doesn't know it takes three deaths to specify it's a serial killer."

"Right. Three," Joe confirmed.

"But you probably know that all ready."

"Yeah."

A sheepish look came across Tucker's face. He knew he was dealing with someone with a lot more experience than he had, and he didn't need to tell him that. He felt embarrassed.

Joe gave Tucker a glance. He sensed his discomfort and sought to make him feel at ease. "A smart investigator will always look at all the possibilities. It appears like things are leaning in that direction at the moment."

"We've never had anything like this happen around here before," Tucker continued. "People usually don't get killed, certainly not like this, you know? We haven't had a murder in this county for years."

"I'm used to dealing with homicides on a weekly basis," said Joe.

"Have you ever worked on these kind of cases? Serial murders, I mean?"

"One."

Who was it? If you don't mind me asking?"

"I don't," replied Joe. "You ever hear of David Eugene Burton? The serial killer in Chicago?" Joe asked.

"Of course. You in on that one?"

"I arrested him."

"No shit," said Tucker, his eyes growing bigger.

"No shit," Joe confirmed.

"How did you break the case?"

"How much time you have?"

Tucker looked at his watch. "Oh, damn, it's seven o'clock. I have to go. Maybe we could get together sometime—for a beer or something."

"Maybe," Joe said.

Tucker set down his cup on the table. He wanted to stay and talk with Joe, pick his brain, see if he could offer any insights into the killings, but it would have to be another time. He was on the clock and had work to do.

"And I'm sorry about the…" Tucker trailed off. "Just doin' my job."

"You owe me," said Joe with a subtle twinkle in his eye.

"Yeah. I guess I do," Tucker confessed as he made his way to the door. "See ya."

As Tucker went through the door, Joe began to think about the logistics of tracking a serial killer. A small county law enforcement bureau in rural Iowa doesn't have the manpower or the expertise to capture one of these elusive predators. Serial killers were generally smart and very cunning creatures, and they didn't screw up very often. That's why they were able to continue to kill for long periods of time. And the more he thought about it, the more his demons started to come back to him. He sat down, elbows on the table, and leaned his head against his hands.

David Eugene Burton was still in his head. The image of Judy Chamber's body lying in the alley flashed in his mind like a recurring bad dream. The girl he could have saved but…didn't. Her porcelain face, her lifeless stare, her manicured, red-painted fingernails, her blood-stained dress. Then Burton's smile. And Burton's mutilated women, morphing into view, grotesque images indelibly imprinted on his psyche like scenes from a horror film. Images he could never unsee. *God, would they always be there to haunt me,* he thought? Would he ever get past having those nightmares that interrupted his sleep, that jolted him awake in the middle of the night in a cold sweat? If he didn't know better, he might think some malevolent spirit bent on driving him insane was at work. But there was no malevolent spirit, only Burton, that smirking, arrogant animal that he should have put down like the rabid dog he was. That he still was.

Finally, he sucked in a deep breath and looked up at the clock. Almost ten minutes had passed since he sat down. *Get your ass moving,* he thought and forced himself to stand up. Wandering into the bathroom, he turned on the shower and removed his clothes. He opened the medicine cabinet and reached for his bottle of antidepressants, his "happy pills." Removing the cap, he tipped the bottle up, and saw the last remaining pill drop into his hand. "Wonderful," he said, popping it in his mouth and chasing it down with a glass of water.

Chapter Seven

Driving along the road to Sioux Rapids brought back memories. Joe could have taken the highway, but a little bit of nostalgia had set in, and he decided to travel via the county asphalt road that he took most often as a teenager. Some things hadn't changed. The old "Dead Man's Curve" was still there, a place in the road that had gotten its name from its abrupt ninety-degree turn to the left that was responsible for more than a few accidents over the years. From there, the road snaked up toward the woods and under a railroad trestle and on into Sioux Rapids.

His thoughts jumped to the years when he was in high school, hanging out with friends from both Sioux Rapids and Webb, and how they used to drive the back roads between those towns, drinking beer and avoiding the law. There were a few kids who were into controlled substances, pot mostly, but Joe and most of his friends were content with drinking beer and pursuing girls. Those were the days, and when he thought back on them, he considered himself damned lucky to have lived through them all. The idea of raising children today, especially in Chicago, was enough to send shivers up his spine. Thankfully, a family was not in his future.

Joe pulled his Camaro into a parking space in front of Grant's Pharmacy. The location hadn't changed in the last twenty years, but everything else had. As Joe pushed open the door and entered the store, he saw that not much of the interior was recognizable. The old tin ceiling remained, the only trace left from the original store. Gone was the marble-topped soda fountain in back as well as the rack of magazines in the front window. He remembered looking at the hot rod magazines to pass time while his mother shopped and would eventually get reprimanded by one of the clerks with the words, "No free reading!"

As he made his way back to the counter, a lavender-haired woman was gossiping to a petite, gray-haired clerk wearing a smock with "Grace" embroidered on it. She was standing next to the cash register. Joe stepped in line behind her and waited for his turn. He couldn't help but overhear the conversation and soon came to realize that gossip had now taken precedence over the servicing of prescriptions. Or so it seemed.

"Oh, Lillian. Isn't that just the berries?" stated Grace.

"Well, I want to tell you that's the least of her worries," cackled Lillian. "Mamie told me that she just found out she has an ovarian cyst the size of a meatball, and her doctor told her he wants to operate right away."

"Dear me," replied Grace.

Running out of patience, Joe tried getting Grace's attention. "Excuse me…"

Lillian shot him a menacing look as she continued talking without missing so much as a beat. Apparently, she was a seasoned professional at evading interruptions.

"But she's afraid if they take out her ovary, she won't be able to have any more children," Lillian continued, "even though her other one seems to be perfectly fine."

Joe spotted a small bell on the counter with a sign that read "Ring Bell for Service." He reached around Lillian and pushed the top of the bell several times which caused it to ring out loudly. Lillian actually fell silent, her self-assertive look morphing into a combination of horror and disdain.

"Sorry. It says, 'Ring the bell for service' and I figured that's what I was supposed to do," said Joe in an innocent voice.

"Well, I never!" said Lillian indignantly.

"Neither have I," replied Joe.

Lillian turned and walked out in a huff, clinging to several white prescription packages.

Joe turned to Grace who looked him straight in the eye and said through semi-clenched teeth, "Polite people wait their turn."

"Polite people don't waste other people's time," Joe replied.

By this time, a thin-faced pharmacist in his early sixties, had observed what had happened and walked out to the counter and stood next to Grace. Dressed in a blue pharmacist's smock with "Richard Grant" embroidered on it, he spoke reassuringly, "It's all right, Grace." And then turning to Joe, he inquired, "May I help you, sir?"

Joe handed him his prescription bottle and explained, "I believe you can. I'm from out of town, and I need this prescription refilled. Could you call my pharmacy and transfer it?"

Grant placed his reading glasses on, and while examining the bottle, he said, "Let see…this is refillable. Ah, there's the phone number." And then looking at Joe, he concluded, "Yes, I can do that."

"Do you know how long it will take?" asked Joe.

"I think I can have this for you in say thirty minutes or so."

"That'll be fine. Thank you," Joe replied with a nod. Before turning to go, he couldn't resist. Out of pure orneriness, he looked at Grace who had been giving him the evil eye for the past few moments, and said, in a perfect Arnold Schwarzenegger impersonation, "I'll be back." Grace's nostrils flared slightly, her expression ice.

It wasn't that he disliked little old ladies. On the contrary, he had interacted with a multitude of older folks as a detective and had comforted many who had been victims of violent crime. But it annoyed him when people had no respect for his time. Oh, well. He would apologize later when he picked up his meds. Maybe she would hate him a little less if he turned on the charm.

He left the pharmacy and began walking down the street. Needing to use up "thirty minutes or so" while his prescription was being filled, he decided to take a walk and see where it would take him. After a block, he spotted a "cafe" and decided to go inside for a cup of coffee.

It was mid-morning and the place was busy. The faux wood-paneled walls and the vinyl-covered floor of the old-fashioned establishment had been well maintained. A long counter with stools ran half the length of the room. It had a cash register at one end and a glass case displaying homemade pies for those customers with a sweet tooth at the other. A row of dark brown booths lined the walls and metal tables and chairs were lined up between them and the counter. A large bulletin board covered with flyers advertising sales and other local events of various kinds hung near the door. The unmistakable scent of grilled bacon and brewed coffee wafted through the air. It brought back memories of the old cafe in Marathon on a Friday or Saturday night eating cheeseburgers and French fries. Spotting a vacant stool at the counter, he walked over to it and sat down.

A worn but still attractive woman of about forty was working as a waitress behind the counter. She was dressed in black jeans, an apron, and a short sleeve brocade denim shirt that was open at the neck revealing a dainty gold necklace and an overabundance of age spots from too much sun worshipping. She wore numerous rings on her fingers, none of which was a wedding band, and her nails had been manicured to perfection. She gave him a quick look-over and seemed to approve. Her nametag read "Karen".

"Whatcha gonna have?" Karen asked in a subtly flirtatious voice.

"Coffee to go," replied Joe.

"Would that be regular or unleaded?"

"What, no premium?" Joe asked, returning the flirt.

"Sorry, hon."

"Make it a regular."

"Small or large?" she asked with a clear double meaning intended.

Joe smiled slightly. "I'd prefer a medium."

Indicating two stacks of styrofoam cups, she pointed. "This one is a large and this one is a small."

"Tell you what," Joe said, "Why don't you fill a large one three-quarters full, and we'll call it a medium?"

In one artful motion that came from years of experience, she set a styrofoam cup down on the counter, filled it three-quarters full, and pressed a on plastic lid.

"There you go," she smiled. She returned the coffee pot to the burner and then returned. "Would you mind if I asked you a question?"

"Depends on the question."

"Are you always this...difficult?

"Well," he said, rising to go. "Sometimes I'm difficult, sometimes I'm easy."

She smiled. "Your 'medium' is a dollar and twenty-five. Same as a large."

As Joe pulled a five-dollar bill from his pocket, his eyes caught the faces of customers, several of whom were staring as if he'd just arrived from Mars.

Noticing, Karen said, "Don't mind them. They've never seen you before, that's all. People are a little edgy about strangers around here these days."

"I can see that," he said and handed her the bill. "Keep the change."

"Well, thank you, hon," she said, giving him a little wink. "Hope to see you again, sometime."

Winking back, he replied, "If you ever get to Marathon…"

"So, you're from Marathon, huh?"

"For a while."

"I don't know. You know what they say about Marathon guys."

"Enlighten me."

"I hear they're Minutemen," she said, referring to the old Marathon High School mascot.

Joe laughed out loud. "Sorry," he said. "That was before my time. I was a Laurens-Marathon Charger."

"A Charger, huh? Well, I'll keep that in mind," she laughed.

She hit some keys on the cash register. The cash drawer popped open and she proceeded to separate the coffee from the tip. Amused by the whole encounter, Joe smiled. As he turned to go, Sheriff Pollock opened the door and two others stepped past him. The first was Jeff Carey. Dressed in a dark suit that was in need of some tailoring, he was a fifty-year-old field operative with the Iowa Department of Criminal Investigation. His ill-fitting suit and stocky frame made him look frumpy, and he smelled of cigarette smoke as he passed by. Following him through the door was Destiny Alexander, a strikingly attractive woman with dark hair pulled into a French roll and blue eyes large enough for a man to drown in. She was dressed in a light taupe linen suit and an ivory chiffon blouse. When Joe locked eyes with her, she suddenly stopped and a surprised look came across her face.

"Something the matter?" Jeff asked, noticing her reaction.

As the sheriff came through the door, Destiny tried to salvage this uncomfortable moment.

43

"Joe! Well, I'll be…"

"You two know one another?" asked Pollock.

"Uh, yes. Yes, we do," she replied. "Excuse me for a few minutes, would you please?"

As Joe walked past, she followed him out the door and onto the sidewalk. "You're the last person I expected to see today."

"Really," he replied coolly.

She clarified, "I mean—It's really good to see you."

His only response was a subtle lift of an eyebrow. Hoisting the coffee to his lips, he took a drink and recoiled slightly. It was hotter than he anticipated.

"What in the world are you doing in Sioux Rapids?"

Avoiding her eyes, "Taking care of my dad's estate over in Marathon."

She went to touch his arm but then retracted it. "I'm so sorry. I didn't know. When did he…?"

"A month ago."

They started walking down the sidewalk and she had to walk briskly to keep up with him as she was six inches shorter and somewhat handicapped by her skirt and heels.

"How are you doing?" she asked in a comforting voice.

"Better."

"That's good. Good to hear."

"Other than the side effects from my medication, I'm doing well."

Noticing he was outpacing her, he slowed and saw an opening to an alley. He decided to turn into it so they could move off the sidewalk and get a little privacy. Destiny followed him in, and after a few steps, he turned to her and was about to speak, but she beat him to the punch.

"Still on leave from the department?" she inquired.

"Uh…yeah. I'm itching to get back to work but…you know how it is."

"Oh, the red tape," she acknowledged. "I know."

"Yeah. The doctors, shrinks, and various police officials, not to mention the high muckety-mucks, all have to review it, approve it, bless it, and genuflect in front of it before they actually sign off on it," he replied.

She smiled knowingly.

44

Joe took a sip of his coffee while neither of them spoke. Five seconds of awkward silence seemed like an hour. Finally, Destiny filled the void. "I...taught a class on the west coast," she said.

"Oh yeah?"

"Santa Barbara."

"Nice place, from what I hear."

"Beautiful."

"I...I would have contacted you, but I didn't want to complicate things."

He could not hide his pain as their eyes met. "I guess I can't blame you. Why would you want anything to do with a crazy person?"

His response nearly brought her tears to eyes, but then her anger kicked in. "Oh, come on. That's not fair. You weren't crazy."

"No?"

"You had a breakdown. It happens to some people."

He looked away as if he wasn't going to acknowledge it, and she wasn't going to let him get away without facing it. Not with her.

"You drove yourself twenty-four hours a day working the Burton case. No one could hold up under the kind of stress you put yourself under."

Looking back in her direction, he said, "When I never heard from you, I..." His sentence drifted off unfinished as he could not find words to describe the feelings of abandonment and loss that had caused him so much anguish.

Her voice quavered a little as she spoke, "I left because I thought I'd been one of the causes."

"Bullshit," he countered.

"Your shrink told me I could interfere with your recovery."

He turned back, his eyes burning into hers. "He told you that?"

"That's what he said. I wanted to be there for you, to help you if I could, but he told me my presence could be detrimental to your recovery. So, when the California gig came up, I took it. I...I had to pay the rent."

After an uncomfortable pause, she glanced at her watch, "Look, I have to get back. I've been called in to consult about the two dead girls—maybe you've heard?"

"Yeah. I read something about it."

45

"Are you staying at your dad's place?" she asked. "Can I find you there?" Joe nodded. "Mm. 303 South Agora Street. Ivory house, blue shutters."

"Good," she said. "Sorry, but I have to go."

She smiled and lightly brushed his arm as she turned to walk away. His eyes followed her out of the alley. As she disappeared behind the building, he took another sip of coffee and began walking back toward the pharmacy to see if his prescription was ready.

Chapter Eight

Destiny Alexander had a lot of things going for her. Not only was she attractive, but she also had an I.Q. over 150. Experience had taught her that highly intelligent women could intimidate some people so she often disguised that side of herself when dealing with certain individuals. It was one of the many tactics she had learned to employ.

When she first met Sheriff Pollock, he invited her into his office. Sitting behind his desk, he read out loud from a folder, summarizing her experience.

"Graduated summa cum laude from the University of Illinois at Chicago with a degree in Criminology, worked in law enforcement in Washington D.C. for four years. Went on to get a Masters in Forensic Psychology from Georgetown University—graduated at the top of your class." He looked over his reading glasses. "Very impressive," he noted.

Pollock continued. "Acceptance into the FBI's National Center for the Analysis of Violent Crime and its Behavior Analysis Unit. Worked as a criminal profiler with the Bureau." He stopped, removed his glasses, and looked up at her. "If you don't mind my asking, why did you leave a job with the FBI to form your own company?"

Destiny wasn't expecting to be interviewed, but she'd dealt with the sheriff's type before and knew how to handle the situation—by telling the truth. "Two other women and I filed sexual harassment charges against a former supervisor. He was eventually fired. But by doing the right thing, you end up poisoning the well for future advancement. So, I looked for options. I found a niche I could fill by working as an independent criminal investigative analyst. I could make myself available to law enforcement agencies needing the services of a criminal profiler. And here I am."

"You sure come highly recommended," said Pollock.

Destiny explained, "Two years ago, Frank Hensley was Head of the Iowa Department of Criminal Investigation. He hired me to work on a serial rapist case in Des Moines. I guess he liked my work so he brought me in to work on this one."

"Well, I've never worked with a profiler before, but if you can help find this maniac, I'm glad to have you on board." Pollock stood up. "Come on, I'll show you a space you can use as an office while you're here."

Two days later, Sheriff Pollock, Destiny, and Jeff were in the building housing the Sioux Rapids Police office. The office didn't amount to much. It was quite small, and rather old. Leftover from the years when small towns used to employ their own police officers, it had a dropped ceiling with fluorescent lighting, and its walls were covered with paneling from the 1970's. The space simply functioned as a place for the deputy in charge to maintain an office and to make phone calls. Pollock chewed on a toothpick looking out the window while Jeff and Destiny were seated around a messy desk poring over files and notes made by Deputy Snyder.

"We have the original notes he made filed in Storm Lake. These are the photocopies that are kept here in case someone needs to access them," clarified Pollock.

"I see. Is Deputy Snyder the only one that works out of this office?" asked Jeff.

"Yeah. Other deputies may use it from time to time if they're called in for some reason, but it's mainly used by Snyder. As you can see, he's not the best housekeeper."

"That's okay. I've seen worse," chuckled Jeff. "Much worse."

Looking over at Destiny, Pollock asked, "How long do you think it will it take for you to complete your profile?"

Still distracted by her earlier encounter with Joe, she was thinking about him rather than focusing on several documents she had on the desk in front of her. "What? Oh, sorry," she answered, somewhat embarrassed that he'd caught her off-guard. "The profile? Normally about a week, but I can have something preliminary for you in a few days."

"Good," he said. He had never worked with a profiler. He knew about them, of course, and the kind of work they did. Thankfully, he had never needed one...until now.

Jeff got up and walked to an old pencil sharpener mounted on the wall and began grinding away on a wooden pencil he found in the desk. "Haven't used one of these in years," he noted.

Pollock grunted an acknowledgement, and Destiny gave him a polite smile.

"How many deputies can you spare on this?" Jeff asked.

"Three plus myself."

"That's not many."

"I only have nine full-time guys out in the field. I have a number of auxiliary deputies, but they're not up to this kind of work."

Destiny looked up from her reading, pushed her chair back and stood. "I have an idea," she said.

"Yeah? What's that?" Pollock asked removing the toothpick from his mouth.

"One of my former colleagues from Chicago is temporarily living in Marathon right now."

"What do you mean 'colleagues'?" asked Pollock.

"He's a detective with the Chicago Police Department, and he does have the kind of experience and expertise we need on this case," she asserted.

"Oh?"

"Who is it?" asked Jeff.

"Joe Erickson."

Jeff's ears perked up. "Joe Erickson? Joe Erickson is here?"

"Joe Erickson. Who the hell is Joe Erickson?" asked Pollock.

"He was the lead detective on the David Eugene Burton case. The guy that killed all those women? Joe practically solved that case singlehandedly. You remember reading about it—it was in all the papers," said Jeff.

"Yeah," stated Pollock. "I seem to recall something about it."

"That's him. He's been on leave from Chicago PD," added Destiny.

"On leave?" asked Jeff, seeking to satisfy his curiosity.

Destiny didn't want to go there but had no choice. "Well…he developed some psychological issues after the arrest and——"

"Oh, Christ!" exclaimed Pollock. "That's all I need."

"He's better now," Destiny insisted. "He's finishing up his medical leave."

"You talked to him?" asked Jeff.

"He was the guy I bumped into at the cafe a couple of days ago. He told me he was getting ready to go back to work," she said.

"What's he doing around here?" asked Jeff.

"He's originally from Marathon, grew up there. His father died recently, and he came back to iron out all the details regarding his estate."

Pollock protested, "I don't know if I want some outsider getting invol—"

"Sheriff," Destiny interrupted.

Jeff stepped to Pollock. "Look, I don't want to tell you how to run your department, Sheriff. But you might want to think about deputizing this guy—if only for a few weeks. He could be a great asset."

"Check with his supervisor in Chicago. I can give you his lieutenant's phone number if you want a reference," Destiny added.

Pollock thought for a minute and sighed. "All right. If you're both that hot on him. But he'd have to come on as an unpaid consultant. The county can't afford to hire people on a whim, and I don't have that kind of authority anyway." Pollock looked to Destiny and then to Jeff. "Hell, if he doesn't work out, maybe he can find the son-of-a-bitch who stole the license plates off my cruiser last month!"

"Someone stole your plates?" asked Jeff.

"Don't ask," growled Pollock. And with that, he tossed his toothpick into the trash and stepped out the door.

Jeff's eyes followed Pollock as he moved toward the door. He was wondering what was eating on the sheriff today. Turning to Destiny he asked "How well do you know Joe Erickson?"

"Reasonably well, I guess," she responded evasively.

"You think he'd be willing to come on board?"

"He might."

"Well, twist his arm."

"I'll see what I can do."

Outside, Sheriff Pollock leaned up against the fender of his cruiser and checked his cellphone. He was nearing retirement and hoped he could coast the final two years and deal with the usual things that faced his department: accidents, burglaries, assaults, illegal drugs, and drunken drivers. But fate had intervened, and that was not to be. Not now. And today, he was distracted. His wife of thirty-five years was experiencing severe back pain and would soon be going into the hospital for tests. That worried him, and it wasn't doing anything to help his disposition.

Chapter Nine

The clear western sky was aglow in roses, oranges and yellows as the sun was setting. Joe was busy preparing a late supper and relaxing with a glass of wine—Pinot Noir, one of his favorites. He wasn't a wine snob, but he knew what he liked. His wine aficionado father started collecting wines following his retirement and had accumulated a good selection of American vintages. Merlots, Pinot Noirs, Cabernet Sauvignons, Chardonnays, Pinot Grigios, Sauvignon Blancs, and a few other varieties he acquired over the years were stored in racks in the basement. It would be a shame to let them go unused. And there were way too many bottles for him to transport back to Chicago. And even if he could, he had no place to store them all.

Water was starting to boil on the stove, and as he was slicing some mushrooms on a cutting board, the doorbell rang. Grabbing a dishtowel, he wiped his hands and walked to the door.

Opening it, he saw someone he didn't recognize. The visitor, a man about forty-five years old, had the polished look of a well-kept, well fed businessman who could have used a few less carbs and a little more exercise as about fifteen extra pounds hung over his belt. He was dressed in khaki slacks, a dark green golf shirt, and penny loafers.

"Hi, I'm Tom Kincaid," the man said. "From down the street. You met my daughter this morning...jogging?"

"Oh, Melissa."

"Yes."

"Nice to meet you," said Joe extending his hand. "Come in."

"Thank you." Tom shook it firmly.

Joe led the way to the kitchen, and as they entered, the water on the stove began to boil over. "Oops, bear with me a second," said Joe as he moved the pan to another burner.

"Sorry, I guess I came at a bad time."

"No, not at all. I usually don't eat this late."

"Normally I wouldn't have knocked this time of night either, but I was out for a walk, and saw your light on so…"

"Would you like a glass of wine?"

"No, no thank you. But I'll take a raincheck, if you don't mind."

"Of course."

"I see you cook."

"Oh, yeah. When you're not married, you have two choices. You can either learn to cook or you can eat out all the time. I got tired of eating out, so I taught myself to cook sometime ago, and I came to enjoy it. You cook?"

"Oh, god no. My wife takes care of that. I'm afraid I'm all thumbs in the kitchen. I can't be trusted to boil water properly."

"I guess that would meet the definition of all thumbs, huh?" Both men chuckled, and before the mirth had gone away, Joe asked, "What can I do for you, Tom?"

Tom paused, looked at the floor for a moment, and when he looked up, his face had taken on a serious expression. Joe noticed and asked, "Is there something wrong?"

"Well, I heard you're a detective, is that right?"

"Yeah. How did you know about that?"

"Word travels fast in a small town."

There was an awkward pause, and Joe repeated, "What can I do for you, Tom?"

"Uh…The thing is…I grew up in Sioux Rapids. Went to high school with the fathers of the two murdered girls."

"Both of them?"

"Yeah, we're all about the same age. We haven't seen each other much over the years, but still—it brings these tragedies pretty close to home, you know what I mean?"

"I imagine it would."

"You can understand that my wife and I have concerns about our Melissa's safety. And I thought…you being a detective and all…you might have some insight or advice to help keep her safe."

"Okay," Joe started out, "I would advise her to avoid going out by herself. If she does go somewhere, she should go with a group of friends. There's safety in numbers."

"I see."

"And she should be wary of strangers, people who seem overly friendly or may want her to accompany them somewhere. In other words, she shouldn't trust people she doesn't know."

"Of course."

"It just comes down to using common sense, so she doesn't make herself vulnerable to any predators that might be out there."

"Her mother and I—well, she's our only child and she's…well…" He didn't finish the sentence so Joe did it for him.

"A little forward, you mean?" That was the most respectable phrase Joe could come up with to describe her.

Tom raised his eyebrow, and looking at Joe, he knew full well he'd had already discovered how precocious she could be. "You've noticed."

"Yeah," Joe smiled. "She's up front about stuff, I'll give her that. Not a bad trait."

"We've been on her about that, but it hasn't been easy. She has a mind of her own."

"Tell me, does she run every morning?"

"Yeah, she's obsessive about staying in shape."

"It's a good practice. Hopefully, she'll be that disciplined her entire life."

"Do you think it's safe for her to run each morning?"

"In Marathon, probably. But there's no sense tempting fate. If she doesn't have a friend or two she can run with, she's welcome to jog with me if she wants."

"I appreciate that. I'll let her know."

There was a pause as if Tom wanted to say something, but then decided not to. "Well, I guess I should leave you to your supper," he said as he stepped to the door. "It was nice to meet you, Joe."

"Same here."

"Have a good evening."

And he was gone. Joe thought there was something rather odd about Tom's manner. He couldn't quite put his finger on it, but he seemed conflicted. His exterior calmness belied an inner anxiety of some kind. Was there something he wasn't willing to tell him? Or was he hiding something? Or, maybe he was just worried about his daughter. He thought for a moment, then began setting out the ingredients to make his vinaigrette.

Everything was prepared and ready for cooking now. Opening the refrigerator, he removed a plate covered by a large T-bone steak. He walked out onto the patio in the back yard where his father's gas grill was hot and ready.

When the steak had reached medium rare, he removed it from the grill. He was preparing to take it inside when he heard footsteps.

"Do I detect the odor of burnt animal flesh?" came a voice from the corner of the garage.

He turned to see Destiny on the patio. Her dark hair was down, and she looked terrific in cutoff jeans, a tie-dyed tank top, and sandals.

"If we weren't meant to eat animals, why are they made out of meat?"

A little smile appeared in the corner of her mouth as her eyes moved from the T-bone to Joe's eyes. "I have to say that's a lot of meat you've got there," she observed.

"I'd be willing to share it with you."

"Really?"

"Really."

"That may be an offer I can't refuse."

"Come on. Let's go in before the mosquitoes find us," said Joe, leading the way into the kitchen.

Turning to Destiny, he said, "I thought you told me you didn't like red meat."

"I make exceptions."

"You do?"

"I do…for you," she said as her eyes locked onto his. She stepped closer to him, and their arms smoothly and effortlessly slid around each other. It felt so good to have her close again. His hands slipped under her tank top, and his fingers slid along her warm, smooth skin. When they came up for air, she placed one hand on his cheek and the other on his shoulder.

"You're shaking," she observed.

"Yeah, I guess I'm a little tense."

"Because of me?"

"Probably."

She looked up at him with a glint in her eye. "I can help with that."

"Oh, yeah?"

"Mm-hm. Wanna get naked?"

He remembered her saying that to him one other time, in her apartment in Chicago, and the memory brought a smile to his face. "Maybe," was his tongue-in-cheek answer.

"What about all this food?"

"It can wait."

Taking her hand, they walked into the bedroom. Making love to her was not a new experience. It was familiar territory: the taste of her skin, the feel of her body against his, the musky scent of love. Back in Chicago, their intimacy led them to know all the little ways to pleasure one another. And given the intensity of her music tonight, Joe knew he'd played all the right notes.

Thirty minutes later they rolled apart and lay side by side on the bed, bodies glistening. After a moment, Joe turned to her and ran his hand through her hair, twisting a lock gently around his finger. She rolled onto her side to look at him.

"It's been a while since I've done this, you know," he said.

"Like riding a bicycle."

"Well, I hope I didn't wobble too much."

Destiny burst into laughter. He loved to hear her laugh. In fact, he loved

56

everything about her. No woman ever turned him on like she could. And no woman ever made him feel the way she did.

"No, no. You were great!" She smiled. "I've missed you."

"You mean you missed this."

"I missed you, wise guy." She kissed him. "And this, too." She ran her finger along his chest. "You remember the first time we . . .?"

"You never forget the first time. You own it for life. I seem to remember we needed to buy some new clothes afterwards."

"Ripped to shreds as I recall," she said, chuckling.

"Yeah. A couple of wildcats."

She moved so her elbow was on the bed and her hand supported her head. After a pause, she looked in his eyes. "Can I ask you a question?"

"Depends."

"You always say that."

"It does."

"Were you serious today?"

"About what?"

"Itching to get back to work."

"Yeah."

"Well, do you think you might feel up to giving us a hand on this case?"

"What do you mean by 'a hand'?"

"I was thinking of…consulting. If we really are dealing with a serial killer, you and I are the only ones with any experience."

Joe sat up, pushing himself back into the pillow. "So, you want me to work with you?"

Sitting up next to him, she said, "Sheriff Pollock said he would be open to getting you on board."

"I don't know."

"We need you," urged Destiny. "I'll give you his number before I leave."

"You're leaving?"

"I should be getting back."

She got up off the bed and he followed. When she bent over to pick up her clothes, he put his hand on her back. When she rose up, she turned to him and their bodies came together in an embrace. When their lips met, her clothes dropped to the floor.

Looking her in the eyes, he said, "What would it take to get you to stay?"

She looked at him and replied, "Food."

"Why don't you take a shower, and by the time you're done, I'll have something for you?"

"I have a better idea. Why don't we both take a shower, and after we're done, I'll help you."

Chapter Ten

The Buena Vista County Sheriff's Office had relocated to a new modern concrete structure built in the industrial area of town. Replacing the old office located in the county courthouse, it afforded more space, a modern jail, and a state-of-the-art communications center in a less congested area.

Sheriff Pollock's office was like a lot of office spaces in new buildings, sterile and devoid of character. A combination of concrete and sheetrock walls, metal shelving, institutional filing cabinets, a large desk with a computer, keyboard, and printer made up the bulk of the office. Additional chairs sat in front of the desk to accommodate deputies and others who had business with the sheriff. In contrast to the cold and utilitarian space, personal items made the office less austere. Plaques, framed certificates of service, and Green Bay Packers memorabilia hung from the walls. Framed photos and other items sitting on his desk and in nooks and crannies around the office suggested a wife's touch.

Seated in front of Pollock's desk, Joe was doing his best to hold his temper as Pollock's condescending attitude was rubbing him the wrong way. *I thought she said he was open to working with me,* he thought to himself.

"I checked with your lieutenant," said Pollock.

"Vincenzo?"

"Yeah. He told me you were damned good. He also told me you're a maverick and a pain in the ass."

"That's one point of view," replied Joe. "I prefer to call it being independent and self-motivated."

"Well, I don't want some cowboy riding in here, doing whatever the hell he pleases. All that's—"

Joe interrupted saying, "Let's get something straight. I'm not a fucking cowboy!"

"Excuse me?" said Pollock, taken aback.

Joe went on. "I'm a decorated detective, and I happen to have experience in an area you don't, that's all. Now, if you want my expertise, I have to be able to work the way I always have because that's how I get results. That way, I won't get in your way, and I expect you'll stay out of mine. I want to be able to carry my service revolver at all times and have special deputy status. I don't expect to be paid, but I want full cooperation from everyone in your department and access to everything that's known about each case. We don't have to be best buddies in order to find out who the hell is killing these girls."

Pollock's face reddened. "I've never been spoken to like this."

"I just want you to know up front where I stand because you'll find I'm a no-bullshit kinda guy."

Pollock rose to his feet. "So am I. Maybe that means I'll eventually get to like you a little."

Joe stood and put it on the line. "So, you want my help or not?"

"If you're as good as they say, yeah. But there's two things you need to remember: One, I'm the boss around here; and two, don't ever mess with me. Understood?"

"Understood." Joe held out his hand, and Pollock reluctantly shook it. "I'll give you the best I've got."

Pollock gestured with his head toward the door. "Go see Delores at the front desk. She'll arrange to get your ID made up."

In a small office, Destiny was typing on her laptop when Joe stuck his head in the door. "Nice office," commented Joe.

"Come in. I had a choice of this or a spare jail cell so…"

"This is not the way to treat—"

"I'm kidding," she cut him off. "How did it go with Sheriff Pollock?"

"He hates my guts. But it's official," he said, flashing his new ID card.

"Well-well. Let's see it."

Joe handed it to her and then leaned down and kissed her on the neck.

"Now, that could be construed as sexual harassment, 'Special Deputy Erickson.'"

"Uh-huh. You gonna swear out a complaint?"

Destiny stood and handed back his ID card, "Not if you accompany me on some official business."

"Where are we going?"

"You'll see."

Joe followed her out of the building and they got into her car and drove to the county medical examiner's office downtown. The secretary behind the desk was a well-dressed, petite woman in her early fifties.

"May I help you?" she smiled.

"Yes, I'm Destiny Alexander, and this is Joe Erickson. I called earlier."

"Of course." She picked up the phone, pushed the intercom button. "A Ms. Alexander and a Mr. Erickson are here to see you." She paused for a moment, hung up the phone and then pointed toward a door saying, "You can go in…right through that door."

Inside, Dr. Milton Fredericks introduced himself. After shaking hands, he went back to his lab table, selected a glass slide and proceeded to arrange it under his microscope.

"Thank you for seeing us," said Destiny.

"I hope you don't mind if I continue working. I'm under a time crunch today," apologized Fredericks.

"We won't take up much of you time, Doctor. I was wondering if you could update us on anything that could help me in creating a psychological profile on our perpetrator."

"Like it says in the report. Each girl had restraint marks on her wrists and ankles, and each one was repeatedly raped. There was considerable vaginal bruising but no trace of semen. Both deaths were due to strangulation." He looked up. "What else would you like to know?"

"Any forensic evidence on the first girl that differed from the second?" Joe asked.

"No. Actually, the forensics team came up dry on that account, I'm afraid. No hairs, no prints. We retrieved some microscopic fibers from the ligature marks that were consistent with a white cotton cord, the type sold in the hardware section of practically every store in the country. The cotton fibers found on Jennifer Callaghan's body matched those found on Tina Olson. Other than that, there was nothing that wasn't consistent with materials from the riverbank."

Dr. Fredericks stopped what he was doing and walked to a cupboard near the refrigerator and removed a drinking glass.

"Whoever this guy is, he knows what he's doing. It's obvious he has some knowledge of forensics. He was smart enough to wear a condom—there were traces of lubricant found in the vaginas of both girls but no DNA. And both victims were washed clean post-mortem. Traces of a common dishwashing detergent were found in the hair of both victims."

"He washed them after he killed them?" asked Destiny.

"It would appear so."

"So, any evidence would go down the drain," Joe concluded.

"Indeed, it would."

"So, what you are saying is, you have no evidence to speak of—nothing but some cotton fibers?" Joe asked.

Offended, Dr. Fredericks said, clearly separating his next two words, "Not quite."

"We're listening," said Destiny, trying to smooth things over. "What else do you have?"

"There was inflammation of the mucous membranes of the eyes, nose, and throat, that suggests both victims were exposed to a chemical agent such as tear gas or pepper spray. So far, the results have been inconclusive on which it may have been. If I were a betting man, I'd lay odds on pepper spray since it's widely available."

"That could have been how he subdued them," said Destiny, glancing at Joe.

"Well, I can't draw that conclusion. All I can say is they were exposed to it at some point."

There was a short pause.

"So, that's it?" Joe pressed.

"I suggest you contact the Department of Criminal Investigation and talk with them. I'm only the coroner. Now, if you'll excuse me, I have work to do," said Dr. Fredericks in a tone that implied "we're done here."

"Thank you, Doctor," said Destiny. "I appreciate your time."

As Joe and Destiny exited Frederick's office, she stopped him in the hallway. "You can't push people like that. This isn't Chicago."

"Hey, I'm the one that grew up around here."

"Then try to remember. Things don't work here like they do in the city. You'll have to adapt if you want to get any cooperation. After all, they're your people, you know. Try to remember how to deal with them."

Silence.

"So, is this my first official ass-chewing?" Joe asked.

She didn't answer, —just shot him a look.

He knew it was time to shut up.

Chapter Eleven

T he late morning weather was warm and sunny. The humidity was typically high, but the temperature was eight-four degrees according to Joe's car, a far cry from the ninety-five degrees it was a couple of days ago.

A white Cadillac hearse was parked in front of the steps leading to the First United Methodist Church in Sioux Rapids. A universal symbol of funerals and death, its presence meant that services were being held for one of the church's members. Today, it was the funeral of Jennifer Renee Callaghan, murder victim number two.

A multitude of cars surrounded the church and were parked along nearby streets, something typical of small-town funerals because everyone knew virtually everyone else in one way or another. When a prominent person dies or a well-known family suffers a loss, people in the community pull together, show their sympathy, and pay their respects by attending either the visitation or funeral service. The Callaghan family was not only active in the community, they were also well liked, so the turnout was quite large.

The service concluded, and the doors of the beige brick church opened. The funeral director and his assistant oversaw the six pallbearers as they carried the casket down the steps to the hearse. The large spray of flowers atop the casket jiggled as the pallbearers carefully slid the ornate silver box into the hearse. Jenny's family, her father, mother, and younger sister appeared first, followed by her grandparents and other relatives. They made their way down the steps and congregated on the sidewalk. Joe spotted Tom Kincaid and his wife among the mourners. A host of Jenny's high school classmates and friends were in attendance, and they assembled on the lawn at the side of the church. Many of them crying or displaying expressions of numbness and disbelief.

Cars began lining up behind the hearse to chauffer family members and close friends to the cemetery where the minister would conduct a short ceremony prior to internment. Joe and Jeff were both dressed in suits in order to blend in with those in attendance. Along with Deputy Snyder, they positioned themselves across the street from the church so they could observe the crowd for any suspicious individuals or unusual behavior. An old red pickup truck with most of its paint worn away slowly drove by on a side street, apparently driven by some morbidly curious individual bent on getting a gander at the proceedings. As it slowly made its way down the street, the funeral director closed the rear door of the hearse and the pallbearers prepared to step into a dark van that would convey them to the cemetery.

Jeff took a couple of steps away from Joe and lit a cigarette. Without any breeze, the smoke hung in the air for a time before it dissipated.

"Bad habit," said Snyder. "Ever thought about quitting?"

"No," replied Jeff, tossing it off. "A person needs a few bad habits."

"This one could kill you."

"Yeah, well…Everybody has to die of something."

Snyder snorted in amusement saying, "Well, I guess that's one way to look at it."

"See anything suspicious?" Jeff asked Snyder as smoke exited his mouth.

"Nothing. Nothing out of the ordinary."

Then he looked at Joe. "Anything?"

"No."

"I suppose it's too much to ask to have the perp show up at the funeral," said Jeff.

"You never know about sickos," corrected Joe. "This could be the kind of opportunity he would seek to give him his kicks."

"It would be nice if we knew who or what we're supposed to be looking for," said Snyder.

"It would be nice if the perp looked like a zombie, too, so he would stand out," Joe replied in a sarcastic tone. "But that's not the way it works. Chances are he looks perfectly normal. So, keep an eye peeled for any kind of odd behavior or some person who looks out of place."

Jenny's father looked across the street at the three men and then said something to his wife. After a moment, the two began walking across the street toward them.

"You know these people?" asked Jeff.

"Yeah, They're Jennifer Callaghan's parents," answered Snyder. "Jack and Carla."

Jack Callaghan was the owner of the local insurance agency, so he was well known around town. He was forty-five with a wiry five-foot-ten-inch frame. His once golden hair had thinned a little and was aging into a silvery blonde with more white through the temples. His wife, Carla, was also blonde, although she looked a few years younger than Jack. She was shorter than her husband by about five inches, and unlike some married women with children, she'd managed to keep a youthful looking figure. Both were dressed in dark funeral attire.

Jack stopped in front of Joe and Jeff. "I'm sorry, I saw you men standing over here, but I don't know who you are."

Snyder spoke up. "These two men were brought in to work your daughter's case."

"I'm very sorry for your loss," said Jeff.

"Thank you," replied Carla.

Jack looked at each of them, trying his best to suppress his anger and grief. Finally, he spoke. "One girl brutally murdered, and now the same thing has happened to my own daughter…" He stopped as his voice started to break.

"I can assure you were doing our best to find—"

Jack cut him off. "If you had done your best, my daughter would still be alive!" said Jack. Carla soothingly put her arm around her husband.

"Jack, honey," she said, "you can't blame them. Come on." She pulled gently on his arm and Jack started to turn. Then he stopped. Looking at the three men with fire in his eyes, he pointed his finger. "You get that son-of-a-bitch!

You hear me?" He paused a moment to regain his composure but his anger melted into grief, and all he could manage was little more than a whisper. "You get that son-of-a-bitch!" With that, he turned and walked back across the street leaving Carla there by herself.

"I'm sorry," she apologized. "It's been hard."

"I know," replied Snyder. He offered his arm. "Here. Why don't I walk you back across the street?"

Carla took Snyder's arm, and they walked to the lead car behind the van, the vehicle reserved for transporting immediate family to the cemetery. Snyder opened the door for her, and once she was seated, he gave her a nod and closed the door.

"Sensitive guy," remarked Jeff, dropping his cigarette and then stepping on it.

"Yeah, give him time," said Joe, still scanning the crowd, "He'll eventually become cynical and insensitive like one of us." Jeff snorted a laugh. "Suppose all three of us need to follow them out to the cemetery?"

"Probably not. Snyder and I can handle it. There will only be forty or fifty people there anyway. Not all that many go to the committal service."

"Fine. I'll meet you back in Storm Lake," said Joe. "I'll check out the church after everyone has left for the cemetery."

"Sounds good. See ya later." Jeff left Joe and walked to his car. He drove to the rear of the line behind the last car in the caravan. Deputy Snyder pulled his cruiser in front of the hearse to begin the police escort to the cemetery. Once the funeral director signaled to him, the cruiser's red and blue emergency lights began flashing and one by one the procession pulled away from the church.

Joe watched as all the cars followed the hearse down the street. After Jeff's car had passed by, he walked across the street and up the steps into the church. He gave it a walk through, trying to avoid being engaged in conversation by some of the people remaining inside. A few individuals sat in pews praying, while some others, primarily older men, gathered at the back near the doors softly conversing.

When he had seen enough and was satisfied there was no one suspicious lurking inside, he gave the men eyeing him a cordial nod and left. Pausing for a few moments at the top of the steps for a last look, he took them down to the sidewalk and walked to his car. He sat for a while contemplating everything he had witnessed. There was little to show for his time today, but that was nothing out of the ordinary. A lot of days were like this during the course of an investigation. He hoped Jeff and Snyder might luck into something, but he wasn't confident the cemetery would produce anything significant. He stuck the key in the ignition and fired up his Camaro. Time to roll.

Chapter Twelve

When Joe got back to Storm Lake, he found Destiny hard at work at her laptop putting the finishing touches on the criminal profile she was scheduled to present in two days. Thinking it was best to leave her alone, he sat in one of the interrogation rooms and began jotting down random thoughts in his notebook. He had found that by writing things down—facts, speculations, questions, random thoughts—he stimulated his mind and that resulted in deeper, more critical thinking. These thoughts often crystalized during his early morning jogs.

Jeff rolled in about forty minutes later and confirmed Joe's hunch. Nothing from the committal service was worth reporting. Jeff's topics of conversation seldom deviated from work, and his conversations primarily stayed focused on the task at hand. As a field agent for the Iowa Department of Criminal Investigation for almost twenty years, he was strictly business, but he did have a couple of weaknesses: cigarettes and food. In fact, he smoked like a chimney and ate what he wanted without regard for its health benefits or lack thereof. It was by the grace of God he hadn't suffered a heart attack and didn't weigh 300 pounds. Or maybe he inherited superior genes.

"The mother, I think her name is Carla, right?" he said.

"Yeah."

"Well, she seemed so gracious in spite of everything. She came over to Snyder and me at the cemetery and asked us if we would like to stay for lunch afterwards."

"That was kind of her," Destiny commented.

"You should have," said Joe.

"Snyder couldn't stay because he was on duty, and I didn't feel comfortable sticking around by myself. I mean, I didn't know anybody, and I didn't want people sitting across the table from me asking who I was, and did I know the young lady, and wasn't it tragic, and blah, blah, blah. And besides that, her husband didn't seem to be in the "'sure, have some lunch with us'" frame of mind. So, I thanked her for the invitation and told her I had to get back to Storm Lake. I feel kind of bad about it though, you know?"

"Lunch afterwards. It's the custom. You missed out, Jeff. Those church ladies can really cook!" said Joe.

"Speaking of lunch…" hinted Destiny looking at her watch.

"Where do you want to go?" asked Jeff.

"Well, I was—"

"I suppose you two are into those leaf and twig diets," Jeff teased.

"Healthy nutrition, you mean?" Destiny asked.

"Yeah."

"And what would you prefer, if I may ask?"

"Pizza. There's a place on West Milwaukee I haven't tried yet."

Destiny sighed but before she could register a complaint, Joe chimed in. "I wouldn't mind pizza." Joe and Jeff looked at each other and then simultaneously turned to Destiny for a response.

"Well, I guess I'm outnumbered," she acquiesced. "As long as I can get one with veggies, I guess it'll be all right."

"So, you don't eat meat?" asked Jeff.

"No." Then looking at Joe with a straight face said, "But occasionally I'll make an exception."

Joe wanted to smile but he suppressed it, and when Jeff looked at him quizzically, he gave him one of those it-beats-the-hell-out-of-me shrugs.

"So…are we agreed?"

"I guess. But next time, it's my choice," she asserted.

"Agreed," smiled Joe.

"Come on. I'll drive," said Jeff. Sense memory impulses in his brain were triggering the smell of pizza. He had the scent, and it was like setting the hounds loose on a fox.

On the ride over, Joe asked, "Do you know all the restaurants in Des Moines, too."

"Most," replied Jeff, and he was serious. "I can tell you the cuisine and rate for each one for you if you like."

"Don't you ever cook?"

"You've got to be kidding. Cooking rates right up there with having a colonoscopy."

"If I did that, I'd weight three hundred pounds," joked Joe.

"Good metabolism, no exercise, and a cast iron stomach," Jeff laughed, patting his belly. "That's all it takes."

They arrived at the pizza place and went inside. The smell of pizza filled the air and energized their appetites. Examining the noon buffet, Destiny was pleased when she saw they offered vegetarian as well as cheese-only pizzas.

They ordered and helped themselves to plates, napkins, and forks before starting through the buffet line.

After they sat down, the waitress brought both Joe and Jeff a glass of beer and Destiny a water with a slice of lemon. Joe had chosen a booth in the corner where they could have some degree of privacy. The noon crowd was beginning to thin out, and the booths on each side of them were now empty, their tables full of plates, glasses, napkins, and uneaten crusts.

Joe looked at his full plate. "I guess I can run this off in the next day or two."

"Yeah, me too," joked Jeff.

Joe laughed.

"What? You think I don't run?" kidded Jeff.

"In your dreams," quipped Joe.

"You got that right. Those dreams keep waking me up at night! Hey, this is pretty good!" Jeff said as he wolfed down a second mouthful.

Joe reached for his glass of beer and looked around to see if it was safe to speak. It wouldn't be good for any of the locals to overhear them talking about the case. He took a swig of beer and then spoke to Destiny in a subdued voice.

"How are you coming on the profile?"

"It's getting there. I told Sheriff Pollock to schedule a meeting for the day after tomorrow. I'll give the presentation then."

"Great," said Jeff as he reached for his beer.

Joe looked around. "Okay, let's discuss what we've got so far."

Destiny glanced quickly left and right. "All right."

"We have a double homicide. Circumstances are virtually the same, so we can presume it's the same killer or killers," stated Joe.

"I think that's a given," agreed Jeff.

"But my question is, do we have a serial killer or could it be something else?"

"What do you mean?" asked Jeff.

Joe picked up another slice of pizza. "Well, is it possible we are not dealing with a serial killer?"

"What are you thinking? Revenge killer? Thrill killer?" asked Jeff.

"What I'm wondering is this: Are we jumping the gun on labeling this the work of a serial killer? Technically, it takes three deaths with the same M.O. for a perp to be labeled a serial killer." Joe had been thinking about this ever since he read about the two cases online in the Marathon library.

"Thrill kills have been known to involve kidnapping, torture, and rape," suggested Jeff.

"I'm aware of that," said Destiny. "But posing them along a riverbank like he has doesn't fit. Thrill killers are usually young people. This person's trying to make a statement of some kind."

"That leaves revenge as a possible motive," stated Joe.

"There doesn't seem to be any evidence for revenge in either of these two cases," explained Jeff. "The families were interviewed and asked that question. No one was able to pinpoint someone with a grievance of some kind or a grudge against a family member."

"Back to square one," said Joe.

"Could this guy be a deviation, a fellow student or classmate who's watched too many horror pictures? Played too many gruesome video games?" asked Jeff. "Kids these days…"

"No. This is not the work of a teenager. It's definitely an adult," stated Destiny. "Each one was planned and executed by a mature mind."

"So, are you convinced, like the sheriff, that this is the work of a serial killer?" asked Joe.

"I wouldn't say that I'm convinced. But it certainly points in that direction. Given the nearly identical M.O.'s, it goes without saying the same person or persons are responsible for both of these deaths. So it's best to move forward on that assumption in case a serial killer has surfaced in this area. If we do have a serial killer on our hands, he is not going to stop until he gets caught. There will be more victims."

"I didn't think serial killers existed in rural areas like this one," said Jeff. "I've always read they typically operate in or around cities. You know, Jeffrey Dahmer in Milwaukee, the Son of Sam in New York."

Destiny took a sip of her water and then spoke. "That's true the majority of the time. That's because a city offers more opportunities, more prey for the predator, if you will. And the city offers the advantage of anonymity. It's easier for a person to remain inconspicuous because people function within tighter circles. For example, many city dwellers don't even know their neighbors. But for every pattern there are always anomalies."

"What kind of anomalies?" asked Joe.

"There are some serial killers who are mobile, like the 'I-5 Killer' or the 'I-70 killer', for instance. Both traveled interstate highways, stopping off in various cities to seek out victims, and then moving on to commit additional murders in other cities. In fact, the I-70 Killer never has been found. So, this case could be one of those anomalies."

Destiny paused for a moment to let that sink in. Then she added, "It's been speculated there are between twenty-five and fifty active serial killers operating in the country right now."

Suddenly she cleared her throat and stopped talking. Joe noticed why. A young, blonde-haired girl wearing the pizza franchise's uniform was pushing a cart over to the adjoining table and began clearing away dishes. The girl glanced and caught Joe's eye. She smiled, and he gave her smile and a nod back. They went on eating their pizza while she cleaned, waiting to resume their conversation once she was out of earshot. It wasn't long until she pushed the cart to another booth farther away and began the same cleaning procedure. Joe looked up and felt comfortable resuming their conversation.

"You said there are between twenty-five and fifty serial killers operating in the country right now? I remember hearing something like that at one point but didn't know if it was accurate."

"It is, according to the FBI," Destiny replied. "Frightening thought, isn't it?"

As they finished eating their lunches, the conversation drifted to more upbeat talk that ranged from the Chicago Cubs to the best way to marinate a steak. Driving back to the sheriff's office, Jeff looked over at Joe and asked, "What exactly led you to suspect David Eugene Burton, if you don't mind me asking."

"Not at all. The fact is…he screwed up. They all screw up sooner or later. That's how they get caught. But with him, it was a minor traffic accident that placed him in the area. It was not unlike the parking ticket that led to the arrest of Son of Sam. A minor, unrelated thing like that is what gave us the lead we needed, and it progressed from there. That's the kind of thing we hope for in these cases."

"So, luck had a lot to do with it," stated Jeff.

"Absolutely," said Joe. "And we're going to need a lot of luck on this one, too."

Chapter Thirteen

His steps were measured and deliberate as he moved silently across the floor from the kitchen through the living room, and down the hallway toward the bedroom. He strategically placed his foot down, transferring his weight to make each step soundless, moving slowly but surely forward in a kind of slow-motion ballet. With the exception of the kitchen and the bathroom, the floors of the house were covered with carpeting, and that helped muffle his footsteps. But the house was also seventy years old, and while it had been well cared for over the years, he couldn't assume the floors would not creak.

He crept to the door of the bedroom. It was halfway open, and the moonlight shining through the window provided enough light to illuminate the bed. The woman, Destiny Alexander, was asleep, her scantily clad body partially covered by a sheet. Pausing at the door, he stared at her for a moment. The house was so quiet and the night so still that he could hear her breathing, including an almost imperceptible little whistle emanating from her nose.

He reached out and cautiously pushed the door, hoping the hinges were well lubricated. His other hand reached into his pocket, pulling out a length of white cotton cord, which he twisted in his fists. With each precise step, he inched closer and closer. Finally, he was there, at the foot of the bed. He paused and observed her. Her head moved slightly, and he froze, holding his breath so as not to make his presence known. She stopped moving and continued breathing just as she had been, a breath in and out about every ten seconds. One more step and she was lying within arm's reach. His grip around the cord tightened with anticipation, and he slowly moved it down, closing in on her neck. And then he struck, pushing the cord hard against her throat. It shocked her into consciousness, and her eyes and mouth opened wide in terror!

"N-O-O-O-O-O-O!" screamed Joe, abruptly sitting up in bed, breathing heavily.

Destiny, jolted awake by his scream, sat up and turned on the bedside lamp. Reaching out to him she exclaimed, "My god, Joe! You're soaked with sweat! What in the—…"

"I'm sorry. I'm sorry. Bad dream." He bent over, his head dropping into his hands. "Another damned nightmare!" he said through clenched teeth. "I'm…I'm sorry."

"It's not your fault," Destiny consoled as she slid over and put her arms around him. "Are you going to be all right?"

He reached down and grabbed his T-shirt off the floor and began wiping the sweat from his face. "Yeah. I am. I'm sorry. I bet that scared the hell out of you, too, huh?"

"Here, let me," she said, taking the T-shirt from him and wiping his neck and back. "That must have been some dream."

"Yeah. It would make a Stephen King story look like *Bambi!*"

"Would it help if you told me about it?"

"No-no. No, I wouldn't wish my nightmare visions on anyone else."

"Do you have them often?"

"Not every night. But it's like a Catch-22 situation. If I take my pills, I can't sleep. And if I don't take them, sometimes I have nightmares." He reached for a bottle of water on the nightstand and took a drink.

"So, you didn't take them?" she asked.

"Not all of them. Damned side effects are as bad having the disease. It's like you're trading one for the other."

She kissed his shoulder. "Is there anything I can get you?"

"How about a new mind?"

"I don't think so. I kind of like the one you have."

"It's broken."

76

"Then, we'll just have to fix it."

"Well..."

"When we get back to Chicago, you should talk with your doctor. See if he can put you on a different medication so you don't have to deal with these side effects."

"Yeah."

"Come on, let's try to get some sleep. You want me to leave the light on?"

"Will it keep the boogie man away?" he joked.

She smiled, knowing he would be all right since his sense of humor was still intact. "No, dear. But I will. Come here."

***

The next morning, Joe slipped out of bed without waking Destiny. He put on his jogging clothes, exited the house and walked down the driveway. Melissa was leaning against a large maple tree in the front yard.

"You're late," she admonished. "I was about ready to give up on you."

"Yeah, I had a late night."

"I'll bet."

"What do you mean by that?"

Melissa answered with naughty eyes. Joe ignored her, and they began to jog side-by-side north toward the main street.

"You think you'll catch the guy who killed those girls?"

"I hope so."

"So do I. Because my dad's being a real dipshit."

"Dipshit?" Joe asked.

"Yeah."

"What do you mean he's being a dipshit?"

"He's become the warden of my prison," she complained. "I can't go anywhere, can't do anything. Except for the Internet, I may as well be in solitary confinement. Thank god he hasn't taken that away yet."

"You can't blame him for being cautious."

Melissa quickened her pace, causing Joe to speed up.

"Can I ask you a question?"

"Uh…I suppose."

"Do you go for younger women?"

"Excuse me?"

"Do you go for younger women?" she repeated.

He knew where she was going with that question, so he asked, "You mean, like you?"

"Maybe."

"You know, if you were my kid, I'd put you over my knee."

She smiled seductively. "Mm. I might like that. But you didn't answer my question."

Joe looked at her, "That's right, I didn't."

"You're being evasive."

"Yeah, I am."

"How come?"

"Can I ask you a question?" Joe asked.

"I suppose," she said, emulating his response.

"Are you really this horny or do you just like messing with people's minds?"

He could see she was surprised by how blunt his question was. So, he decided to call her bluff.

"Look, would you really want to get it on with a guy your dad's age?"

Melissa stopped jogging and Joe turned back to her. Her face had melted, and the sexy facade was gone. Standing there was a vulnerable eighteen-year-old girl.

"Well…no."

"Good. So why don't you cut all the sexual innuendo crap, and try acting like an adult. Because what you're doing isn't funny."

"Okay."

"Someday that kind of talk with the wrong guy will get you in some deep shit. And I would hate to see you beaten up, raped, or even worse. I've seen it happen, and I can tell you the results aren't pretty."

Silence.

It appeared he had left Melissa in a state of shock. She was completely taken aback by Joe's response. Finally, he broke the silence. "Come on, let's finish our run."

She matched his pace but neither of them spoke. He could hear her sniff once in a while, but he didn't check to see if she was crying. He could see that she had when they stopped running. Joe noticed a shiny red Honda Civic was sitting in Melissa's driveway.

"Something new?" Joe asked.

"What do you think?"

"Yours?"

"Yeah. My dad got it for me."

"The warden, you mean?"

"Well..."

"Congratulations. I'll bet you enjoy it. Once you're out on parole, that is," Joe said as he tried to use a little humor to play down the rebuke he gave her earlier. It made her smile.

"Maybe I'll give you a ride one of these days."

He recognized the possible double entendre, but it seemed like an innocent remark so he let it slide. "Drive with care. And make sure you wear that seatbelt."

"I will," she said. "And thanks for, you know.....I'm not mad at you or anything. I guess I sorta deserved it."

Before he could answer, she gave him a peck on the cheek and ran into the house.

For god sakes, he thought as he quickly looked around to see if anyone was watching. Thankfully, no one was. He took in a deep breath and let it out.

As he walked back to his house, he noticed Destiny's car was gone. When he opened the door and went inside, he smelled fresh coffee. There was a note on the table that read, *Thanks for last night! Coffee is made. I have to prep for my presentation this morning. See you later! Love you, Destiny.* He held it for a few moments and then read it again. The texture of the paper felt slick in his hand, and he ran his finger over her name. After a moment, he poured himself a cup of coffee, and carried it along with the note into the bedroom. He saw she had made the bed and folded his clothes. The sight of it made him smile at her thoughtfulness. Placing the note on the chest of drawers, he sat on the bed drinking his coffee and thinking about last night. Looking up, he thought he heard the shower calling his name. He picked up his watch and confirmed he was running late.

Chapter Fourteen

L ater that morning, Joe, Jeff, Sheriff Pollock and his senior deputies, Matt Wilson, Jon Taylor, and Phil Barnes, were standing around a table in a conference room drinking coffee and comparing notes about the two murders. A laptop was set up at the head of the table and an image of the Chicago skyline graced the screen overhead.

Destiny opened the door and walked to the head of the table. Sheriff Pollock announced, "If you'll all take a seat, we can get started." The deputies moved to their respective seats and sat down.

"By now, you all know Destiny Alexander, a criminal investigative analyst, better known to most of us as a criminal profiler. She was brought in by the Department of Criminal Investigation to help us on this case, and we're lucky to have her with us. Before we proceed, I should remind you this information is confidential and none of what you are about to hear can leave this room. Understood?"

Various mumbled notes of agreement and head nods came from the men as Pollock moved to one of the chairs and sat down next to Deputy Taylor.

"Thank you, Sheriff," Destiny said, acknowledging each of them with a look. "Sheriff Pollock will determine if and when to inform the media about this."

With a few strokes of the keyboard, an image from her computer appeared on the screen above and behind her. "I have to tell you that I'm pleased the county has this kind of technology. It makes my presentation much easier."

"Taxpayer money well spent," responded Pollock.

The sheriff and his deputies each produced small notepads and prepared to take notes.

"I'd like to go over this profile with you," she began. "Please keep in mind that a profile is not what you have been led to believe on television. Simply put, a criminal profile provides an outline to help focus the investigation. It's not definitive. One other thing. Feel free to ask questions as I move through this, okay?"

She touched a key on her laptop and an image with the words "Organized Offender" appeared on the screen.

"The man we are dealing with here exhibits characteristics of an organized offender. In other words, he plans and chooses his victims ahead of time, possibly stalking them to determine their vulnerability. He will often wait patiently until the moment is right before acting."

Once again, she touched the keyboard, and images of Ted Bundy and John Wayne Gacy appeared.

"Ted Bundy and John Wayne Gacy are two well-known examples of organized serial killers. It's possible for an organized serial killer to transition into a disorganized killer or vice versa, but at this time our perpetrator is highly organized."

Destiny reached for the keyboard, pushed a key, and the screen changed to a heading of "Characteristics" with a numbered list beneath it.

"What we are dealing with is a white male between the ages of twenty-five and thirty-five. He has average to above-average intelligence and has either attended college or attained a degree. He would appear normal to anyone encountering him. He is more than likely married or in a relationship of some kind. He is mobile, probably drives a nice car. He'll be following the news accounts of his exploits. He functions primarily as a day person, even though he commits these crimes at night. His signature is leaving the dead girls nude and posed along a riverbank, so we have to assume he has intimate knowledge of the river and surrounding area. The lack of any forensic evidence shows he is either well read on the subject or has had some law enforcement training. He wants his victims found as he believes he is making a statement by posing them the way he does."

She paused and looked around the room. "Are there any questions?"

Deputy Taylor was the first to speak up. "Do you think he has killed elsewhere and has recently moved to this area?"

"I can answer that," said Jeff. "We contacted the FBI, and they ran the M.O. through VICAP. There weren't any matches."

Destiny added, "It's possible that he has worked his way up to committing murder from other crimes like rape and assault. These could be his first two victims."

"You said he's making a statement," said Pollock. "What kind of statement?"

"I have no way of knowing that. But he definitely wants his victims found," she replied. "And given the nudity and the posing, there is a definite sexual connection of some kind. The majority of the Hillside Stranglers' victims were found nude in and around Los Angeles. But as far as the psychology of this killer, you'd have to ask a psychiatrist."

"Could he simply be screwing around with law enforcement personnel?" asked Wilson.

"Yes. It's not unusual for this type of killer to taunt police in some way. Dennis Rader, the BTK killer in Kansas, sent letters to law enforcement as well as the newspapers. But so far, there have been no such communications."

Joe had been listening intently but was not taking any notes. He was well read on serial killers and knew all about the characteristics of organized killers. Most of what Destiny was presenting was nothing new to him. Finally, he spoke.

"The first girl...there was a phone call, right?"

Pollock responded, "Anonymous call to nine-one-one from a burner phone near Albert City. Male voice. Short message. We have it on tape."

"We sent a tape of the call to Des Moines for voice analysis. So, if another call comes in, it may be possible to do a voice match," Jeff interjected.

"What was the nature of the call?" pressed Joe.

"The caller stated he had a tip," Pollock explained, "and he said, and I quote: 'The river holds the body near the Grove of Linn.'"

"That was it?"

"Yeah. Then he hung up. At first we thought it was a crank call, but we didn't have any other leads so we began searching the river near Linn Grove.

I'll be damned if the body wasn't found the next afternoon."

"The river holds the body near the Grove of Linn," Joe repeated. "That was a rather odd, poetic hint, don't you think?"

"I searched for it all over the internet thinking it may have been a quote from a book or something. If it was, Google didn't find it," explained Jeff.

"It's a strange thing to say," added Destiny. "Maybe it didn't have any significance in that way. Maybe he didn't think his victim had been found in a sufficient amount of time and needed to provide a hint about where the body was."

"Maybe he didn't want the body to decompose," offered Deputy Barnes. "Maybe he wanted her to be found while she was still recognizable."

"Or attractive," added Destiny.

"That could also mean their identities were important to him in some way," said Jeff.

"I thought we checked that out," said Pollock. "We'd better look at that aspect again."

"There's no logical reason someone would make such a call from a burner phone twenty miles away from the scene unless he was trying to disguise his location," Joe pointed out.

"He took pains to remain anonymous," said Pollock.

"Do you think this guy is someone who's always lived in this area and who's progressed from torturing animals to killing humans?" asked Wilson.

"There's no way to know that for sure," replied Destiny. "But it may be worthwhile to investigate any complaints of animal abuse. You're right about progression, though. It can start with abusing animals, then move on to the killing of animals. It doesn't take much to make the leap from killing animals to killing humans. We know Jeffrey Dahmer started out that way."

"You said he appears normal," said Barnes.

"Yes," Destiny replied. "He could look like any of you sitting in this room."

"Jesus," mumbled Pollock.

"Great," said Barnes.

The deputies looked around at each other, and after seeing the looks on their faces, Destiny intervened. "Don't think of it as hopeless. Let the profile help you in narrowing the range of suspects. Use the characteristics I've outlined for you."

Joe chimed in. "It's going to take time and some good police work and a little luck. That's what it took to nail David Eugene Burton. That's what it'll take to get this guy, too. But we'll get him."

After a few more questions, the meeting broke and the deputies dispersed. Sheriff Pollock thanked Destiny for the presentation, and he and Jeff adjourned to his office for a conference call they had scheduled with the Jay Thompson, Jeff's supervisor at the Department of Criminal Investigation.

Later that morning, Joe and Destiny were looking over 8" X 10" color photos on a table in her makeshift office. The two of them made an interesting duo when it came to working on an investigation. She was highly analytical while Joe was highly intuitive. In their previous roles on the Burton case, they found they worked well together. They also found they were capable of annoying the hell out of one another.

Tina Olson's senior picture, Jenny Callaghan in a cheerleading outfit, and crime scene photos were spread over the desk. Joe was comparing photographs of the two girls' abandoned cars. Then he looked at Destiny.

"Both cars stopped on county roads. Why would they stop?"

"They both knew the perpetrator?"

"But how would they recognize someone at night? His car?"

"Maybe his car was parked alongside the road and he flagged them down so they stopped to help. Or maybe he was hitchhiking and they both recognized him."

"Maybe," acknowledged Joe.

"The motive couldn't have been robbery," Destiny said. "Both of the girls' purses contained money and debit cards."

Joe thought for a moment and was struck by an idea. "Do you have photos of the inside of both Jenny and Tina's cars?"

Destiny started shuffling through photos. "Uh, yeah. Just a second." She found photos of the cars and handed them to him. "Here."

He took them from her and began scrutinizing each one.

"God, don't girls ever clean out their cars?" he asked as he viewed the messy interiors.

Destiny didn't comment, but instead pointed to each photo.

"Look. Here and here. See. Purses and wallets."

She paused as she thought about it. After a moment, she said, "That's odd."

"What is?"

"Nothing was taken but both wallets are out of their respective purses. They should be inside."

"Why would they both be out?" asked Joe.

"I don't know. Even if a purse tips over, a zipper or a clasp should keep everything from spilling out."

"Hand me the magnifying glass."

Destiny complied and Joe began studying the photo of Tina Olson's car. "Hmm."

"What is it?"

"Is there another photo of this from a different angle?" asked Joe.

"Yeah…uh…right here," said Destiny, handing him another photo.

Joe looked at it under the magnifying glass and declared, "It looks like…"

"What?"

"A driver's license."

He picked up the other photo of Jenny Callaghan's car and began looking at it. "I don't see one here."

Destiny handed him another photo. "Here's another shot."

He took it from her and began scrutinizing the photo.

"Maybe her driver's license is still in her wallet," Destiny suggested.

"Maybe." He examined some of the contents on the floor of the car. "That looks like it might be a document of some kind. The glove compartment's open."

"Wait a minute!" she said in a moment of inspiration. "Here's a shot from outside the car."

As he slid it in front of him, her finger pointed to something on the asphalt road. "Here's something!"

Joe looked closely but the resolution was not good enough to determine what the object was.

"Can't tell," he said. "Wait. What's the report say?"

Destiny pulled the report from the file and began reading. "Uh...let see...Here it is. Ah! *Victim's driver's license was found on the road next to the car.*"

"Does the list mention anything about an insurance card or the car registration?"

Destiny looked through the long list of items found inside the car. "Let's see...uh...yes! On the floor...insurance card...and vehicle registration. Both!"

"Damn!" he exclaimed, hitting his fist on the table.

Destiny turned to Joe and said, "Omigod. It's a cop."

He looked up at Destiny. "It's a cop."

"That's right. You'd pull over for a police officer. And what's the first thing the officer asks for when he comes up to your window?"

"Driver's license, registration, and proof of insurance. Was there anything in addition to the driver's license for Tina Olson?"

"Let me look." She went through the list of items from Tina Olson's car. "No, only the driver's license."

"Maybe he didn't ask for the rest of it. Maybe she didn't know enough to produce it beforehand," said Joe, leaning forward in his chair.

"And a cop would know all about forensic evidence," Destiny added. "We'd better take this to the sheriff."

Sheriff Pollock was sitting in his chair looking across the desk at Joe and Destiny. He took a sip from an oversized coffee mug with "World's Best Grandpa" imprinted on the side.

"Are you trying to tell me the killer is one of my own deputies?"

"Not necessarily," said Destiny.

"No?"

"It could be a state patrolman or—" Joe started to explain.

Pollock cut him off mid-sentence. "And you're basing this on a couple of drivers licenses."

"Isn't that enough? Look, they both voluntarily stopped alongside the road. Why? They had their driver's licenses out of their wallets. Why? They were both handcuffed and apparently subdued with pepper spray."

"Anybody can buy that stuff," said Pollock argumentatively.

That caused Joe to blow his cool. He suddenly rose from his chair, a move that took Pollock by surprise.

"Jesus Christ! Didn't your people check the crime scenes for parallel evidence?"

Pollock stood and handed it right back. "Don't get all uppity with me, god damnit! We're not a bunch of know-nothing rednecks around here!"

"That's not what I—"

Again, Pollock interrupted, "Maybe they missed something, okay. It happens. I have good men working on this, and I'll check with them. But I can add two and two, you know. And in my opinion, what you're saying is not equaling four."

"Then get out your calculator because we have to subtract nine deputies from the suspect list."

"We need something called evidence if I'm not mistaken," growled Pollock. "They cataloged over sixty items in the Callaghan car and over a hundred items in the Olson car. It looked like Tina Olson used her back seat as a trash barrel. And driver's licenses were only part of all the stuff found. That's pretty flimsy evidence to accuse one of my deputies, don't you think?"

"Okay," he said, taking a deep breath, "I'm sorry I got a little intense. There was no offense intended. But let's look at this in a rational way, all right?"

Destiny stepped in, attempting to salvage the situation with a little charm. "Look, Sheriff, if I can explain. All we need to do is to eliminate your deputies so we can move on. The question we need to answer is who had opportunity. That's all we need to know right now. Is it possible you can pinpoint where each of your deputies happened to be at the time of the abductions?"

"I suppose," answered Pollock, starting to cool down some. "They call in at regular intervals, write citations, take calls to investigate…yeah, we could do that."

Joe could sense her charm was beginning to work and she was beginning to win him over. She continued, "If you could create timelines for all of your deputies, I can work with you to see if any of your men fit the profile. If nothing else, it's a starting point. Because right now we have nothing to go on."

Pollock thought for a moment. "All right...All right, I'll do it so I can eliminate my men. I know these guys. Hell, I hired most of them, and I don't like the idea of treating them as suspects."

"I know how you feel about loyalty, and that's an admirable thing. I think they'll all come up clean, but wouldn't you agree it would be negligent not to do it, given the circumstances?"

Reaching for his coffee cup, he looked at her and then glanced over at Joe. "Yeah, you're probably right."

They left Pollock's office, and as they were walking down the hall, Joe said, "Honey rather than vinegar, right?"

"Catches 'em every time."

Chapter Fifteen

Saturday afternoon, Joe was at the house. The garage door was up and so was the hood of his Camaro. He was reinstalling the K&N air filter after rinsing the dirt out of it. While he didn't work on cars as much as he would like, he still got his hands dirty on occasion. You can't work on new cars like you can the old ones. You don't fix things anymore, you replace them. You don't tinker with a car using wrenches and screwdrivers these days. Today you tweak a car's performance by employing a computer. That takes most of the fun out of it. Someday he thought he would buy a project or build something from scratch, but living in an apartment in the city made that next to impossible. He never lost his desire to work on cars, and he'd owned some beauties over the years. Despite the frustration associated with working on cars, he always seemed to be happiest when he had a wrench in his hand and a project to work on.

Just as he finished tightening the clamp on the air filter, he heard a vehicle pull into the driveway. Looking around the hood, he saw an old seventies C10 Chevy pickup pull to a stop. Tucker stepped out followed by a young boy. Joe stuck the screwdriver in his back pocket and began wiping his hands on a grease rag as the boy ran up to him.

"Well, who are you?" Joe asked.

"Jimmy," was his reply as he began looking over the car.

"This is my boy," said Tucker. "Now, don't touch the car, okay?"

"Okay."

"I thought you were supposed to be on duty," said Joe.

"Had a root canal done this morning so I took the day off."

"Fun, aren't they?"

"Sure are." Then taking a look at the Camaro's engine bay he blurted out, "Holy shit! This thing has a supercharger?"

"Yup. A little something I bolted on for fun." Seeing Jimmy straining to see the engine, Joe picked him up. "Here you go. What do you think?"

"Holy shit," said Jimmy, imitating his father's reaction.

"Jimmy!" Tucker admonished.

Joe laughed. "Pretty cool, huh?"

"Yeah, pretty cool!" Jimmy parroted back.

Joe put Jimmy down and looked at Tucker. "So, what's up?"

"I've been thinking."

"Yeah?"

"There weren't any tracks where either of those girls were found."

"Tire tracks, you mean?"

"Tire tracks or footprints. Seems odd, doesn't it? The only tire tracks at the scene were made by the police cruisers. There weren't any footprints found at the first scene, either. None on the shore and none on the road. And the only footprints we found at the second scene were on the shoreline, and they belonged to the two boys."

"Where are you going with this?"

"I'm thinking the bodies might have been brought to the scenes by boat. The river would have washed away any signs of a boat ever having been there. It hasn't rained for almost a month so the ground away from the shoreline is hard and wouldn't leave good prints. But even if there were a few footprints near the bodies, the perp could brush any indications away with a branch or something."

Joe thought for a minute as he considered the possibility. *Tucker may be on to something.* "Good thinking. So, you believe it could be someone who knows the river, maybe lives along the water?"

"They wouldn't necessarily have to live there. You see, the river is good for cat fishing. I know. I've fished there myself. There are a lot of places I could launch my boat from and never be seen, especially at night."

"So, what do you think ought to be done?"

"Well," said Tucker, pausing to rub his jaw, "somebody ought to be checking the opposite bank for tire marks and footprints. Gotta launch a boat from somewhere. Chances are he didn't take the bodies all that far up or downstream."

"Have you mentioned this to the sheriff?"

"No, I just thought of it while I was sitting in the dentist's chair all gassed up."

"Maybe you should get gassed up more often," joked Joe as he looked at his watch. "I've got three hours before I have to be in Storm Lake. You think your boy might like a trip to the river?" At that moment his cell phone rang.

"Joe Erickson," he answered. It was Jeff.

"We just got a missing persons report," Jeff said. "A teenage girl in Rembrandt has been reported missing by her mother. We're driving there now."

"What's the address?" asked Joe.

"Two ten North First Avenue. You can't miss it. You can't get lost in Rembrandt."

"I know. I'll meet you there in twenty minutes."

Joe ended the call and turned to Tucker.

"Looks like it'll have to wait. A girl in Rembrandt has gone missing."

Chapter Sixteen

Rembrandt was another one of those small Iowa towns like Marathon that had become a casualty of progress. In the 1940's and 50's small farms of 160 acres known as quarter sections were the standard-sized farms. But starting in the 1960's with the advent of bigger, more powerful machinery, farmers acquired larger farms, which in turn were acquired by even larger farms. A single farmer could now do the work that four or five farmers had done a decade or so earlier. Fewer farmers meant fewer families and fewer children, and with fewer children it was no longer feasible to sustain a school in a small town. Schools were forced to consolidate to form larger schools in neighboring communities. When a school moved away, it devastated a town's economy. Stores closed because the people who used to support local businesses were gone. Over a period of forty years, the once bustling main streets of small towns were reduced to little more than a tavern, a post office, and a grain elevator.

As Joe turned onto First Avenue and passed Main Street in Rembrandt, he could see two police cruisers and Jeff's sedan parked at the address they'd been given. He parked and got out. A few neighbors had gathered on the lawn and in the street, drawn to the home by the arrival of the police.

The white turn-of-the-century house with its large wrap-around porch was the residence of Chuck and Rita Van Allen. Chuck worked as a long-haul trucker who was only home a couple of days a week. The rest of the time he was on the road driving a semi back and forth to the West Coast. Rita worked as a clerk in a grocery store in Storm Lake.

Sheriff Pollock was questioning Rita, an emotional mess. She was a small, thin woman in her early forties with sharp features and auburn hair that was a couple of shades too dark to look natural. She sat at the dining room table, dabbing her eyes and blowing her nose into a handkerchief while Jeff, Destiny, and Deputy Wilson took notes.

"I know this is difficult," said Pollock, "but the best—"

"How much longer are you going to let this go on?" she interrupted, wiping her eyes.

"Ma'am, we don't know for sure she's been abducted. That's why—"

Again, she interrupted him. "What's it gonna take? Another body?"

"Ma'am, please."

"I don't want to be the mother of a victim," she said as she started sobbing.

"We need your help if—"

"She's such a sweet girl, such a sweet girl. How could anyone—"

This time Pollock interrupted her, his frustration beginning to show.

"Mrs. Van Allen, you have to help us do our jobs."

Her sister, Meg McElroy, a somewhat younger, shorter, and rounder version of Rita, entered from the kitchen carrying a glass of water.

"Here, honey. Here," she said as she handed Rita the glass.

Then she held out a light blue pill. "I want you to take this. It'll make you feel better."

"I don't want to—"

"Take it. It's one of my valiums. It'll help."

Rita rose from her chair. "I think I'm going to vomit."

It was like the parting of the Red Sea. Immediately, everyone backed away to give her space as she rushed out of the room with Meg trailing after her.

"I need some air," sighed Destiny. "If you'll excuse me."

"I'll join you," said Jeff as he reached in his pocket for a pack of cigarettes.

Joe was walking up the sidewalk as Destiny and Jeff walked down the porch steps. As soon as they met on the lawn, Jeff's Zippo lighter clicked as he lit his cigarette and looked at Joe. "The girl's the same approximate age as the previous victims." Jeff was interrupted when his cell phone rang. "Sorry, I have to take this," he said and walked out into the street for some privacy.

Joe looked at Destiny. "What's the story?"

"Her name is Suzanne Van Allen, eighteen, hasn't been seen since early last evening. She told her mother she was spending the night with a friend but she never showed. Her mother found out this afternoon and called the police. There's a deputy interviewing the girl's friend right now."

"She driving a car?" asked Joe.

"Yeah. A white Dodge Challenger. There's a BOLO out on the car."

"What do you think?"

"The location isn't consistent with the other two victims. There's no river around here. But it's always possible he may have expanded his range and taken advantage of an opportunity."

"Before I got the call, Tucker dropped by to see me. I think he may be on to something. He thinks the perp may have used a boat to transport the bodies to the crime scenes."

"Deputy Tucker?" Destiny said with an inordinate amount of concern in her voice. Joe picked up on it.

"Yeah. Why?"

"The sheriff and I finished running checks on all the deputies…"

"And?"

"He's the only deputy who had opportunity. So, I started putting together a profile on him."

"Don't tell me…"

"Certain elements fit. I haven't dug any deeper but—"

She stopped talking when she saw Sheriff Pollock and Deputy Wilson quickly exit the house, bound down the porch steps, and get into their cruisers.

Jeff, still holding his cell phone, ran over to them. "Get ready to roll. They've spotted the girl's car in a parking lot at the SouthSide Motel in Spencer."

"Come on," Joe said to Destiny.

Sheriff Pollock pulled out first, followed by Deputy Wilson, Jeff, and then Joe. With emergency lights flashing on the two cruisers, they sped up Highway 71, the main link between Storm Lake and Spencer.

"Why would the car be at a motel? It doesn't make sense."

"No, it doesn't," said Joe. "And this stuff about Tucker doesn't make sense either. Why would he make a point to talk to me about elements of the case if he was the perp?"

"To throw you off?"

"I don't think so. He doesn't strike me as cunning and devious."

Rolling at seventy-five miles per hour, twenty miles over the posted speed limit, it didn't take them long to reach the city limits.

The two-story SouthSide Motel was located on the south side of town, just off the highway. They drove onto the access road leading to the motel, and a Spencer police officer waved them into an adjacent lot where members of the Spencer police force had gathered.

"Who's in charge here?" asked Pollock.

A large-framed, prematurely gray-haired man of forty-five stepped to Pollock.

"I am," he said. "Bill Rousch."

"Vince Pollock. What have you got?"

"We have the white Dodge Charger you're looking for over there." He pointed toward the car parked in the motel lot. "It was driven by a man who registered last evening. He's in room seventeen."

"Anyone go in or out while you were here?"

"Not as far as we know. One of my officers listened at the door and heard the television, so we assume someone is in there. What do you want to do?"

"None of this fits the perp's M.O., Sheriff," offered Destiny.

"Listen," said Joe. "Why don't you let me pose as the manager? That way I can knock on the door and get a look."

"We don't know if he's armed," replied Pollock. "What if he has the girl tied up in there and you spook him?"

"He'll have no reason to suspect the manager," reasoned Joe. "I can ask about the air conditioning. Maybe do a check."

"Too risky." He turned to Rousch. "What do you think?"

"It's your call."

"We're better off with the element of surprise. Break the door in."

"You heard the man," said Rousch to his officers. "Break the door in."

Pollock's decision infuriated Joe. He glanced at Destiny and shook his head. He couldn't believe the Sheriff would refuse a tactical approach that made more sense.

The Spencer police officers moved silently over to the room. Their guns were out of their holsters now, and they were poised to enter. A burly officer named Lutz walked up to the door with a battering ram and positioned himself to breach the door. He looked at Rousch who gave him a nod.

Lutz swung the battering ram, striking the door. It made a loud crunching noise as the door splintered and flew open. Two officers along with Sergeant Rousch entered, guns drawn and ready to use them if necessary.

"Police! Freeze!"

A naked young woman screamed and jumped off the young man she was having sex with. She instinctively covered herself with a sheet.

"Freeze!" yelled Rousch.

"What the......" was all the young man could get out as he froze, horrified by the intrusion.

An officer looked in the bathroom and yelled, "Clear!"

At that point Sheriff Pollock and Deputy Wilson came through the door.

"Suzanne Van Allen?" asked Rousch in a demanding voice.

"Yes," answered the girl as her fright began turning to anger.

"Who's this?" asked Rousch, indicating the young man.

"He's my boyfriend!"

"What's your name?"

"Uh, I'm...Sean McCarthy," the boyfriend said timidly.

After a moment, the officers lowered their service weapons, realizing the two kids were not a threat. The room smelled of sex, and they looked at each other, not knowing quite how to proceed.

"Have you seen enough yet?" asked Suzanne indignantly.

"All right. Everybody out," Rousch said with a mixture of anger and disgust in his voice.

Suzanne pulled hard at the sheet to cover more of her body. As the officers began filing out of the room, she yelled, "I'm eighteen years old! So is he! We have a right to fuck if we want to!"

Lutz, still holding the battering ram, looked at a fellow officer and said, "She's got a point."

"Could be a lawsuit over this," he said in reply.

"Let's hope not."

Deputy Wilson and Sheriff Pollock were the last to leave. As Wilson tried to close what was left of the door, Suzanne screamed, "You assholes!"

Wilson looked at Pollock, and mimicking Rita Van Allen, he said, "She's such a sweet girl."

"Knock it off," was Pollock's response. He was in no mood for humor after this debacle, knowing that blame would land square in his lap. He walked up to where Jeff, Destiny, and Joe were standing.

"God damned false alarm," he muttered.

Joe's anger was supplanted by a feeling of gratification at Pollock's rashness and poor judgment. He had to suppress a smile as he looked the man in the face. But he couldn't resist a little dig.

"Maybe the manager should have tried knocking," he said calmly.

As the sheriff walked to his car, the hotel manager walked over and inspected the broken door. Seeing it was beyond repair, he walked up to Rousch and demanded, "Hey! Who's going to pay for this door?"

Joe and Destiny slid into the Camaro. They were both annoyed by the embarrassing scene at the motel. It was a ninety-degree day and the sun made the interior of the car almost unbearable, and that did little to help their temperaments.

Joe chuckled incredulously, "That guy is a piece of work."

"Ignore him. He doesn't like you."

"I've noticed."

"Oh, for god sake," begged Destiny, fanning herself. "Turn on the air conditioning. I'm roasting in here."

"I was just waiting for you to turn medium rare."

"I'm already fried on the outside and pink on the inside! Now turn on the freakin' air conditioning!"

"All right, already," Joe said. He turned the key and the engine rumbled to life. Reaching for the A/C controls, he turned the fan up to maximum and revved the engine a couple of times. After a few moments cool air blew from the vents.

"Oh, that's much better," she sighed.

"What is it with women, anyway? They complain when they're too cold and they get bitchy when they're too hot."

"And you don't?"

"No, we do something about it." She gave him the evil eye in response. On any given day, most guys would have realized that some things are better left unsaid. Today, he wasn't one of those guys.

When Destiny had buckled her seatbelt, he put the car in gear, and after they drove out the parking lot, his foot hit the accelerator and squealed the rear tires a bit as they drove onto the access road. Neither spoke until Joe turned onto the highway and had shifted the Camaro into fifth gear.

"All right, tell me about Tucker."

"All right," she sighed. "He patrols the area adjacent to where the abductions occurred. And he had a sixty-minute block of time unaccounted for on each night the abductions took place."

"Okay, he may be able to explain his whereabouts during those times, but for the sake of argument let's agree that he had opportunity. But you said something about his profile?"

"He possesses characteristics of an organized offender. He's socially competent, average to above average intelligence. He's employed in a skilled position, and he follows crime reports in the media."

"How do you know that?"

"The sheriff told me he's always carrying around a newspaper, and he's always talking about crimes that appear in news articles."

"Oh. Okay. Go on," said Joe.

"Well, needless to say, I haven't been able to do any research into sexual aberrations or family history. That won't be easy, and it will take some time to do that."

"Anything that doesn't fit?"

"Most organized offenders tend to be married or in a relationship, and they tend to drive nice cars. He lives with his young son and drives an old pickup. But those may be anomalies."

"This could fit a lot of people, even me."

"Oh, so you have a young son I don't know about?"

That annoyed him further and he gave her a look saying, "It's improbable but not impossible."

"I said this is all preliminary until I can do further research. Jesus, what's gotten into you?" she said defensively.

Joe ignored her question and asked, "How long will it take?"

"Two or three days. Answer my question."

"He doesn't feel right to me," Joe said.

"Feel right? Are you psychic now or some—"

"I don't think he did it," Joe snapped.

"Maybe he didn't. But right now, it's the most promising thing we've got!" she snapped back.

"Hey, I'm just voicing my opinion. What the hell's the problem?"

"The problem is your tone."

"My tone?"

"Yes, your tone."

"Really? Have you considered your tone?"

She paused for a moment and then said, "Take me to Storm Lake."

"Storm Lake. Why?"

"Because you're unfit for human companionship."

"Oh, for…" Then he remembered what Will Rogers once said. *Never miss a good chance to shut up.* It was good advice. Especially now. Then there was silence. It was a long forty-minute drive back to Storm Lake.

Chapter Seventeen

The antique clock on the wall chimed twelve times and Joe was once again suffering from insomnia. All alone tonight, he stood in the kitchen, lit only by the light coming in through the window over the sink. He poured himself a glass of Merlot from his father's stock. His doctor had offered to write him a prescription to help him sleep, but he refused. The idea of using a drug was not an option because he feared he could become addicted to it. It was bad enough he had to take medication for his depression. The thought of drinking a glass of wine was appealing because it might help him feel drowsy enough to nod off for a few hours even though he had read there was evidence to the contrary. Besides, he wasn't about to let all that good wine go to waste. After re-corking the bottle, he lifted the glass to his lips, and the first sip stimulated his taste buds and palate in a most pleasing way.

Carrying the glass into the living room, he stood next to the window. It faced the street, and the glow from the streetlight reflected off Joe's brooding face and into the windowpane. His eyes refocused from the street to his own ghostly image. He gazed upon his face, tracing the lines, studying the intensity of his eyes, and thinking about the tiff he had with Destiny that afternoon.

"Erickson, you're such an asshole!" he said to his reflection. It didn't answer back. A good thing. If it had, he would have punched it because what he saw pissed him off.

The more he thought about his prickly behavior that afternoon, the worse he felt. True, she hadn't helped matters any, but why had he reacted the way he did? He knew better. The suppression of emotions is something that you learn early on in police work. It works as a survival mechanism because the stress of police work coupled with the horrific acts of violence encountered on the job can take a psychological toll. That's why some cops he had known had problems releasing those pent-up feelings. And it's also why many of his experienced colleagues had typically resorted to using alcohol as a form of self-medication. Unfortunately, a few of them had allowed those pent-up feelings to evolve into demons that eventually drove them to tragic ends. But many in law enforcement succeeded in discovering their own unique outlets for purging those feelings. Hobbies, families, and community involvement could often provide a release and a way to distance a person from the job. Joe believed that adhering to his running regimen had kept him from becoming a functioning alcoholic like some of his colleagues. But it was not quite enough to prevent his nervous breakdown or as his doctor called it, "stress-related depression." Maybe nothing could have prevented that. But he was convinced the physical exercise was instrumental in his recovery.

His eyes started to moisten a bit, and he choked back a tear by taking a drink. He needed to find a way to make amends to this woman. Losing her again would prove unbearable. For a good fifteen minutes he stood there. His thoughts clicked back to reality when a car passed by. He looked at his watch. 1:45 a.m. He wondered what someone would be doing out so late at night on a weekday. Heading home from a night at the tavern? Taking his wife to the hospital to have a baby? Delivering drugs? All sorts of scenarios ran through his head.

And then the alley with Jamie Chambers' lifeless body appeared to him as she had so many times before. Joe shook his head as if to shake her out of his memory. *No, damnit! I'm not letting you in! I'm not letting you mess with my head tonight!*

Looking into his wine glass, he saw there was one swallow remaining. He downed it and then returned the glass to the kitchen. As he made his way back to the bedroom, sleep was foremost on his mind, and he hoped that calm sea of contentment would not elude him. Lying on the bed, his thoughts drifted until he revisited making love with Destiny. Sleep came to him.

The alarm woke Joe at the usual time the next morning. He had slept for only a few hours but he escaped experiencing any nightmares. He knew that his morning jog would sharpen his mind. Jogging down the street, he turned into Melissa's driveway just as she was coming out of her house.

"Good morning," he said.

They began jogging up Agora Street. As they turned from Agora onto Athens, Melissa broke the silence.

"Who's your girlfriend?"

"Excuse me?"

"Who's your girlfriend?" she repeated.

"My girlfriend," he said. "That's what you said, right?"

"You know it is."

"I don't know if I would call her my girlfriend."

"Lover, then?"

"God, you are something else."

"Inquiring minds want to know."

"Inquiring minds should mind their own business."

They continued running and Melissa didn't ask any more questions for a few blocks. But her curiosity got the best of her, and she could not resist reopening up the conversation again.

"She's pretty," she remarked.

"Who is?" he asked, messing with her a little. He knew her well enough by now that she would not let him off the hook easily.

"You know who!"

"And how would you know that? Have you been window peeking?"

"Of course not. I have eyes."

He gave in. "Yeah, you're right. She's pretty."

"What's her name? If you don't mind me asking."

"Destiny."

"Cool name. Are you going to introduce me?"

"Introduce you?"

"You have this annoying habit of repeating my questions, you know that?"

"Is that a fact?"

"Yeah. So, are you going to introduce me?"

"Maybe. If you don't bug me about it."

"Promise?"

"Promise."

"When?"

"Well…when the opportunity presents itself, I'll introduce the two of you. How's that?"

"Great!"

It seemed that was all she wanted—enough information to satisfy her curiosity. She apparently understood what was and was not socially acceptable as well. Her inquisitive nature could have pushed her to probe into the realm of personal intimacy, but she chose not to. His initial rebuke may have had made a lasting impression. She had cut all the blatant innuendo and had been acting more mature—at least around him. She had begun to grow on him since they started running together. And why not? She was smart, clever, and well-spoken. He liked this kid. Not in a sexual way although he wasn't blind to her good looks. Perhaps it was because he was old enough to be her father. For some reason he couldn't explain, his paternal instincts had begun to seep out. He wasn't used to interacting with teenagers in this way. The teens he usually encountered were associated with violent crime in one way or another. Befriending Melissa was a new experience for him, and he found it gratifying to jog with her each morning. He would probably miss her when he moved back to Chicago.

They ended their run as they usually did, with a cool-down walk to Melissa's house. The topics of their conversation always seemed to appear out of thin air, and it was hard to tell what direction they would take on any given day. Most of the time they were rather banal. Today, they discussed what to look for in a good pair of running shoes.

"See you tomorrow," she said before turning and heading toward her front door.

"You bet," replied Joe, using one of his father's favorite expressions. As he began to turn, his eye caught Melissa's mother standing in the kitchen window and gave her a wave. She smiled back, and with that he walked down the driveway and onto the sidewalk leading to his father's house. A tractor pulling a wagon drove past, belching black smoke from its diesel engine's exhaust pipe as it accelerated south out of town. But he hardly noticed. His mind was focusing on what he was going to say when he saw Destiny.

Chapter Eighteen

The mid-morning sun beat down mercilessly as Marv and Lorraine Koehler, a farm couple in their early sixties, paused outside the doors leading to the sheriff's department. Marv was a thin, wiry man with a deeply wrinkled tanned face thanks to many years of exposure to the sun. Lorraine was a thickset woman with rather masculine features and silvery gray hair worn short. Both were dressed for farm work: jeans, cotton shirts, and leather work shoes.

"You're going to be wasting their time, Marv. They'll probably think we're meddling," she said in her usual overbearing way.

"What can it hurt? It might even help," he replied.

"They'll probably lock you up."

"Good! I could use some peace and quiet."

"You old turd!" she countered.

Bickering was a constant in their marriage, and although it disturbed people who didn't know them, friends familiar with their squabbles believed it was actually their own peculiar way of showing affection for one another.

Joe had just parked his car and was walking toward them. They were too focused on each other to notice him approaching.

"Well, let's get it over with," Lorraine said as she put her hand on the door.

"Is there something I can help you with?" asked Joe as he reached them.

"Oh!" exclaimed Lorraine. "I didn't see you."

"Who are you?" Marv asked somewhat defensively.

"Joe Erickson." He extended his hand to Marv as he said, "I'm a special deputy working with the county."

"Oh. Marv Koehler," said Marv, shaking his hand. "And this is my wife—"

"Lorraine," she interrupted, smiling and extending her hand. Joe shook it and felt she had the grip strength of a small bear.

"We need to talk to someone about the murders."

"What do you mean?" asked Joe.

"She means we may have seen something," explained Marv.

"Okay, why don't you follow me?"

Joe escorted them into the small lobby inside the main door. He spoke to Delores Simms, one of the deputies whose desk was behind a large glass window, and she activated the door that led to the office area. She met them on the other side and led them down a hallway and into an interview room.

"Make yourself comfortable. Can I get you anything…coffee or…" asked Simms.

"No, thank you," said Lorraine.

"I wouldn't mind a cup of coffee—black please," said Marv. Lorraine gave him a disapproving look.

"Have a seat and one of our officers will be with you shortly."

Simms left the room, and both Marv and Lorraine pulled out chairs and sat down at the table. Lorraine glanced over at Marv with an annoyed look on her face.

"What did you have to get coffee for?"

"Because they offered, and I wanted it. Besides, my taxes have already paid for it."

"Their coffee doesn't come out of tax money."

"How do you know that?"

"Because I know."

"How do you know?"

"Because I do."

"Oh, I forgot. You know everything."

"That's right."

Silence. After a few minutes, Marv began drumming his fingers on the table.

"Will you stop that?

107

"Stop what?"

"That infernal drumming?"

"What drumming?"

"Your fingers."

"Oh."

He stopped drumming his fingers, but a minute or so later, he unconsciously started doing it again. Lorraine looked at him and cleared her throat.

"Marvin! You're going to put me in a homicidal rage if you don't stop that!"

"Sorry."

Silence. A minute later, Marv began tapping his foot. Just as Lorraine was about to say something to him, the door opened and Deputy Simms brought Marv a cup of coffee and set it on the table in front of him. As she was leaving, Joe, Destiny and Deputy Wilson entered the room and introduced themselves. Joe seated himself across from the Koehlers while Destiny stood back in one corner and Wilson sat next to Joe, preparing to take notes.

"You said you may have some information about the murders?" asked Joe.

"Maybe," said Marv. "You see, we were coming back from my brother's place. He lost his wife a while back, and we spent most of the day visiting with him."

"Get on with it," interjected Lorraine. "They don't want to hear about Harold."

"Well, like I said, we were coming back on that county road where they found that girl's car."

"It was her car all right. No doubt about that," said Lorraine.

Marv shot her a look that conveyed his annoyance. "Right. And we saw that a deputy had a car like hers stopped alongside the road."

"A deputy?" asked Joe.

"A county deputy?" asked Wilson.

"Yeah. He looked like you—the uniform, I mean."

"Could you see this officer's face?" asked Wilson.

"Not very well," said Lorraine.

"He was talking to me," admonished Marv. "No, I didn't get a very good look. It was like he made a point to turn his back to us as we went by. Thought that was kind of odd."

"What time was this?" asked Wilson.

"Oh, it was around midnight, a little after."

"Can you describe the police cruiser?" asked Joe.

"It was black," said Lorraine.

"Typical police car. It had those spotlights near the windshield—and those blue and red flashing lights...you know."

"Emergency lights," corrected Wilson.

"Yeah, those."

"Were you able to identify the make and model?"

"Yup. Chevy Impala. I know because I wanted to buy one like it but wound up settling for a Malibu."

"Too expensive," she said, bringing up a sore subject.

Marv let out a sigh. "It wasn't that expensive," he replied. "It could have been a lot—"

"Uh, pardon me," interrupted Wilson, attempting to fend off an argument. "Why did it take you this long to come forward?"

"We were visiting our son in Omaha for a few days. We didn't get back until day before yesterday," answered Lorraine.

"That was when we heard about that other girl," said Marv. "Then when I read about it, I realized that we may have seen that very same car on that county road while we were on our way home."

"Are you sure it was black and not dark blue or dark green? It was late at night," Joe inquired.

"I may be old, but I'm not blind," replied Lorraine.

"It was black all right," assured Marv. "There was a moon out that night, so with the headlights, I could see what color it was."

"Did you get a look at the girl?" asked Wilson.

"Not really," said Lorraine.

"She was inside her car," clarified Marv. "I couldn't see anything. I couldn't even tell if it was a boy or girl to be honest."

"I could. It was a girl. I could tell that much," said Lorraine.

"Can you describe the deputy? Tall, short, heavy, thin?" asked Joe.

"Well…kind of medium, I guess. I didn't look all that close because I was driving. Who knew it was going to wind up being something important?"

"Did you notice anything about the deputy?" Wilson asked Lorraine.

"Well, not really. He was…like Marv said…sort of medium-sized, wasn't real tall, wasn't real fat. Just sort of …regular, I guess. He wasn't small by any means. Marv thought it might have been a stop for drunk driving or something so we drove on. If it was an accident, we would have stopped but the deputy waved us on," added Lorraine.

"He waved you on by?" asked Joe.

"Yeah."

"But he did so with his back turned?"

"He did," said Lorraine.

"Seemed kind of odd to me," added Marv.

"Like he didn't want you to see his face?" asked Joe.

"I don't know. Maybe."

"Is there anything else you can think of?" asked Wilson.

"I can't think of anything else. Marv?"

"That's about it, I guess. I hoped this helped."

"It did, it definitely did," said Joe.

Wilson pushed back his chair and stood up. "Well, if there's nothing else, we won't take up any more of your time. Thank you for coming in." Marv and Lorraine rose from their chairs. Since Marv was holding his coffee, Wilson handed Lorraine his card. "And if you do think of anything else, you can call the office. You never know. Any little thing you can remember might help."

"Thank you," replied Lorraine, placing the card in her breast pocket.

"There, you see," said Marv, "it wasn't meddling after all, was it?"

Lorraine looked as Wilson. "I'm never going to hear the end of this."

Wilson opened the door and escorted them out while Joe and Destiny remained behind. Destiny walked to Joe, strictly business.

"I know, I know," said Joe in a low voice.

"And just what is it you know?"

"Tucker's cruiser is black."

"It is. And there's only one black Chevy Impala in the fleet," she added.

"Yeah."

Chapter Nineteen

A meeting was set up with Sheriff Pollock, Deputies Taylor and Wilson, and Joe and Destiny to discuss the new evidence. Wilson summarized what came out of the interview with the Koehlers, and Destiny gave an overview of Tucker's profile. Joe was uncharacteristically quiet as he took it all in. By the time they finished, Pollock was not happy.

"Jesus Christ," Pollock muttered under his breath. He looked at his deputies and then at Destiny. "You're telling me one of my own deputies is responsible for these murders?"

"I said he could be," Destiny clarified. "I'm not saying he is. We simply have to entertain the possibility."

"What bothers me most are those two sixty-minute gaps in time on the nights of both abductions. What the hell was he doing during those two hours?" asked Wilson.

Taylor spoke up. "I'll admit this looks bad, but I think we have to give him the benefit of the doubt. After all, he's one of us. He deserves some consideration."

"True, but we need to bring him in for questioning so he can account for those gaps in time," said Wilson. "We have to eliminate him as a suspect if he's not our guy."

"All right," sighed Pollock. "I don't like it, but we've got probable cause. Let's bring him in. He started vacation this week, so I'll have Delores call him on his cell phone and tell him I need to see him right away. When he comes in we'll take him into custody. That's the best way to do it."

Over an hour had passed, and Deputy Delores Simms reported to Pollock that she could not reach Tucker. She had tried several times but her calls were going to his voicemail.

"Shit," responded Pollock. "Get Taylor and Wilson in here." Fortunately, they were still in the building, and they were in Pollock's office in a matter of minutes.

"Well, Tucker's not answering his phone. I don't know if it's by choice or whether it's for some other reason but he can't be reached."

"You want to wait, see if he answers later?" asked Taylor. "I mean, we could bring him in tomorrow, couldn't we?"

"He started vacation today, didn't he? What if he takes off? It'd be the perfect opportunity to flee," said Wilson.

"Why would he flee? How would he know he's a suspect?" Taylor countered.

"I don't know, but what if he does? This would be the perfect opportunity to get a week's head start. How would it look if he turns out to be guilty and we had the opportunity to bring him in and we didn't?"

"What do you want to do?" Taylor asked Pollock.

Pollock weighed both their arguments carefully. "Before we do anything, let see if he answers his phone. I'll tell Delores to keep trying. Stick around, you two. I may need you."

Pollock walked to Deputy Simms' desk. "Delores, I want you to try Tucker's phone a couple more times. If you don't get hold of him, call his mother. We have her number on his contact sheet. Ask her if she knows where he is because he isn't answering his phone. Play down the urgency so she doesn't think it's anything important, okay? Say it's a question about insurance or something like that."

Half an hour later, Deputy Simms walked into Pollock's office. "I tried calling Tucker and it went to voicemail. Then I called his mother. She told me he's in Laurens right now watching his son play Tee-ball. I decided to try him one more time and he finally picked up. He said and I quote, 'Hell, no, I'm not coming in. I'm leaving on fishing trip tonight and I don't have time.'"

"God damnit," Pollock fumed. "Get Taylor and Wilson in here. And call Laurens and find out when that damned Tee-ball game will be over."

"That doesn't leave us with many options," offered Wilson.

"I know," replied Pollock. "Let's take him into custody the hard way. We'll set up an intercept when he's en route home. I'll speak to the county attorney and get his take on this. Call Laurens," he said to Wilson. "We'll need their eyes on this."

Deputy Wilson contacted the Pocahontas County deputy sheriff in Laurens who verified Tucker's pickup was parked at the game. Deputies Wilson and Barnes, and Sheriff Pollock would set up a traffic stop once Tucker crossed back into Buena Vista County. The Pocahontas County deputy would inform them when Tucker's vehicle left Laurens and approached the county line.

***

Following Jimmy's Tee-ball game, Tucker stopped at a convenience store for gas. After getting Jimmy an ice cream cone, he drove out onto Highway 10 expecting to be home in ten minutes.

They drove on heading for home. When the car crossed the county line, Tucker glanced into his rearview mirror and his eyes widened. "What the hell...?" he muttered. Jimmy saw is dad's reaction and stopped licking his ice cream.

Three police cruisers, Sheriff Pollock, and two deputies converged on his pickup with their lights flashing. Deputy Barnes pulled in front, forcing Tucker to stop while Deputy Taylor pulled up close to his rear bumper to prevent him from backing up. Pollock's cruiser pulled alongside, parallel to Tucker's pickup.

They all exited their cruisers with guns drawn but pointed downward. Pollock moved around his cruiser, and seeing that Tucker already had his window lowered, yelled, "Will. Shut off the truck and place your hands on the windshield."

"What the hell is this?" Tucker yelled.

"Do it!" commanded Pollock.

Tucker turned off the key to the ignition and reached forward, placing both hands on the windshield. He knew the drill but could not comprehend why he was being apprehended. It made no sense.

"I have Jimmy with me. Be careful!" Tucker cautioned with a desperate tone in his voice.

Jimmy sensed his father's despair and froze in fear.

Pollock moved to the driver's door of Tucker's pickup saying, "You know the drill. Get out and place your hands on the hood."

Jimmy's ice cream cone dropped from his hand and onto the floor. "Daddy…"

Tucker turned to look at Jimmy. The look on his son's face was enough to make him cry. "It's all right, Jimmy," Tucker said quietly. "It's okay."

Tucker got out and placed his hands on the hood. When Pollock moved to him, he saw a wide-eyed Jimmy sitting inside with ice cream running down his chin. He had grandchildren his age, and it made him feel lousy. As he was pulling out his handcuffs, Tucker spoke.

"Can I ask what the hell you're doing?"

Pollock grabbed Tucker's left wrist, pulled it behind his back, and cuffed him. Through the ratcheting sound of the handcuff, Pollock said, "Will, I'm taking you into custody. We want to question you about the murders of Tina Olson and Jennifer Callaghan."

"Are you nuts?" protested Tucker. "Am I under arrest?"

"Not yet."

"You've got to be kidding!"

Pollock grabbed his right wrist and pulled it behind his back. "Don't make this any harder than it already is." The second cuff ratcheted closed. Taylor assisted Pollock in placing Tucker into the back of Pollock's cruiser, holding his hand on top of Tucker's head as he ducked down into the seat.

"What about Jimmy?" asked Tucker.

Pollock glanced over at Barnes and nodded toward the pickup. Barnes understood. He had kids of his own and knew what to do. He grabbed a bottle of water from his cruiser, walked to the passenger door, and opened it.

"Hi, Jimmy," Barnes said in a calming voice. "Remember me?"

Near tears, Jimmy gave a nod.

"Good. I'm your daddy's friend, Phil. How would you like to go for a ride in a police car? Would you like that?"

"Am I going to jail?" Jimmy asked in a pathetic little voice.

"No, Jimmy. You're not going to jail. There's nothing to be scared of, okay?"

"Okay."

Barnes pulled a handkerchief from his pocket and wet it with water from the bottle. "You have some ice cream on your chin. Would it be all right if I wiped it off?" Jimmy nodded. "Good, cuz it'll get all sticky if we don't, and your hand might stick to your face. Like this." Barnes put down the bottle and demonstrated sticking his hand to his chin and not being able to remove it.

"Oo, ow!" clowned Barnes as he pretended pulling sticky fingers off his chin. Jimmy managed a smile. "See, we wouldn't want that to happen to you now, would we?"

Barnes wiped Jimmy's chin and hands and took a swipe at the blob of ice cream on his T-shirt. Then he held up the bottle of water. "Would you like a drink of water?" he asked. Jimmy nodded and Barnes handed the water bottle to Jimmy who took a swig.

Barnes saw the melting ice cream cone on the floor and reached down and picked up. "You like dirt ice cream?" he asked. Jimmy shook his head. "Good. I think we'd better let the birds have it." Then he tossed the dripping mess out onto the shoulder of the road.

"You want to go for a ride in a police car now?"

"Uh-huh," Jimmy replied timidly.

Taylor had called for a tow truck for Tucker's pickup, and he would stay with the vehicle until it arrived. It would be impounded and checked for any forensic evidence. Pollock's cruiser had already driven away from the scene. After buckling Jimmy into the passenger seat of his cruiser, Deputy Barnes and Jimmy were on their way down Highway 10 heading for Storm Lake.

Chapter Twenty

Melissa was in her bedroom, sitting on the bed with her laptop. Since her father had curtailed her social life by forbidding her to travel outside of town alone, the Internet was her only link to the outside world. She was active on Facebook and was a passive contributor to several website forums. She was checking her email when she heard the front door open downstairs.

"Jean! Melissa! You home?" said her father in a voice meant to be heard throughout the house.

"Ye-es!" Melissa yelled back, splitting the word into two syllables.

"Come down here! It's important."

She sighed. "O-kay!"

It was unusual for her father to be home this early. Melissa closed her laptop, placed it next to her on the bed, and went downstairs. Her mom had joined him in the living room and had a strange look on her face.

"What is it?" Jean asked.

"You're not going to believe this. They arrested Will Tucker today for the murders of those two girls."

"Oh my god!" gasped Jean. "Will Tucker?"

"The deputy? You're kidding," uttered Melissa.

"I can hardly believe it. Are you sure?" asked Jean.

"Yeah. It sounds like they have him dead to rights."

"He always seemed so nice," murmured Melissa. "He spoke at our school."

Tom removed his suit coat, and Jean took it from him. "Who'd have thought."

"Hard to believe, isn't it?"

"How could he do such a thing?" asked Melissa.

Tom shook his head in amazement. "I have no idea."

"How did you find out?" Jean inquired.

"Bill Anderson heard it on his scanner. And then he called his brother-in-law who has a golf buddy who knows one of the deputies in the sheriff's office."

Tom walked over to the bar and poured himself two fingers of scotch. He took a drink, turned, and saw Melissa facing him.

"Does this mean I can finally go somewhere on my own now?"

"Well," he hedged, "he hasn't been convicted of—"

"Da-ad!" she protested.

"Tom, you can't continue to keep her prisoner in her own home."

"Please?"

He hesitated a few moments as he weighed his options. Melissa was beside herself with anticipation, having crossed the fingers of both hands behind her back.

"Oh, all right," he sighed, giving in to both of them. It was two against one and he knew from past experience that he was outnumbered and outgunned.

"Oh, thank you! Thank you!" Melissa exclaimed, and she gave him a kiss on the cheek and ran upstairs.

He chuckled a bit at her reaction. Looking at his wife he confessed, "Maybe I've been a little over-protective."

"A little?" she said with a hint of a smile.

Back in her room, Melissa sat back on her bed and picked up her iPhone and checked her email. She was pleased to see a message from Michael, a guy she met through the University of Northern Iowa. She'd enrolled to attend college there in a couple of months, and she wanted to get to know more about the business department. He was an upper-class representative serving as a liaison between the business department and new students who had listed business as a possible major. Their email communications began merely as an information exchange, but it had grown more personal in recent weeks. His message read:

Hi. Thanks for sending me your picture. I saw you when you and your parents were visiting the campus last spring but didn't get a chance to introduce myself. My loss. Your father must be a thief, because he stole the stars and put them in your eyes! I have attached a photo of myself. Hope you are not disappointed! Later, Michael.

She thought the "stole-the-stars" line was kind of corny, but when she opened the attachment with his picture, her jaw dropped. The photo revealed a twenty-one-year-old blonde-haired god. *Omigod!* she thought. *He is gorgeous!* She wrote him a return message that read:

Loved your picture! Wow!! Maybe we should try to get together sometime this summer. I know it will be hard, but I think we can work it in. Ha-ha!!

Melissa.

She clicked on send and her message went out into cyberspace. She leaned back on her pillows and wondered how long it would take him to answer. Then a thought occurred to her—maybe she came on a little too strong with that message. That was a tease, not an offer. She considered it some more and concluded it was okay. His previous messages had contained some subtle flirting, too. So, if he was put off by it or assumed too much oh well...too bad!

Chapter Twenty-One

Tucker was sitting in the interrogation room with Sheriff Pollock and Jeff taking turns questioning him. Behind the two-way mirror in the adjacent viewing room stood Joe, Destiny, Deputy Taylor, and James Rickert, the Buena Vista County Attorney. They had been observing the proceedings for the past half-hour.

Rickert was a vain man of fifty, tall, tanned, and trim. Dressed in a tailored pinstriped suit and Italian shoes, he would have appeared quite at home on Wall Street. What was most striking about him today was his Straight to Heaven "men's perfume," a scent that was a bit too strong for such an enclosed space.

"If he's innocent, why the hell won't he say what he was doing during those sixty-minute gaps?" asked Rickert.

"I don't know. He must have good reason," said Taylor.

"His good reason might be that he killed those girls."

"If he did, you'd think he'd be trying to cover his ass with some kind of explanation."

"You'd think."

"There's got to be another reason," stated Joe. "He's not stupid."

Rickert's eyes moved from Joe and then to Taylor. "You worked with him. What do you think?"

"I would never have suspected him. It surprised the hell out of me. To be honest, I still have trouble believing he did it."

They watched for a while longer as Jeff questioned and cajoled him in an attempt to extract information. Tucker was not forthcoming, and the questions about his whereabouts were met with silence.

"He's not helping himself, that's for sure," said Rickert. "Look, we don't seem to be getting anywhere here, and I have to be in court tomorrow morning. Call me if anything eventful happens, okay?"

"Got it."

Their attention turned to the interrogation room, and they listened as Pollock was now questioning Tucker. Taylor looked at Destiny and said, "The sheriff's pretty good at interrogating suspects. You know he was a big city cop before he moved here?"

"Oh?" Destiny said.

"Yeah. He came from Ft. Dodge." He chuckled at his own joke. Destiny did not find it particularly amusing, but she smiled politely. Joe ignored him.

Joe could see and hear that Pollock and Jeff were getting frustrated with Tucker's refusal to cooperate. They were doing a good job trying to get him to talk, but they had been questioning him for over an hour and were still getting nowhere. Tucker continued to deny being at the scene of the abductions, even though eyewitnesses placed his cruiser at the second one. And he continued to remain silent when asked to account for his whereabouts at those times.

"Excuse me," said Joe, and he left the room. Destiny followed him out into the hallway. She was still harboring some resentment over the tiff they had in Spencer, so her approach to him was cautious.

"What's the matter?" she asked.

"I think I know why he's not talking."

"Why's that?"

"He's protecting someone."

"Are you still thinking...he's not the one?

"Uh-huh. I am."

"What about the evidence that points to him as the perp?"

"I know. The evidence doesn't look good."

"And the black police cruiser the two witnesses saw at the scene?" she pressed.

"I don't know. I haven't figured that one out yet."

"So, this is your gut feeling?"

"More or less. It just doesn't feel right."

"Joe..."

"I know, I know, feelings aren't evidence."

"No, that's not what I'm saying."

"Then, what?"

"What I'm saying is, he isn't acting like a perp. His nonverbal communication, his eye placement, they don't demonstrate deception. You may be right. He could very well be protecting someone."

Joe looked at her, and he could see that she was moving toward his point of view. "He is, I'm sure of it."

"But who? And why?" she asked. "And what could be so important that he would risk his career over it?"

"That would be the sixty-four-thousand-dollar question, now wouldn't it?"

At that moment a rumpled Jeff opened the door of the interview room and stepped into the hallway. As he did, he let out a huge sigh and reached for his cigarettes.

"What's going on?" Destiny asked.

"The sheriff got frustrated and leaned on him a little hard so he decided to lawyer up," he replied. "Not surprised. We weren't getting results with any other method we tried." Destiny looked at Joe. "I guess that means we're done."

"Appears that way."

"Quite a day, huh?"

"That it was."

"You...want to go somewhere for a drink?"

This caught Joe off guard. He'd been reticent about approaching her given her cool demeanor, so her invitation came as a pleasant surprise. This thaw in the ice was what he'd been hoping for.

"Yeah. Yeah, I'd like that."

"There's a nice little bistro on Erie Street."

"I know the place. Works for me."

Fifteen minutes later they were seated at a table by the window. No one was sitting at the tables near them so they had some semblance of privacy. The bistro was a trendy place with oak and brass decor. A leggy, middle-aged waitress named Corie took their order and brought Destiny a glass of Pinot Grigio and Joe a Glenlivet on the rocks.

"Would you like anything else?"

"Not right now, thanks," Destiny replied.

"Let me know if you do," she said with a smile. And she turned and walked back to the bar.

Joe took a drink of his scotch and resisted the temptation to check out Corie's ass as she walked away. Not a good thing to be caught doing given the circumstances so he kept his eyes glued on Destiny.

"Thanks," he said. "I needed to mellow out after all this."

"Me, too."

He took another drink, and then looked her in the eye. "I'm not good with apologies, but I owe you one. I behaved like an asshole the other day."

"You did."

"And I've been kicking myself ever since. I'd show you the black and blue marks but…"

"Not in public, please. You can stop with the kicking now. Apology accepted."

"Thank you."

"You're welcome. To tell you the truth, I probably didn't help matters, either."

Choosing not to comment, he gave a little shrug and asked, "How's the wine?"

"It's good. And the scotch?"

"Great."

"Well then, I guess we're all good, huh?" she smiled.

He smiled back. "Everything's good."

And she smiled back. "Good." She looked at him and they both burst into laughter. "That's way too many 'goods' isn't it?"

"Most likely."

They both looked out the window at the passing traffic for a few moments, and then Destiny broke the silence by posing a question.

"So…what's your theory about Tucker protecting someone?"

"He has to be. You'd think if you committed a criminal act you'd try to cover your ass by having an alibi or creating some sort of story to account for your time. He knows all about this kind of stuff, but he's refusing to talk."

"Who could he be protecting?"

"A friend? A relative? I don't know. Does he have any brothers?"

"No, two sisters."

"I plan to have a talk with him. Maybe I can get him to open up to me. I'm counting on the fact he respects me enough to confide in me…at least, I hope he will."

"What I'm afraid of, Joe, is another girl is going to be kidnapped because no one is looking for the perp anymore. For all intents and purposes, this investigation has come to a stop."

"I know. But it hasn't stopped with me. This guy is still out there, and I intend to find him."

Chapter Twenty-Two

At seven o'clock Melissa stepped out of the bathroom, her makeup and hair done to perfection. Dressed in jeans and a chic floral print sleeveless blouse, she was the epitome of every teenage boy's dream. Preparation complete, she bounded down the stairs.

Her father entered from the garage carrying a small hammer, a punch, and an oilcan. His intention was to fix a squeaking door hinge that had finally become so annoying he couldn't stand it anymore. He stopped in his tracks when he saw Melissa all dressed up.

"Where are you going?" he asked.

"It's taco night at the cafe in Webb. I thought I would drive up there and hang out with Emily. I haven't seen her for a while."

"Oh."

"Mom said it would be okay."

Emily, her cousin, was a year younger and lived on a farm a couple of miles north of Webb. They had always been good friends as well as cousins. And Emily's older brother, Zak, would let them swipe beer from his refrigerator whenever they wanted it.

"All right," said Tom. "Be careful."

"Don't worry," she replied. "I'll be home by midnight. Probably sooner."

As she left the house and walked to her car, she glanced down the street and saw Joe leaving his Camaro and walking toward his house. She waved, but he failed to see her. Oh well. She noticed Destiny wasn't with him. *Wonder what he's doing tonight,* she thought. *Maybe she'll be coming later,* and then she snorted a laugh when she realized the unintended double entendre.

She opened the door of her red Honda and plopped down in the seat. Fastening her seat belt, she started the car. The air conditioner kicked out hot air before the cool began to flow through the vents, and she rolled down the window to let the oppressive air escape. Then she cued up her iPod, and a Katy Perry song started blaring from the speakers.

Once it began to feel cooler, she rolled up the window and backed out of the driveway. She cruised through town, ending up at the stop sign next to the cemetery. She turned north onto the Buena Vista County Road M-54 blacktop that would take her to Webb.

She met Emily and they hung out at the cafe after indulging in a few tacos. Melissa had arranged a meeting there with Michael who was home visiting his parents in Spirit Lake, about forty miles away. When 9:00 rolled around, it became apparent he was not going to show up. So, she and Emily went to her brother's house and drank a couple of beers over the next two hours. By 11:00, Melissa wasn't having any fun and decided to call it a night and drive back to Marathon. She said goodbye to Emily, got into her car, popped a couple of breath mints, and headed home.

About two miles outside of town, Melissa noticed headlights coming up fast in her rearview mirror. As fate would have it, Deputy Wilson was coming back from a call north of Marathon at the same time Melissa was returning from Webb. Both were traveling on M54 and met at the corner where M54 curves to the east.

Wilson's headlights illuminated the black cruiser following Melissa's Honda, and he immediately hit his brakes. *Tucker's black cruiser has been impounded. How the hell could it be back in service?* he thought. When Melissa turned east toward Marathon, the black cruiser turned west toward Sioux Rapids, accelerating away at high speed. That looked suspicious as hell. Wilson whipped his cruiser around and pursued the mystery cruiser with his emergency lights flashing. The two cruisers were a blur as they flew past the lighted farmyards and dark fields of corn and soybeans.

The pursuit soon hit ninety miles per hour and Wilson reached for his radio's microphone.

"Buena Vista County eleven-three," he spoke into the microphone, identifying himself to the dispatcher in Storm Lake.

"Go ahead eleven-three," said the female dispatcher on the other end.

"I am in pursuit of—" He stopped mid-message. "Stand by."

The black cruiser had slammed on it brakes, slowing to make a quick turn onto a gravel road, one of many country roads throughout the area. Wilson hit his brakes as well and turned his cruiser onto the gravel road and continued to pursue.

"Shit!" he said out loud. The cloud of dust generated by the black cruiser completely obscured his view. All his headlights showed were clouds of dust and he had to slow down.

"Buena Vista County eleven-three."

"Go ahead eleven-three."

"Buena Vista County eleven-three requesting back-up."

"What is your location?"

"Approximately five miles west of the M-54 on a gravel road south of County Road C-13. I am in pursuit of—"

He stopped talking. For a moment he saw the cruiser's taillights. He seemed to be gaining on it, and then they disappeared. The reason was the gravel road curved sharply to the left and the black cruiser had slowed and made the turn. Because of the dust cloud ahead of him, Wilson didn't see the curve until it was too late to react. His cruiser left the road and came down with a loud bang as its suspension bottomed out in a steep, rugged pasture. The airbags deployed as the vehicle flipped into the air and came down on its side, rolling over and over toward the bottom of the gully. When the cruiser collided with a huge boulder, a section of the roof buckled and caved in, striking Wilson in the head. The car eventually came to a stop upside down, a mass of twisted steel and shattered glass, its only remaining headlight shining aimlessly into the darkness.

"Buena Vista County eleven-three," said the voice female dispatcher over the radio. No response. "Buena Vista County eleven-three, acknowledge," the voice repeated to no avail. The accident left Wilson unconscious and upside down inside his cruiser, held firmly in the driver's seat by his safety belt.

When there was no response, the dispatcher alerted Deputy Barnes who was the closest officer to Wilson's last specified location. She alerted Sheriff Pollock and the state patrol.

Fifteen minutes later, Barnes and State Patrolman Marks were on the scene. Marks was the first to find the wreckage, thanks to the cruiser's headlight acting as a beacon. Wilson was hanging upside down and Marks crawled inside the wreckage to check on Wilson's condition. Fortunately, it didn't appear he was pinned inside. Wilson was semi-conscious, and he tried to speak, but Marks couldn't make out what he was trying to say. Then Wilson passed into unconsciousness. When Barnes reached the scene a couple of minutes later, the two men released Wilson's seat belt and administered first aid as they waited for the EMTs to get there.

An ambulance and a fire truck arrived from Sioux Rapids, and two Emergency Medical Technicians went to work checking Wilson's vital signs and getting him on a spinal board. Fire personnel inspected the wrecked cruiser for fuel leaks and other possible sources of fire. Once Wilson was secure, the EMT's and fire fighters transported Wilson up the steep pasture to the waiting ambulance.

Sheriff Pollock drove to the scene, getting there just as Wilson was being loaded into the ambulance.

"How is he?" asked Pollock.

"He's alive, but his vitals aren't good. We've got to get moving," replied the EMT.

"I'll give you an escort to the hospital," said Pollock.

The two vehicles pulled away with lights flashing and sirens wailing.

Outside the emergency room at Buena Vista County Hospital in Storm Lake, State Patrolman Marks, Deputy Barnes, and Sheriff Pollock waited to hear news about Deputy Wilson's condition. Grim faces. No one was talking.

Joe and Destiny entered the room.

"We heard from Jeff about twenty minutes ago," said Destiny. "How is he?"

"Not good," answered Pollock in a low voice.

"He's beat up pretty bad," added Barnes.

A nurse entered the room and walked up to Pollock.

"Sheriff, his wife is here," she said.

"Thanks," replied Pollock.

Barnes looked at Marks and said, "Bill, this is Joe Erickson and Destiny Alexander. They're consulting on the murder cases."

Extending his hand to Destiny and then to Joe, he introduced himself, "Bill Marks. Good to meet you."

"Bill was the first on the scene. I got there a few minutes later," said Barnes.

Looking at Marks, Joe asked, "Was Wilson able to say anything?"

"Not really. He mumbled something but it didn't make any sense."

"What was it?"

"Well, it sounded like 'blag rooz.'"

"Blag rooz," Joe repeated. "You sure that's what he said?"

Marks shrugged. "Yeah, that what it sounded like. He said it a couple of times and then lost consciousness."

Joe looked at Destiny seeking some kind of insightful answer. "Blag rooz?"

She looked at him sadly and shook her head.

At that moment the ER doctor entered and approached them.

"We have him stabilized. But given the extent of his injuries we're transporting him to Sioux City where they have more extensive trauma facilities. Life Flight's on its way."

"Is he conscious?" asked Joe.

"No, and he might not be for some time. Now, if you'll excuse me...I need to speak with his wife."

They all stayed at the hospital keeping Wilson's wife, Sarah, company until the helicopter landed. Once it did and Wilson was aboard, it was back in the air within minutes. Sarah's brother arrived and drove her the hour and twenty minutes to the Mercy Medical Center. But there was nothing more the rest of them could do now except hope and pray for his recovery. So one by one they left the hospital.

Destiny and Joe walked outside. He was bothered by the words that Marks said Wilson had muttered. "What do you suppose he could have meant by "blag rooz?"

"It's hard to tell. It's possible it was only incoherent rambling."

"Yeah. But he said it a couple of times, that's what Marks said, right? It sounds to me like he was trying to communicate something important but couldn't quite form the words."

"You're not going to leave this alone, are you?"

"I can't. It has to mean something."

"Come on, it's late. Maybe in the morning, when we have clearer minds, it'll come to one of us."

"Yeah. Blag rooz...Blag rooz." It was going to be hard for him to sleep tonight.

Chapter Twenty-Three

The next day, Joe knew he had to visit Tucker and try to find out why he was refusing to talk. He set up an interview and was waiting in the visitor's room when Tucker was led in, dressed in a standard orange jump suit and slip on canvas shoes. Joe stood as he entered.

"Have a seat," Joe said.

Tucker walked to the table and sat down opposite Joe. He didn't look at Joe nor did he speak. He just sat there looking beaten down, tired, and depressed.

"How are you doing?" Joe asked, breaking the ice.

Tucker shrugged. "All right, I guess."

"Where's Jimmy?"

"Staying with my mom."

"Ah," Joe acknowledged.

After an awkward pause, Joe decided to cut to the chase. He took a deep breath and said, "I don't believe for one minute you're guilty."

"That makes you and me," said Tucker.

"That's not true."

"No?"

"There are a lot of people who have a hard time believing you're guilty of these crimes, including the deputies that work with you."

Tucker took a deep breath but didn't respond.

"Look, you're not helping yourself by refusing to clear up those sixty-minute gaps. Why don't you just tell Pollock where you were?"

"I have my reasons."

"I know you didn't commit any crime. How important could your reasons be, anyway?"

"Pretty damned important."

Joe's patience had worn thin, and he slammed his fist down on the table. "Bullshit!" he yelled.

"I can't!" Tucker replied, matching Joe's volume.

"Why?"

"Because…"

"You know what I think?" said Joe. "I think you're protecting somebody. But what I can't figure out is why."

Tucker rose and stepped to the wall. His frustration was apparent and Joe could read it.

"I'm trying to help you here, man. You've got to trust me."

"It'll cost me my job," he admitted in a soft voice.

"Your job? For god's sakes, man! Your job is the least of your worries. They're filing murder charges tomorrow. If they convict you, you're going to lose a lot more than your job! Think of your son."

Tucker sighed and turned away again. Joe sensed his hard-edged approach may have caused Tucker to clam up so he decided to change tactics and try a more sensitive manner of inquiry.

"Tucker, look. I'm not your boss. I don't give a rat's ass what you may have been doing for those two hours, okay?"

"Christ."

"Really, I don't. If you're protecting someone, you must have good reason. Look, I'll do my best to stand up for you. But as you know, I don't have a lot of pull around here, and the powers that be don't like me a helluva lot."

He heard Tucker take a deep breath and felt he was making progress so he pushed further.

"You and I both know the perp is still out there, and right now, no one is looking for him because they think it's you. We have to get this investigation back on track or chances are, another girl is going to die. Come on. You don't want that on your conscience, do you?"

Tucker's eyes avoided Joe's as he looked down at the floor and contemplated whether to spill his guts.

Finally, he took another deep breath, looked up at Joe and said, "All right...All right. I've been stopping off at a place south of Marathon...I've...I've been seeing someone."

"Okay...and that would be?"

Tucker paused obviously not wanting to name her, but he knew he had no choice. "Amy Greene," he acknowledged reluctantly.

"And this was during your shift."

"Yeah. When I was on nights."

"I see."

"Her husband works second shift at the packing plant down in Storm Lake, and she and I...well..."

"Hit it off."

"Yeah, that's one way to put it."

"How'd you meet her?"

"Got called out to her place on a domestic disturbance call."

"Her husband?"

"Yeah. A real piece of work."

"How often have you been seeing her?"

"Any chance I can get. But it's tricky because her husband's got family around so we have to be careful."

"What about on duty?"

"Once a week for the last couple of months. I know it was dumb, but..."

"Hey, you don't have to explain to me. I'm no angel."

"She wants to leave her husband and be with me but...this has all turned into one giant cluster fuck."

"Well, maybe it has. But the most important question right now is can she provide an alibi for those two gaps in time you have on the nights of the abductions."

"Yeah, she can."

"Then why hasn't she come forward?"

Tucker's voice took on a tender, rather sad tone.

"Because she's afraid of her husband. He's a real asshole. If he ever finds out about us, he'll go ape-shit and beat the hell out of her. It wouldn't be the first time."

Joe thought for a few moments. "Does she work somewhere during the day?"

"Yeah."

"Where?"

"Why do you want to know?"

"What if I contacted her and arranged a meeting with the sheriff? We could have you out of here."

"What about her husband?"

"He wouldn't have to know. She could come in while he was at work."

"What about her job? What if they find out she's been having an affair? Her boss is her husband's cousin. That could create a big to-do. Her husband would find out and she could wind up getting fired."

"How are they going to find out? This doesn't have to be made public."

"I don't know..."

"Come on, Tucker. Tell me where she works. I can find out with or without your help, but it will save me time if you just tell me."

Pause.

"She works at the convenience store in Albert City. Stop and Go."

Joe pulled a small notebook and pen from his pocket and put them in front of Tucker.

"I'll need her phone number."

Tucker picked up the pen, wrote down her phone number, and pushed the pen and notebook back across the table. Joe grabbed them, eased back from the table and stood.

"That's her cell phone number. I don't know if they have a land line."

"Thank you. You've done the right thing."

"I hope so."

Leaving the visitors area, Joe was thinking about how he might approach Amy Greene. Then an idea popped into his head. He walked to Destiny's office and poked his head in the door. She was alone working on her laptop.

"Gotta minute?" he asked.

"Sure. What's up?"

"I just finished talking with Tucker and I got him to open up to me. He has an alibi for those hour gaps, but it's a tricky situation."

"Oh?"

"He's been seeing a woman while on duty, a married woman," revealed Joe.

"So, you were right. He has been protecting someone."

"Yeah. He told me her husband is an abuser, and if he finds out about his wife's infidelity, she'll be at risk."

"Great," said Destiny. "So, where do we go with this?"

"Well, I think it would be best if you were the one to speak with her, don't you? Woman to woman?"

"You may have a point. From a view of empathy and understanding, a woman might be a better choice than a man in this case."

"I'm sure you can use your power of reason to motivate her into corroborating Tucker's whereabouts on the nights of the abductions."

"I see. No pressure."

Joe snorted a laugh. "Yeah, no pressure."

"How do I contact her?"

"She works at the convenience store in Albert City, Stop and Go. We should probably avoid walking in on her at work. Her boss is her husband's cousin so we have to be careful. But her husband works nights in Storm Lake so try calling her in the evening."

"Got it."

"See if she'll agree to set up a face-to face meeting with you."

He pulled out his notebook. "Here's her cell phone number. I made a copy for you."

"Thanks. Do they have a land line at home?"

"Not that I know of."

"Let's hope she answers. People see a call from a strange number, and they think it's a solicitation and don't pick up."

"I guess we need a little luck then, huh?"

"Luck is when opportunity meets preparation. So, I guess I'd better prepare just in case."

135

Chapter Twenty-Four

Destiny tried calling Amy Greene on her cell phone but as she feared, Amy didn't answer so she had to resort to a different tactic. The next morning, she made a phone call to the Stop and Go convenience store in Albert City. A middle-aged woman answered.

"Stop and Go. Pam speaking...Hold on." She covered the receiver and yelled, "AMY! SOMEBODY WANTS TO TALK TO YOU!"

Amy Greene came out of the back room and took the phone. "This is Amy," she answered in a soft voice.

"Hi, my name is Destiny Alexander, and I'm working with the Buena Vista County Sheriff's Office."

"Um, I can't really talk to you when I'm at work," Amy replied nervously, turning to see if Pam was watching her. Pam had taken the coffee pot into the restroom to dump the contents and get water to brew a fresh pot.

"I realize that. What I'd like to know is if there is a time we can meet that's convenient for you."

"Oh," she said nervously. "I don't know."

"It's very important," emphasized Destiny. "I think you know what this is about. I can work around any conflicts you might have."

"Well...I work from six until two-thirty, and then I have to be home right away so..."

"I could meet any evening if you like," Destiny reassured her.

"Well, would it be all right to meet at say, seven o'clock tonight?"

"Seven o'clock is fine. Where would you like to meet?"

"How about the town swimming pool?"

"Okay."

"We could maybe sit and talk at one of the park benches."

"That sounds fine to me. How will I find you?"

"Oh, yeah, uh...I'll be wearing an orange T-shirt." Seeing Pam coming back with the coffee pot, she said, "I have to go."

"Okay. I'll see you—" Click. The line went dead. Although relieved she didn't have to twist Amy's arm in order to get her to agree to a meeting, Destiny got a rather weird vibe from talking with her. Meeting at the swimming pool was a little unusual but maybe she could have had a good reason for wanting to meet there. The weird vibe came from the character of her voice. It was soft and seemed like that of a meek individual who was afraid of expressing herself. Calling her at work may have had something to do with it. Destiny wanted to give her the benefit of the doubt until she met her face to face.

Destiny drove back to Storm Lake and reported her plans to Joe.

"Hey, nice going! Did you have to do much persuading?"

"No, she seemed willing to meet with me. I was a little surprised, actually. We arranged a meeting for tonight at seven o'clock by the swimming pool in Albert City."

"Swimming pool?"

"I know, it's kind of a strange place to meet."

"Maybe she has kids."

"I didn't think of that. Is the swimming pool even open at night?"

"I don't know. Guess you'll find out, huh?"

"Well, I'm going to do some research. You going to be around for lunch?" she asked.

"Don't know yet. If I'm not, I'll call you."

Destiny walked down to her office and began researching domestic abuse online. While she'd learned from her training at the F.B.I., it had been a while since she had needed to delve into it. She wanted to refresh her memory about the nature of domestic abuse.

When Joe came down to her office at noon, she was surprised to discover over two hours had passed. Time often flew by when she was immersed in a subject.

"Lunchtime, already?" she questioned.

"Sure is. Why? You busy?"

"Yeah, I am. Would you mind picking up something for me?"

"Sure. What are you in the mood for? Vegetable matter, animal flesh, or a combination thereof?"

"Vegetable matter, please."

"Okay. A salad, it is."

"Don't forget the Italian."

"If I can't find one, will a handsome Swede do?" he teased.

"In a pinch." she smiled back.

She worked most of the afternoon researching the characteristics typical of domestic abuse victims: depression, low self-esteem, poor self-image, stress-related disorders and social isolation among other things. Not all of them applied to every individual. *But for god's sake,* she thought, *I'm going to come away from this with a case of depression myself if I continue reading about these victims.* She looked at the clock. Almost four. She got up and walked down to the main office where Deputy Simms handed her a message from Joe. He was running down a lead in Linn Grove with Deputy Snyder and wouldn't be back until after six, so she decided to go to her motel and rest. She was paying for the room and the rental car herself now, as the state only covered her expenses for two weeks. Maybe a shower and a change of clothes would snap her out of the negative funk she was in.

When she entered her motel room, she fell onto the bed and stared at the ceiling. What kind of woman was she going to be meeting tonight? Was she going to be up to the job of convincing her to meet with Sheriff Pollock? Feeling a headache coming on, she kicked off her shoes, removed her clothing, and stepped into the shower. She stood under the pulsing stream, enjoying its warmth.

Noticing her fingertips had begun to wrinkle and turn white, she realized she had once again lost track of time. She shut off the water, and when she stepped out of the shower, the cold air of the room shocked her body, and she grabbed a towel and covered up.

After she dressed, fixed her hair, and put on makeup, she glanced at her watch. Ten minutes to six. *Hm,* she thought. *I have time for a glass of wine before heading to Albert City.* Hoping for a late supper with Joe after she returned, she left her motel room and cruised downtown to the little bistro she liked on Erie Street. That same table near the window she and Joe shared the last time they were there was waiting for her. Once again, Corie came over to take her order.

"Hey, where's that good-looking guy you were with the last time you were here?" she asked with a smile.

"You remembered."

"I have a pretty good memory for people."

"I don't know. I think I misplaced him."

"If I find him, can I keep him?"

"Well, it depends on the day," Destiny replied.

Corie laughed. "I know what you mean. What'll you have?"

"A glass of Pinot Grigio."

"Coming right up." And she turned and walked to the bar.

Destiny looked around the bistro and noticed a couple of men giving her the greasy eyeball. It was nothing new; it was something she'd become used to, and as long as they weren't lewd about it, it amused her more than it bothered her. Men. It's in their genes—and their jeans.

Corie brought over her wine. "Would you like a menu?" she asked.

"No, thanks. We may be in later tonight."

"Great. Enjoy." And with that, she moved on to another table.

Destiny was hoping that would be the case. But if she and Joe would not be having supper here this evening, that would be all right. She could use some alone time to digest the information she hoped to get during her meeting with Amy Greene. Savoring her wine, her thoughts drifted to how she would convince this woman to provide an alibi for Tucker. Would it be a hard sell? What if she failed?

Before she knew it, she realized that twenty minutes had somehow passed. Tipping up her glass she drank the last remaining swallow.

Her GPS took her north on Highway 71, then east on Highway 3, and finally a short two-mile stretch north on County Road N14 to Albert City. Mostly fields of corn, soybeans, and the occasional farm place during the thirty-minute drive.

When she reached the city limits, she found the swimming pool and parked nearby. It was open, and she could hear children and teenagers enjoying themselves jumping off the diving boards and splashing around in the water. Wooden picnic benches were placed near the pool.

Destiny had arrived a few minutes early and thought maybe she might not see Amy Greene, but as she rounded an evergreen tree, she spotted a woman in an orange T-shirt sitting at one of the picnic tables. At least, she hoped it was her. Walking up to the picnic table, she asked, "Amy Greene?"

The woman turned. "Yes. Are you Destiny?" Amy asked with a little Missouri twang in her voice.

"I am," Destiny replied, extending her hand. "It's nice to meet you." Amy stood and they shook hands.

Amy Greene was a small, thin woman in her late twenties with red hair and freckles. Her green eyes projected a sense of sadness that was noticeable even though she tended to avoid eye contact much of the time. Destiny noticed some old bruising on her arms. And when Amy gave her a brief smile it was apparent that her two front teeth were dental crowns. After they both sat down across from one another, Destiny was the first to speak.

"I'm here to ask for your help. I suppose you've heard that Will Tucker has been arrested and jailed for the abduction murders?"

"He isn't a murderer."

"I know. But they're filing murder charges tomorrow."

"He isn't that kind of person."

"I don't think he is either. But the problem we're facing is this: he's refusing to account for his whereabouts during certain times on the nights of the abductions."

"I don't understand."

"We've found that he does have an alibi for the times in question, but he's been refusing to say who it is. You see, he'd rather remain in jail than to reveal her name and risk having her abusive husband find out."

Tears welled up in Amy's eyes. "Is that true?"

"I'm afraid it is."

"Oh, god. I......" And she broke down crying. "I...I had no idea..." she whimpered.

"We know Will's a good man, a man of integrity, and he must think a great deal of you to sit in jail rather than to put you in any kind of danger."

"He's protecting me because he loves me," she sobbed.

"I know."

"I'm sorry," she said as she reached into her purse for a tissue to dab her eyes.

"So, he stopped by to see you on certain nights while he was on duty?"

"Uh-huh."

"I see."

"No, you don't see. It wasn't just for sex. Sometimes it was just to talk, you know? I'm not a whore."

"I wasn't thinking that."

"I needed somebody nice to talk to. Somebody to love. Everybody needs to have somebody like that."

"I understand, I do," Destiny consoled. "I know how you feel."

"You do?"

Destiny could feel sympathy tears beginning to well up and choked them back. "Uh-huh. I do."

"I married a man—Dwayne, that's his name—and he turned out to be a monster. At first, everything was okay. And then he started drinkin', and he would get mean and start hitting me. I didn't know any better, I thought everything was my fault."

"But it wasn't your fault."

"No."

"What was he like when he wasn't drinking?"

"It wasn't much better. He made me feel stupid...like I was worthless. Called me names...put me down every chance he got."

"You're not stupid and you're not worthless," Destiny reassured her. "You know you're not."

"I know. I thought someday he would grow up, you know? Thought he would change. But he never did. He only got worse."

"I'm sorry," said Destiny. "How bad did it get?"

"One time Dwayne started hitting me, and I had enough of it so I decided to fight back, and he beat me so bad he knocked my front teeth out. I managed to get out of the house and call nine-one-one, and that's when Will came out. He arrested Dwayne and hauled him off to jail. I wound up in the hospital that time. That's how I first met Will. He was so nice and kind, and he checked up on me in the hospital to see how I was doin'. He even saw to it I got to a dentist. He and I…well, it sort of took off from there. I mean, it wasn't something either one of us planned, it just sort of happened. I don't know why he'd be attracted to somebody like me, but…I guess…well, we just like to talk, and he's such an easy guy to be around, if you know what I mean."

Destiny thought of Joe and smiled, "Yeah, I do." But a question came to mind, and she had to ask. "Can I ask you a question?"

"I guess so."

"Why did you go back to Dwayne after he got out of jail?"

"After he came home, he was all sorry, and he acted nice and treated me like he did after we first got married. I thought that time in jail would've given him time to think and maybe change because of it. But that only lasted just so long. And then it all just started again. Little things, and then little things turned into bigger things. And it got worse after he would go out drinkin'. And then after a while it didn't matter whether he was drinkin' or not. Now, he's just mean to me all the time."

"Why don't you leave?"

"Where would I go? I don't have anybody around here. All my relatives live in another state. And I don't want people around here to know about my problems. It's embarrassing. I have a job. I can't just pick up and leave. How can I? I don't even have a car."

"So, you're going to keep living with this guy?" Destiny asked.

"Will and I've been talking. I've come to the end of the line with Dwayne. I don't love him anymore. I hate him! Will wants me to get a divorce so he and I can be together. I want that too, but I'm afraid they would never leave us alone."

"They?"

"It's not only Dwayne, it's his whole family. He has a bunch of brothers and sisters that all live around here. I even work for his cousin. That family of his could make our lives miserable."

"They might think twice if you were living with a deputy sheriff."

Amy pulled another tissue from her purse and wiped her eyes. "I don't know what to do. I just know things can't go on the way they are." She blew her nose and apologized, "Sorry." And after sticking the tissue in her pocket, she looked at Destiny, "You said you needed my help?"

"The first and most important thing we need to do is to exonerate Will and get him out of jail. You think you can verify the nights that Will visited you when he was on duty?"

"I think so. Yeah, I used to put a little mark in my personal calendar when he was planning on coming over."

"Good. Would you be willing to speak with Sheriff Pollock and provide an alibi for Will on those nights?"

"I would but if Dwayne finds out, he'll kill me."

"What if we could do it in a way that Dwayne would never know? We could have an unmarked car pick you up somewhere and bring you to the sheriff's office. It could bring you back when you're done. And what you tell the sheriff would never have to be made public."

"Can you do that?"

"I'm sure Sheriff Pollock would agree to keep what you say confidential. Does that sound okay to you?"

"Well, yeah. I guess. Will can't stay in jail because of me. I can't let that happen."

"Is it all right to call you on your cell phone?"

"Don't call me when I'm at work. But it's okay to call me at home after 2:30. I'm off by then, and Dwayne, he works second shift in Storm Lake so he's always gone by that time unless he happens to call in sick or something."

Destiny smiled and stood. "Fine." Amy stood as well. Destiny handed Amy her card. "My phone number is on this card, so you'll know a call is coming from me."

"Okay."

"Thank you, Amy. I'm sure that Will is going to be grateful you've decided to step forward. If you need anything, or if you need to talk to someone, call me. Feel free to call me anytime, okay?"

"Thank you," Amy replied, looking Destiny in the eye for a moment. "Nobody's really taken an interest in me before. I mean, not like this. Not somebody like you, anyway. Most people, they don't seem like they care much."

"Well, I care," responded Destiny, "I want you to know that."

Destiny watched Amy walk toward the sidewalk and out of sight. She sat back down at the picnic table feeling depressed, thinking about what years of marriage to a man like Dwayne Greene must have done to leave such scars on this young woman. Despite all the training she'd received and how she'd disciplined herself to remain emotionally detached, she put her elbows on the table and supported her head with her hands. As she let out a deep breath, a sympathetic tear rolled down her cheek. She sat up and brushed it away. There would be no supper with Joe tonight. Not after this experience. Alone time was a must.

Chapter Twenty-Five

The morning sky was gloomy, a perfect reflection of Joe's state of mind. Once again, he had not slept well, having awakened in the middle of the night from a nightmare that made further sleep impossible. Stepping out his front door, he saw Melissa sitting on his front step. She looked up at him and spoke unfiltered as she often did.

"You look like crap," she said.

"Well, good morning to you, too."

"What's the matter?"

"Nothing you can fix, I'm afraid."

"Oh, I don't know about that," she smiled.

Joe shook his head. "You ready?"

"Whenever you are."

They walked down the sidewalk and onto Agora Street. From there they began jogging toward the main drag, turning on Attica and following a route that had now become routine.

Joe noticed the usually talkative Melissa was silent this morning so he decided to ask why.

"You're not your usual loquacious self today. Something wrong?"

"Loquacious," she repeated. "Are you testing my vocabulary?"

"Not at all. It's just that you're rather subdued this morning, that's all."

"Okay. Can I ask you a question?"

"I suppose. It hasn't stopped you before."

"What if a girl wanted to meet you, and she set up a place and time. Would you not bother to show up?"

"Depends on the girl," he replied.

She looked at him in disbelief, and the look on her face made him chuckle.

"I'm kidding," he said.

"I would hope," she protested.

"As a matter of fact, that would be pretty rude and inconsiderate in my opinion."

"That's what I think, too."

"What happened? Did you get stood up?"

"Yeah. Night before last I was supposed to meet this guy named Michael up in Webb, and the dickwad never showed."

"Really."

"Yeah, really. He said he was going to meet me for tacos at Taco Night. So, it was just me and my cousin Emily."

"So, is that so bad? Spending time with your cousin instead of some guy?"

"No. But you'd think he could've at least texted me or sent me an email or something if he couldn't make it."

Suddenly, Joe stopped jogging. A revelation! Melissa turned, and walked back to where he was standing.

"What's the matter?" she asked, seeing he was transfixed, staring off into space. "Are you all right?"

"Email."

"Yeah. What about it?"

"You've got email."

"Well, yeah," she said, kindly substituting "yeah" for the more sarcastic "duh" she might have used with someone else. "Doesn't everybody?"

"Private? I mean, your own email you don't share with anyone else?"

"Of course."

"Ah-hah."

Melissa didn't understand his odd behavior. It was like his mood went from overcast to sunny in a matter of seconds. "Are you all right?" she asked again.

"Oh, yeah! I am now."

Something had jolted Joe out of the doldrums, and he was now fully energized. "Come on, let's finish our run." They took off and Melissa had to push to keep up with him.

"What's gotten into you?" she asked, breathing harder than usual.

"Nothing. Well, not nothing exactly. I've thought of something, that's all."

"Well, think slower, I can't keep up!"

When they finished their usual course, and with only an abrupt goodbye, Joe hustled home, leaving Melissa standing bewildered in her driveway. After a quick shower, he got dressed, and was in his car driving out of town in half an hour's time.

The gloomy skies had turned darker and storm clouds were churning when he turned into the driveway at the home of Jenny Callaghan's parents shortly after 8:30 a.m. They lived in a ranch-style home situated on a large parcel of land about five miles outside of town. It was an attractive place with a landscaped yard and a lawn that had no sign of a weed anywhere. Joe walked to the door and rang the bell.

A moment later Carla Callaghan faced him. "May I help you?" she asked.

"Yes, I believe you can," replied Joe, showing her his identification. "I'm Joe Erickson, special deputy working with Buena Vista County."

"I know. I remember you from the day of Jenny's funeral. You were standing across the street with Deputy Snyder and another man."

A wry smile appeared on Joe's face. "You have an excellent memory."

"I do."

"I know it's early in the day, but I was wondering if I could have a few minutes of your time?"

"Is this about my daughter?"

"Yes, it is."

"I don't think I can answer any more questions."

Joe could see the pain in her face and hear the fragile emotional quality in her voice, something he had experienced so many times before when interviewing the survivors of murder victims. But information is crucial in solving cases and he needed to follow up on something that occurred to him that morning.

"I'm sorry to bother you, especially so early, but I wouldn't have come if it wasn't very important."

Carla saw the intense look in his eyes, paused a moment, and then opened the door and invited him in. She escorted him into the living room, a tastefully arranged room decorated with mementos of death. Flowers and sympathy cards were interspersed with photographs of Jenny, and the closed drapes created a depressing atmosphere. No wonder the woman felt sad if she spent time each day in this makeshift funeral parlor.

"Please, have a seat," she said indicating the sectional that dominated the corner of the room. Joe thanked her and sat.

"This has been like living a nightmare over and over again," she confessed. "I don't know if I'll ever get over it."

"I can tell you from past experience you don't ever get over it," Joe said. "But you'll learn to deal with it…in time. Right now, you need to give yourself time to grieve. For your mental health if nothing else."

"You seem to know a lot about it."

"More than most people will ever know." He paused and took a breath. "It may not seem like it now, but you'll eventually come to terms with it and find peace."

"I hope you're right."

Joe segued into why he was there. "I have just one question for you."

"And what's that?"

"Did Jenny have a computer?"

"Why, yes. She was on the Internet a lot doing homework and talking with friends and relatives. She was a very social girl."

"So, I assume she had her own email account."

"Yes."

"Did the police check into her email?"

"No…no they didn't. You think it might have something to do with…?"

"I don't know, but I think we need to investigate the possibility. Do you suppose we could check her messages?"

"I suppose so," she said. "She had a laptop. It's still in her bedroom. You want me to bring it out?"

"If you could, yes."

Carla got up and walked out of the room and down a hallway. A few moments later she returned with the laptop.

"Is there a table where we could sit?"

"Why don't we move to the dining room?" she suggested.

Carla led the way to the dining room and cleared an area on a large, round oak table for the laptop. Joe pulled out a chair and Carla moved one close to him and they both sat down so each of them could see the screen. Carla plugged it in, and before long it booted. It was Jenny, smiling and holding an orange tabby cat.

"That's Jenny with Buddy," said Carla, her voice cracking slightly.

"Do you know how to access her email?"

"Yes, we both have the same system." Carla took control of the keyboard and began typing. A window popped up asking for a password.

"Uh-oh," reacted Joe. "Do you know her password?"

Concentrating on the screen, she said, "No, but I happen to be a computer programmer so…"

As her fingers danced around the keyboard she continued, "I should be able to hack my way into this. You simply have to know what to do."

Joe smiled. "You don't fit my image of a hacker, if you don't mind me saying so."

"So you're saying, I don't look like a nerd, is that it?"

"Not like any I've seen."

"That's a rather back-handed complement, but I'll take it."

More keystrokes.

"You're good," Joe observed.

"There's something to be said about experience…here we go."

And with a final keystroke, the screen revealed Jenny's messages. Carla began reading down the list of senders.

"Jane…Diane…Linda…" She looked at Joe. "Her close friends."

"I see."

"Junk, junk, junk…I'm not seeing anything out of the ordinary."

"Did she archive any mail?" he asked.

"Let see." Carla clicked the mouse several times, and more messages appeared.

"Hm. Several here from someone named Jess."

"Who's Jess?"

"I don't know. She never mentioned him."

"Open the last one," said Joe.

Carla clicked and the message opened up. It read:

> *You said you were dying to meet me. Now's your chance—if you have the nerve! LOL!! I'll be at the softball game in Peterson around 9:00 tonight. I'll be wearing a Black Fast T-shirt. Do I have a surprise for you!!! -- Jess*

"That's where she was going the night she was…" Carla trailed off as tears welled up in her eyes.

"This message would appear innocent enough at the time. But when you read it now, there is an ominous quality that is really disturbing. When was it sent?"

"Oh, dear," murmured Carla. "That morning."

"Can you check to see when he sent the first email to her?"

Carla scrolled down and found the earliest one. She looked over at Joe.

"A month ago. "Do you think this Jess person could…?"

"I don't know. It looks suspicious but it could turn out to be nothing. We need to have a forensics technician comb through her messages, see if he can trace any of these back to their source. Would it be all right to take her laptop in for evidence purposes?"

"Of course. Take it," she said. "Anything that will help."

"Thanks."

"I wish there was something I could do to help catch this monster."

At that moment, a light bulb lit up in Joe's brain. "As a matter of fact…there may be something."

Chapter Twenty-Six

J oe's car pulled into the driveway of a turn-of-the-century Queen Anne-style house on the edge of Linn Grove, a small town of around 150 residents located seven miles west of Sioux Rapids. The house had undergone restoration, and its delicate gingerbread trim had been painted in tones of gray with white and red accents. Had it been painted in bold colors it would have looked right at home in San Francisco among the "painted ladies." It had been the home of Tina Olson.

Thunder rumbled as Joe and Carla stepped from the car and climbed the porch steps to the front door. Before Joe had a chance to ring the bell, the door opened revealing Tina's father, Mike Olson. A large, stocky man, he had the outward aspect of a jock gone to seed. He was dressed in chinos and an untucked blue plaid shirt that did little to disguise the beer gut overhanging his belt. His face was red and puffy with broken capillary lines on his upper cheeks.

"Carla?" he said, obviously surprised by her presence. He opened the screen door and stepped onto the porch.

"Hi, Mike," she said. "We were hoping you'd be home."

"Well, I am today."

He looked at Joe inquisitively and she noticed. "This is Joe Erickson. He's a special investigator brought in by the county."

"I see."

Joe reached out his hand. "Pleased to meet you." Mike gave his hand a firm shake.

"What can I do for you?" Mike inquired.

"I wonder if we might have a few words with you about Tina," said Joe.

Mike gave a subtle nod of his head, and without saying another word opened the door for them and followed them inside. He confirmed that Tina had a computer as well as an iPhone. After Joe and Carla explained what they were looking for, he went into Tina's room and retrieved both items and gave Carla permission to access her email.

Carla went into the family room to begin hacking into Tina's computer. Joe stayed with Mike in the kitchen.

"Actually, I'm not working at the moment," Mike explained. "I've taken some time off. My supervisor told me to take as much time as I need so......"

"It's good to have an understanding boss," Joe replied.

"Yeah. Well, he lost a son over in Afghanistan, so he knows what I'm going through. I do most of my work online anyway so I only have to travel to meetings about once a month or so. I've been seeing a counselor, and he figures it may be time for me to go back to work soon—at least part time. Help get my mind off things. You just can't sit around doing nothing, you know? Not healthy."

"Yeah. Where's your wife?"

"She and our other two kids are clearing out Tina's apartment in Mankato. Her roommate was going to summer school and was living there so she never bothered to bring her stuff home for the summer."

"I'm sorry."

"You want something to drink? Coffee, beer, pop, ice tea?"

"No, thanks. I'm fine."

"You don't mind if I..."

"Go right ahead."

Mike got up and opened the refrigerator door and pulled a bottle of beer from the shelf. He twisted off the cap and sat back down in his chair and took a drink. Ten o'clock in the morning was pretty early to start drinking beer, confirming Joe's suspicion that Mike was an alcoholic.

Joe didn't ask him about Tina since Mike didn't choose to volunteer any more information about her. Instead, they talked sports, and found they were both Chicago Cubs fans. So, they wound up discussing the season, the coaches, and players until Carla appeared twenty minutes later.

"Did you find anything?" asked Joe.

"Yes," replied Carla. "She received the same kind of email."

"What's that mean?" asked Mike.

"It means that Tina and Jenny's abductions are related," confirmed Joe. "We need to take your daughter's computer and phone for forensic analysis. Is that all right?"

"Yeah. If it helps catch whoever did it. Yeah, by all means."

"We'll make sure you get them back when we're done."

Joe wrote Mike a receipt for the items. Minutes later, he and Carla stepped out the front door with Joe holding Tina's laptop and iPhone. Mike followed them down the porch steps and out to the car.

"You'll keep us informed, right?" asked Mike.

"Absolutely. If we make any progress, I'll be sure to let you know."

"We'd appreciate that."

"I want to thank you for your cooperation. This could be the kind of break we've been looking for." Joe offered his hand and Mike shook it.

"Take care, Mike," said Carla, giving him a hug. "Say hello to Judy for me, okay?"

"I will."

Joe drove Carla back to her house, thanking her for hacking into Tina's email. Before leaving, she wrote down the passwords for both Jenny's and Tina's computers and email programs. He thought about that as he pulled onto the street. It struck him as odd to be thanking someone like Carla for hacking into another person's computer. It seemed akin to thanking a kindly lady for doing some shoplifting for him. But circumstances sometimes made things like that necessary. And it wasn't like it was illegal or anything.

As he drove onto Highway 71 south toward Storm Lake, the sky opened up and it began pouring rain. He switched on his wipers but they barely kept up with the torrents of rain from one of Iowa's summer thunder storms.

He used his car's cell phone to call Destiny. She picked up after the second ring.

"Hi."

"Hi."

"Where have you been? I've been trying to reach—?"

"Not now," Joe interrupted. "I can barely see to drive, it's raining so hard."

"Maybe you should pull over."

"I'm okay. I've got something, something important. Where are you?"

"In Storm Lake. At the motel."

"Call Jeff. I'll meet you two there in twenty minutes.

"What is it?"

"It's too complicated to explain on the phone."

"Okay."

"See you in a bit."

Twenty-five minutes later, Joe drove into the motel parking lot on Lakeshore Drive. He pulled in next to Destiny's room, honked his horn, got out, and ran to door. She opened it, and he ducked inside, wet from the rain. Jeff was sitting in a chair drinking a Diet Coke.

"Wet out there," Jeff said. "This better be good."

"It is."

Destiny walked into the bathroom and came back with a hand towel and tossed it to Joe.

"Destiny said you discovered something important but she didn't give me any details. What have you got?" asked Jeff.

"I think we have our first big break," he asserted.

"Yeah?"

"Emails."

"Emails..." repeated Jeff.

"Omigod!" realized Destiny.

"No one bothered to check to see if our two victims had personal email accounts."

"And you found they did," concluded Destiny. "And you found something!"

"Yeah. I met with Carla Callaghan, and she was able to check her daughter's email account. And then we went over to speak with Mike Olson and got his permission to access Tina's account. We found that on the nights of their abductions, each girl was traveling to a neighboring town to meet a good-looking young man they had met over the Internet. Jenny was meeting a guy named Jess, and Tina was meeting a guy named Brad."

"Okay, so…" commented Jeff. "They both met some hot guy. Was it the same guy?"

"Not according to the photos they received. The guys looked totally different. Now that could be chalked up to coincidence. But thanks to Carla, we found both Jess' and Brad's email messages originated from the same IP address."

"Interesting," commented Destiny.

"What's Jenny's mother got to do with all this?" asked Jeff.

"She's a computer programmer. She was able to hack into both her daughter's and Tina Olson's email accounts and found the same type of messages. She provided me with the passwords so our computer tech person can access their laptops and cell phones."

"Do we know if the girls met this guy?"

"We have no way of knowing that. But the two girls were both spending time with friends on those nights, and none of them stated anything about Tina or Jenny meeting some new guy."

"We'd better question them again," said Jeff.

Destiny's eyes lit up. "So, you think the perp may have lured them to fictitious meetings using photos of attractive young men in order to intercept them while they were driving home?"

"Bingo!" Joe exclaimed. "You see, one was a meeting scheduled to take place in Peterson while the other was scheduled in Albert City. Both were supposed to take place at night. In order to return home, the girls would have to drive at night on less traveled county roads, and it was on these type of roads that both of their cars were found."

"You have the sender's IP address?" asked Jeff.

"Yeah." Joe pulled out his notebook, tore out a page, and handed it to Jeff.

Jeff looked at the address and then to Joe. "We're going to need those two computers."

"Already have them in my car. If it wasn't raining so hard, I would have brought them in with me."

"Do you have a computer crime technician who can retrieve this data and trace the IP address to its source?" Destiny asked Jeff.

"We have a guy. He's good. In fact, he's better than good. I'll have him here tomorrow. You'll bring the computers to the office in the morning?"

"Yeah."

Jeff rose from his seat. "I'd better make some phone calls." He walked to the door and saw the torrents coming down. "I'm gonna get soaked. Again." Turning, he looked back into the room. "Joe? Great work." and gave him a thumbs-up. He pulled his sport coat up over his head, hesitated a moment, and then shot through the door, disappearing into the rain.

"How'd you come up with the email idea?"

"It came to me while I was jogging this morning. Something Melissa said, and it was like a light bulb suddenly flashed on in my mind."

"Imaginative problem-solving. You experienced what's called a 'eureka moment'."

"Yeah, whatever it was, it happened out of the blue."

"Those moments are great, especially when they turn into something worthwhile."

"Did you have any luck with Amy Greene?" he asked.

"I did. She's willing to provide an alibi for Tucker on those nights. The poor girl's scared to death of her husband, and you can't blame her. He's abusive, physically and psychologically. I saw bruises on her arms, and they weren't the result of an accidental bump. She told me he beat her so bad he put her in the hospital on one occasion."

"God, I hate those guys."

"But she agreed to meet with Sheriff Pollock tomorrow afternoon. I told her I'd arrange to have an unmarked car pick her up and drive her down here since she doesn't have any transportation of her own."

"Good."

"So, how are you doing?"

"Oh...I think I may be fit for human companionship again," he confided.

She smiled. "Well, in that case, how about some supper? Jeff told me about this nice little Chinese restaurant on the north side of town. He gave it a

156

great review."

"Do they deliver?"

"What's the matter? Afraid of getting wet?"

With a glint. "No."

"Oh," she laughed, "I know what you're thinking, mister."

Destiny grabbed her umbrella. "Come on." He rose from the chair and she nudged him toward the door.

"I just thought..."

"Not so fast," she smiled. "You haven't proven yourself quite yet."

"Okay, okay. I probably wouldn't trust me yet either."

"Let's go, I'm hungry for some shrimp with lobster sauce."

"Who's driving?"

"You are."

Chapter Twenty-Seven

The next morning, Jeff informed Joe that the department's computer crime technician would not be arriving in Storm Lake until the next day due to a scheduling problem. Joe brought in the two laptops along with the girl's cell phones. Deputy Simms tagged them, and placed them in the evidence locker where they would be secure until the next day.

That afternoon Joe walked into the outer office of the sheriff's department. For some time, he'd been feeling that he'd been sidestepping Sheriff Pollock on this case. He knew it would be in everyone's best interest if he would make amends and fill him in on what they had found exploring the dead girls' computers. Deputy Simms was sitting at the front desk.

"Is Sheriff Pollock in?"

"Yes, he's is," she replied. "Go ahead and knock on his door."

Joe gave the sheriff's door a knock and heard a muffled "Come in" from inside. To his surprise, there was a woman standing next to Pollock. She was in her late fifties with well-coiffed salt and pepper hair, neatly dressed in a pink blouse and khaki slacks. She wore a double string of pearls around her neck and a wedding ring on her finger.

"Oh, I'm sorry," said Joe, "I can come back later."

"I was just leaving," said the woman in an accent reminiscent of the Georgia-Carolina region.

"See you at two-thirty then?" asked Pollock.

"Two-thirty," confirmed the woman who walked up to Joe and put out her hand. "I'm Georgia Pollock, Vince's wife."

Joe shook her hand. "I'm Joe Erickson.

"Oh, I've heard all about you!"

"I'll bet you have."

"Vince speaks very highly of you, says you're one of the best."

"Does he now?"

"He does indeed. Well, I have to go. Nice meeting you, Mr. Erickson."

"It's Joe."

"All right, then. Nice meeting you, Joe." She looked back at Pollock and said, "You didn't tell me he was so good looking."

"That's not something that shows up on my radar," replied Pollock.

"No, I don't suppose it does." She reached for the door, gave a little wave to Pollock, and said, "Bye dear." And she was out the door. Joe turned to look at Pollock and there was a rather sad smile on his face that he quickly disguised with his usual gruffness.

"Southern girl," Joe observed.

"Yeah. South Carolina. Met her when I was stationed at Fort Jackson. Don't know what she saw in this Yankee boy, but it must've been something. Have a seat, Erickson."

"Thanks," Joe said as he pulled up a chair in front of the desk.

"What's on your mind?" Pollock asked as he took a drink from a coffee mug, the one that had "World's Best Grandpa" printed on the side. Joe had seen it before, and he thought to himself, *Maybe this guy isn't such a prick after all.*

"Been busy," replied Joe. "I wanted to start off by saying that I wish we had gotten off to a better start, you and me. It was probably my fault, it usually is. I don't always play well with others, as you've most likely noticed."

"I have."

"You know, we've both spent years doing the same sort of job. We have different work habits and methods, but we're both after the same thing, so I figured it doesn't make a lot of sense for us to keep butting heads. Besides, I'm a guest in your house, and you've probably been thinking I just trotted in here like a stray dog and started pissing on the furniture."

"Well, to tell you the truth, I didn't want you here to begin with, but a state guy twisted my arm, and I gave in. And as a result, I resented your presence here. But…I've come to realize you're good. Damned good, as a matter of fact. And besides that…you work your ass off. Anytime I can get someone with your expertise and your work ethic on a case like this…aw, hell, I don't mind telling you I'm out of my league on this and I need all the help I can get. If it's all right with you, maybe we should just start over, you and me. The way I look at it, if we work together, there's a better chance we can catch this son-of-a-bitch."

"I agree."

Pollock rose from his seat. "How about it?" And he held out his hand. Joe stood, and he shook his hand. "Nice to meet you, Sheriff."

"Likewise." They returned to their chairs.

"Speaking of catching this son-of-a-bitch, I think I'm on to something."

"Yeah?"

"I would have called you last night but it was late, and I figured it wasn't something that couldn't wait until today."

"What have you got?"

"This idea popped into my head about emails when I was out jogging the other morning…" Joe went on to explain about what he found when he looked into Tina's and Jenny's emails, the discovery of messages from two boys that originated from the same IP address, and how both girls were lured to meetings with these "fake boys" before their kidnappings.

"That's some damned good detective work, Joe," said Pollock. Joe realized this was the first time Pollock had ever called him by his first name, and that seemed to confirm a major breakthrough had occurred in their relationship. Then the intercom rang and Pollock picked up.

"Yeah? Okay, send them in." He looked at Joe. "Destiny says she has some important information I need to hear. When it rains, it pours, huh?" He rose from his chair, as did Joe, and both men made their way to the door. Joe opened it and saw Destiny standing there with a small, young, red-haired woman. Joe stepped past her into the main office area as Destiny moved to Sheriff Pollock who was standing in the doorway.

"Sheriff, this is Amy Greene. She has some important information."

Pollock looked at Amy. "You do, huh?"

"Yes," replied Amy meekly.

"It's regarding Deputy Tucker," Destiny clarified.

At this point, Pollock's voice changed to a more serious tone. "Well, step into my office," he said indicating the open door.

"Is it all right if she comes with me?" asked Amy, indicating Destiny.

"If you like. Come on in." Pollock held the door open for them and they entered and then closed the door behind them. Ten minutes later the office door opened, and Amy and Destiny emerged. Amy held several tissues in her hand, and it was obvious she'd been crying.

"Thank you for coming in," acknowledged Pollock.

"You're welcome, Sheriff," she said in a barely audible voice. She sniffed back tears and turned to Destiny who gave her a reassuring nod. As the two left, Pollock picked up the outer office phone and pushed a button. After a moment he barked an order into the phone.

"Charlie. Vince. Get Tucker in here."

Jeff, who had finished sending a fax, overheard and knew something had happened but didn't know what it was. He saw Joe standing at the front desk conversing with Deputy Simms and motioned him over. "You want to fill me in on what just happened?"

"Yeah. Let's step outside."

"Good, because I'm confused." Joe followed Jeff out of the office and down the hall.

***

Deputy Charles "Charlie" Warner was the oldest deputy on the force. He was a rough-hewn man of sixty with a shock of gray hair, a large physique and an equally large mustache. For years, his job had been supervising the jail and monitoring the prisoners. When he stopped in front of Tucker's cell, Tucker sat up in bed.

"Sheriff wants to see you," announced Warner in a sympathetic voice.

"You know what he wants, Charlie?"

"Didn't say."

Tucker stood up and stepped to the door. He knew the drill. He stuck out

161

his arms so Warner could apply handcuffs. After the door opened, Warner led him down the hall toward Pollock's office. It was humiliating for Tucker to be incarcerated by a fellow officer he considered a friend. And Warner felt awkward as hell having to treat a fellow deputy the same way as the scumbags and perverts that occupied his jail cells over the years. In his own mind, he didn't believe for a minute this baby-faced kid was a killer, but no matter what he thought, no exceptions could be made in the way prisoners were handled. He was by the book through and through.

***

Standing outside, Jeff had finished a cigarette and excused himself to go to the restroom. It was one of those perfect Iowa days without a cloud in the sky and a temperature around eighty-eight degrees. As Joe stood there taking it in, a green Dodge pickup pulled up, and out slid a big man in need of a shave who was dressed in a dirty T-shirt and worn-out blue jeans. Greasy hair stuck out from under a sweat-stained camouflage cap, and his surly disposition was evident from the moment he stepped from his truck. He walked to Joe.

"I need to talk to somebody," he said in a threatening voice.

"What about?" asked Joe.

"I wanna know what the fuck my wife is doin' here."

"Your wife?"

"Yeah. Amy. Amy Greene."

Joe thought, *Oh, so this is the worthless piece of shit that beats his wife.* But before he could say anything, Destiny and Amy emerged from the building. Amy gasped when she saw her husband, and she cowered as he approached.

"What the fuck did you do?" he demanded. "My brother calls me and says he saw you get hauled away by the cops!"

"Come on," said Destiny. And she started guiding Amy back into the building. But Dwayne grabbed Amy so hard by the arm she winced and cried out in pain.

"I asked you a question, god damnit!"

At that point Joe stepped in. "Excuse me," he said calmly, and grabbing Dwayne's wrist, he forcibly removed his hand from his wife's arm.

Dwayne looked at him with disdain and snarled, "Who the hell are you?"

"I'm a special deputy with the county. I can explain everything if you'll just step over here, please."

Joe motioned him away from the entrance giving time for Destiny to get Amy back inside. Dwayne followed Joe who made sure they would stop around the corner of the building.

Now safely inside, Amy was in tears. "Oh, god!" she cried, "It wasn't supposed to be like this! What am I going to do? He was supposed to be at work! He never told me he was taking the day off."

Destiny tried her best to console Amy knowing full well that this unfortunate turn of events could turn out badly for her. Even so, she knew that Joe was well aware of Amy's situation and had experience handling bullies like Dwayne Greene. "It's all right. I'm sure Joe will explain things to Dwayne."

"I hope so, because Dwayne, he's going to go ballistic when he gets home. And I don't want to be there when he does."

"Amy...Amy, look at me," she said in an attempt to calm her down. Destiny spoke to her in a cool, composed manner, "I know Joe really well, and he understands how to talk to men like Dwayne. I'm sure he can give him a reason why you had to come here today and convince him there is nothing to be concerned about. So, let's just wait and see what happens after Joe talks with him, okay?"

"All right, but..."

"Come on, let's go down to my office and wait. Maybe you'll have a chance to see Tucker later on." That seemed to be enough to convince Amy to go with Destiny and get her mind off Dwayne for the time being.

***

Back outside, Dwayne had followed Joe around the corner of the building. Turning to Joe, he belligerently demanded, "What the fuck is going on here?"

"Well, it's like this," said Joe. And he delivered a powerful punch to Dwayne's gut that doubled him over and made him gag. As Dwayne began to rise up, Joe slammed his hand into his groin, grabbed him by the testicles, and squeezed so hard Dwayne's eyes nearly popped out of his head. With

163

his other hand, Joe shoved him back against the wall of the building, his arm pushing against his collarbones. As the big man was uttering some indistinguishable sounds from deep in his throat, Joe spoke.

"Your wife's here because she witnessed something related to those two girls' murders, and she is not allowed to talk about it to anyone. It's confidential, so you don't ask her any questions, you understand?"

Unable to speak, Dwayne managed a little nod as tears welled up in his eyes and saliva dripped from the corner of his mouth.

"And I hear you like to beat her up, too. I even heard you put her in the hospital. I don't like guys that beat up women. So if I hear you've laid a hand on her again, in fact, if you so much as even mess with her in any way, I'm gonna track you down and pull these fucking things right off! You got that?"

Dwayne uttered some primitive guttural sounds of affirmation as tears rolled down his cheeks. Joe squeezed even harder. "What? I didn't hear you?"

Dwayne managed an almost inaudible, high pitched, "Uh-huh."

"Good! And if you're dumb enough to think you and your idiot brothers can come after me for payback, I want to tell you something. I've got ways of making you disappear so the worms won't even find you. Now you get your sorry ass home!"

And with that, Joe let him go. Without a word Dwayne slowly walked, thighs together with one hand holding his testicles, back to his pickup. With some degree of difficulty, he managed to climb into the cab. And after a moment, he hit the starter, shifted into reverse, backed out of the parking space, and slowly drove away, hunching over the steering wheel as he rolled down the street.

Unbeknownst to Joe, Jeff had stepped back outside and witnessed the incident. "What do you call that back in Chicago?" he asked with a sniff.

Joe looked at him and replied matter-of-factly, "Marriage counseling."

***

Back inside, Tucker was standing before his boss. Pollock had his hands on the back of his chair, visibly annoyed.

"So, tell me. Is it true? Were you screwing Amy Greene while on duty?"

164

"Yes, sir," a humiliated Tucker replied.

"And that's why you refused to account for those sixty-minute gaps."

"Yes, sir. I didn't want to get her in trouble with her husband."

"Well, I think you've already done that. You have anything to say for yourself?"

"Not really...other than it was wrong, and I'm sorry it happened," said Tucker.

"I see. Well, I guess that settles it." He looked over Tucker's shoulder into the outer office and called out.

"Warner!"

Deputy Warner, who had been waiting in the outer office, stepped in.

"Yes, sir?"

"Take his cuffs off. He's free to go. I'll send over the paperwork later."

Warner removed Tucker's handcuffs and gave him a pat on the shoulder. As Tucker turned to leave, Joe and Jeff entered the outer office.

"Oh, and Tucker..." said Pollock. Tucker turned back to face him.

"Yes, sir?"

"You're suspended."

Silence.

"Come on, kid," Warner said to Tucker, and the two men walked dejectedly out of the office to the property room to pick up Tucker's belongings.

"Sheriff," protested Joe.

"He violated policy. It's in the regulations. There's nothing I can do about it," stated Pollock.

Joe started to go toward his office when he felt Jeff's hand on his shoulder.

"Let it go," he advised softly. "He has no choice."

"He arrests the wrong guy, and then suspends him on top of it," Joe vented. "He could have made an exception."

"Look," said Jeff confidentially, "I wasn't supposed to say anything so keep this under your hat. He just recently found out his wife has cancer. Pancreatic. She's supposed to start chemo today, so you might cut the guy a little slack."

Joe let out a loud sigh. "Ah, shit."

"And to make matters worse, he's been feeling like a limp dick on this investigation. He's got a lot on his plate, and he's due to retire next year so...come on, let's get out of here. I'll buy you a beer."

As they walked out into the hallway, they ran into Destiny and Amy Greene.

"Were you able to square it with my husband?" she asked.

"I explained the situation to him, and I'm pretty sure he got the message. If he bothers you in any way, you let me know and I'll have another talk with him."

"Oh, thank you."

"I should probably tell you, he had a...a little accident outside—nothing serious mind you—but he may be a bit sore for a while. I might avoid asking him about it, though. It's a little embarrassing."

"Oh...okay. Do you suppose I could see Will?"

Joe didn't want to tell her about Tucker's suspension and the unintentional consequences resulting from her alibi so he felt a little prevarication was in order. "He may be a while. There are papers to fill out and he has to gather his things. So, I'll tell you what, Jeff is taking us out for a beer. He wouldn't mind if you came along—would you, Jeff?"

"Uh, no, of course not."

"Well, I..."

"Oh, come on, Amy. I'm buying," said Destiny. "You can always have a soft drink if you don't want to have something with alcohol in it."

"Well...okay," agreed Amy, giving her a rare smile. "I guess I can see Will later on maybe. It's been a long time since I got to go out anywhere."

Chapter Twenty-Eight

D el Woodward, a computer crime technician for the Iowa Department of Criminal Investigation, fit the stereotype people often associate with computer geeks. Looking almost anorexic, he was in his early thirties and saw the world through glasses with Coke-bottle lenses. His unruly hair, Hawaiian shirt, thrift store suit pants and blue sneakers with made him a perfect candidate for one of those television shows that teach people appropriate ways to dress. Most of his colleagues ignored his eccentric attire because he was a genius when it came to computers.

Del had driven the two-and-a-half hours to Storm Lake from his home in West Des Moines early that morning, arriving a few minutes before eight o'clock. The sheriff's staff set him up in the conference room, and he had wasted no time investigating each of the laptops and tracing the suspicious email messages. He was sucking down his third can of Diet Dr. Pepper when Joe and Jeff walked in shortly after ten o'clock. The two laptops were plugged in and running with each one displaying its screensaver image. After introductions, Del began talking.

"Both email contacts came from the same IP address, so I think you can assume that Brad and Jess are the same guy using two different aliases."

"Can you trace him?" asked Jeff.

"Well, I have to tell you this guy is smart. I'm impressed! I mean, he really knows how to cover his ass," he said with admiration.

"You can't just trace him through his internet service?" Joe asked.

"His IP address, you mean?"

"Whatever."

"Well, yeah. But if someone sets up an account in Budapest by way of Amsterdam by way of Melbourne, etcetera, etcetera, like this guy has done, there's no way on god's green earth you're going to trace him back to an actual site address in Iowa or wherever the hell he lives."

"So, you're telling us that the perp can send and receive email anonymously, and there's no way to find out who he is?" asked Jeff.

"Yeah. More or less."

"Christ," muttered Joe under his breath.

"Tell me you have some ideas," insisted Jeff.

"Ever been to Budapest?" quipped Del.

Joe was getting frustrated. "You mean to tell me there's nothing—"

"Now, wait a minute. Wait one minute." Del cut Joe off before he could finish his sentence. Sensing his anger, Del changed his tone. "Let me explain what he's done. You ever heard of a Chinese puzzle box?"

"What's that got to do with it?"

"Do you know what it is?" he asked calmly and slowly.

"Yeah," Joe replied. "A box inside of a box inside of a box."

"Right. Essentially, that's what this guy has done with his Internet connections. His email bounces from server to server in numerous foreign countries. I only traced three—Melbourne, Amsterdam, and Budapest—but he could have a dozen for all we know, and tracing them is a complete waste of time."

"Why's that?" asked Jeff.

"You can't serve an internet service with a search warrant in Budapest. Are you kidding? Even if you got Interpol involved…I told you, this guy is smart."

Destiny entered the room and announced, "Sheriff Pollock just received a call from Wilson's wife. He's recovered to the point they're going to transport him by ambulance back to the hospital here in Storm Lake. He'll be doing the remainder of his convalescing here."

"When?" asked Jeff.

"Today. He should be back in town sometime this afternoon. She said she'd call when he's is in his room."

Joe felt relieved he'd finally be able to speak with Wilson and maybe discover what "blag rooz" meant, if it meant anything at all. For all he knew, it could wind up being the incoherent ramblings of an injured brain. But his father taught him at an early age not to assume anything. "Remember," he used to say, "there's a reason the word assume begins with 'ass' so don't be one."

They spoke with Del for another half-hour. He said he would follow up on the two laptops and see if he could find anything that could provide any clues to the suspect. But he wasn't hopeful and told them not to expect any breakthroughs.

"Unless he screwed up really bad, and I don't think he did, he's going to remain a ghost."

***

At about five o'clock, Sheriff Pollock received a call from Sarah Wilson saying her husband was settled in and had permission from the attending physician to receive a few visitors. Destiny relayed the message to Joe and Jeff, and they piled into Jeff's car and drove across town to the hospital. As they got off the elevator and rounded the corner, they saw Sheriff Pollock waiting in the hallway outside Wilson's room.

"The doctor's in there, now," Pollock stated. "His condition's been upgraded to fair."

"That's good to hear," replied Destiny.

It wasn't long until Dr. Harrington came out. He was a youthful, fifty-year-old with a jovial personality. When he saw the four of them, he asked, "Are you waiting to see Matthew Wilson?"

"Yes," answered Pollock.

"Five minutes, no more," ordered Harrington in a serious tone, and then countered with a quip. "Any more than that, and you'll be talking to Nurse Ratched."

"Understood," replied Jeff. "I always wondered whatever happened to her."

"She works for me now," said Dr. Harrington. "Five minutes, that's all." And with that, he walked away down the hall.

Sheriff Pollock pushed the door open to Wilson's room and the others filed in behind him. Sarah was sitting in the chair next to the bed. Gauze bandages covered much of Wilson's head and he was hooked up to a digital monitor. An I.V. drip hung from a stand with a line leading to his arm. He saw them enter and managed a smile.

"Hey," he said in a weak voice.

Pollock leaned in, "You gave us quite a scare."

"Yeah. I feel pretty lucky."

"You feel up to answering a few questions?"

"Sure."

"Do you remember anything about the chase?"

"I was after a...phantom cruiser."

"A what?" reacted Pollock.

"A black crui-ser," he winced.

Joe's eyes went to Destiny. "Blag rooz......"

"Black cruiser," she said.

"Damn! I should have figured that out!" Destiny thought he was going to literally slap his forehead.

"I thought I saw...Tucker's cruiser."

"But it couldn't have been his. It was impounded," added Pollock.

"Tail light..."

"Tail light?" asked Jeff.

"Wasn't...wasn't broken."

"Oh, yeah. Tucker's cruiser has a broken tail light that he temporarily mended with red tape," clarified Pollock. "We hadn't had a chance to have it repaired."

"Black Chevy Impala," confirmed Wilson.

"What was it doing when you first saw it?" asked Joe.

"Following a...a red Honda...Civic, I think. Coming from Webb."

Joe's forehead suddenly broke out into a cold sweat and his stomach practically jumped in his throat. He bolted from the room. His behavior was so sudden that Destiny followed him out into the hall.

"What is it? What's the matter?" She had never seen him like this before. The color had drained from his face, and if she didn't know better, she would have thought he was becoming ill.

"Joe...?"

He had his cell phone up to his ear.

"Shit! No answer," he growled.

"Tell me! What's going on?"

He began punching a phone number into his cell phone.

"The red Honda. He was following Melissa! She told me she was meeting someone in Webb that night and he never showed. Sound familiar? Wilson must have interrupted the abduction."

"Omigod!"

He held the phone up to his ear once again, waiting with a sense of urgency.

"Come on. Answer!"

After a couple of rings, Melissa's mother answered, "Hello."

Using a calm voice so as not to upset her unnecessarily, Joe said, "Jean, it's Joe Erickson."

"Yes, Joe?"

"Could I speak with Melissa?"

"She's not here. She's meeting some boy in Storm Lake tonight. The one that stood her up before. I told her—"

"How long ago did she leave?"

"I don't know. I wasn't here when she left. If you need to reach her, you can call her cell."

"That's all right. I'll catch her another time. Thanks."

He ended the call and punched in Melissa's cell number. The call went to voicemail. He grabbed Destiny by the arm. "Come on!"

"Joe, I—"

"There's no time! Melissa's in danger! Hurry!" And the two of them hustled out of the hospital and into the parking lot where they got into Joe's Camaro and sped out onto the street.

As he was driving, he explained the situation to Destiny.

"Why are we going this way?" asked Destiny.

"Because it's the back way from Marathon to Storm Lake. Quicker with less traffic. It's the route most Marathon people take traveling to Storm

Lake. Odds are this is the route she took."

"You think we'll meet her?"

"I don't know. In case we don't, you watch the side roads on your side, and I'll watch them on mine. If you see a red car, yell."

"It isn't night."

"I know. We have to catch her en route or make sure she made it to Storm Lake before we go looking for her down there."

Joe was pushing his Camaro up to eighty-five miles per hour, hoping desperately to see Melissa's car. At the junction of County Road M-54 that led to Marathon, he hit the brakes and made a hard left-hand turn going north. Again, he ran the car up to eighty-five miles per hour. The fields and side roads were flying by.

"Slow down," implored Destiny. "If I blink, I could miss it. It's hard to see the road when the corn is so high."

"All right," he agreed and slowed to sixty-five.

Two miles later, Destiny cried out, "Red car!"

Joe slammed on the brakes and pulled a tire-burning U-turn in the middle of the road. He turned off onto the gravel road, and there sat Melissa's red Civic about thirty yards in. He knew it was her car from the license plate number. He parked his car so it blocked any other vehicle from entering the road, thus preserving a possible crime scene.

"Stay here. I want to get a look," he said to Destiny. "If someone stops, don't let them past the car." The Civic's door was partially open, and from the look of the gravel on the surface of the road, tire tracks revealed where another vehicle was parked. He felt sick to his stomach. He wanted to see the inside of her car but knew that could compromise the crime scene. He walked back to his car, opened the door and sat down sideways in the seat, his feet on the road. He sat forward resting his elbows on his knees.

Destiny walked around the car. "Should I call it in, Joe?" But she got no response. She knelt next to him and placed her hand on his arm in an effort to comfort him. He responded to her touch and looked over at her.

"He's got her," he sighed.

"I'm so sorry...my god, Joe. I don't know what to say."

"Why? Why her? I don't get it!"

Then he abruptly stood up, almost knocking Destiny over. He took a couple of steps, and picked up a rock from the road. In an act of frustration and anger, he let out a growl and threw it far into the cornfield.

"DAMN IT!" he yelled. "DAMN-DAMN-DAMN-DAMN-DAMN!" Then he turned and stepped back to his car, and at that point his knees began to buckle. As he collapsed, he slid down the side of his car, the seat of his pants landing on the graveled surface of the road. With his knees now pulled up, he leaned his head down against them clenching and re-clenching his fists in frustration as Destiny stood by feeling helpless.

David Eugene Burton's victims flashed through his mind, and then the crime scene photos of Tina Olson and Jennifer Callaghan's death scenes appeared. He shuddered when he saw the bodies had Melissa's lifeless face. He started to tremble and hyperventilate. Would that be her fate, too? Her naked body found along a riverbank? Victim number three? Another Jamie Chambers to haunt him? He had to get that image out of his head or he was going to lose it. *Can't afford to fall apart now. Not when you need to be your best,* he thought. *For god's sakes, Joe! Get your shit together!*

Destiny had never seen him like this before and didn't know what to do. Was he having a panic attack or nervous breakdown? Should she comfort him? Talk to him? Leave him alone? Fortunately, he rose and moved toward her, his arms opening, seeking her embrace. Always self-sufficient, never relying on anyone, always able to fly under his own power. But not this time. He needed to find strength and reassurance at this moment, and he found it in Destiny. Nothing was said for some time as they stood there holding one another. Finally, Destiny broke the silence as her soft voice asked, "Are you going to be all right?"

Releasing her, he looked in her eyes. "Yeah...yeah, I am."

She gave him a little smile. "Good." And after taking a breath she took a step back. "I'd better call this in, huh?"

He nodded. Pulling her cell phone from her pocket, she asked, "What's our location?"

"Four miles north of the junction of County Roads C-49 and M-54."

After calling nine one one, she took Joe's hand and they walked out to the edge of the road to signal the first responding law enforcement officer.

In less than ten minutes, Deputy Taylor arrived on the scene. Ten minutes after that, the scene was lit up with red-and-blue flashing lights. Deputies and state patrolmen set up roadblocks a mile in each direction, and the gravel road had been cordoned off with crime scene tape. Sheriff Pollock, Deputy Taylor, and Jeff were speaking near Joe's car, which had been moved off the gravel and onto the blacktop road.

"If we have a phantom cruiser, where did it come from?" asked Jeff. "He has to have a place to hide it. Could have multiple places for all we know."

"It would have to be out in the country somewhere. People would notice if it was in town."

"It wouldn't be hard to find the same make and model car and modify it to look like a police car. Hell, for all we know that could be where my stolen license plates wound up," Pollock asserted.

By this time, Joe had pulled himself together, and overhearing the conversation, he stepped in. "Wait a minute. If I remember correctly, Marv Koehler described the vehicle he saw as having red and blue flashing lights and spotlights."

"So?" reacted Pollock.

"Think about it. Would you go to all the work of installing spotlights if you were going to clone a police car? That's a lot of work."

"What are you getting at?" asked Jeff.

"The state of Iowa sells its retired state patrol cruisers at auction, don't they?"

"Yeah," replied Pollock, now interested in where this line of thought was going.

"And they remove everything but the spotlights because they don't want to repair the holes drilled through the fenders and into the passenger compartment. You've seen these cars running around, right? The spotlights may be disabled but are still attached."

"That's right. I've seen them," agreed Taylor.

Joe looked over at Jeff. "Suppose we can get a list of people who purchased

Impala cruisers over the last two years?"

"I'm on it," responded Jeff who made a B line for his car.

"Good point, Joe," said Pollock.

"Sheriff! Over here!" called out a state patrolman standing over by Melissa's Honda.

"Excuse me," Pollock said to Destiny.

Destiny said to Joe, "I've been asking myself, why Melissa? Is it random or is there a connection to the other two victims?"

"Yeah. You know, Tom told me he knew the fathers of the other two girls. Went to high school with them."

"Three men, three teenage daughters. That's no coincidence, Joe."

"Yeah. But what the hell could it be?"

"You know what's different about this abduction? It didn't take place when it was dark. He didn't wait until she was returning home late at night when there was no traffic. He intercepted her while it was still daylight. Why?"

"He had opportunity but didn't care if he was seen."

"Right. Why would he be emboldened like that? It's reckless."

Chapter Twenty-Nine

Melissa lay spread-eagled on the mattress of the old iron bed, the same bed that once confined Tina Olson and Jenny Kincaid. Like the other victims, her hands were cuffed to each post at the head of the bed while her ankles were shackled to the posts at the foot. A blue bandana covered her eyes.

She thrashed and fought against the restraints and vented her animosity when her abductor took a scissors and cut off all the clothing she had been wearing. But to no avail. Completely bare, with nothing but an old woolen army blanket to cover her, thoughts of the other two victims ran through her mind. She wondered if they had found themselves in this exact predicament, feeling the same anger, the same fear, the same desperation.

She'd pulled so hard against her restraints that the skin around her wrists and ankles was rubbed raw and beginning to bleed. But she kept fighting anyway, hoping something would give way so she could free herself. She wasn't about to end up dying like the other two girls.

Melissa didn't know where she was. But the sounds of locusts and crickets and the lack of any human noises suggested a rural area. Odors told her she was in a place that once held farm animals.

The door latch scraped metal against metal and she stopped pulling on her cuffs to listen. The sound of her abductor's footsteps grew louder as he walked closer and closer to the bed.

"Tsk, tsk, tsk. Look what you've done to yourself," he remarked as he observed the abrasions to her wrists and ankles. The sound of that voice repulsed her. "You should stop what you're doing because you're not going to break loose no matter how hard you try. You'll only continue to hurt yourself." Seeing the blanket on the floor, he remarked, "Look here. You've lost your blanket." And he proceeded to pick it up and place it back over her. "There you go."

So thoughtful. What's he want, a thank you? she thought.

"Do you have to use the facilities?"

Melissa shook her head no.

"You tell me if you do and I'll see to it. We wouldn't want any ugly accidents now, would we?"

He walked to the table and began his ritual of swallowing a Viagra tablet and washing it down with a few gulps from a water bottle. "Thirsty?" he asked.

Melissa didn't answer his question, but she chose to ask a question. "Why are you doing this? Just who are you, anyway?"

"You can call me...Michael."

She stopped breathing. *Oh my god!* she thought. "You're Michael?"

"Are you surprised?"

She could hear the leering smile in his voice and she felt nauseous.

"'It might be hard, but maybe we could work it in. ha-ha?' Isn't that what you wrote in your email message? Well, I think we can make that happen."

She'd been played, and she knew it. All the flirting and teasing she had done in emails with someone she thought was a blonde-haired god. It was all bogus. She wanted to cry, but she knew she had to be strong if she was going to survive this. Strategies and tactics were buzzing through her mind like bees swarming around a hive. What to do? What to do?

"We're going to make that happen all right. But until then, I'm going to have a little appetizer," he said, moving back the blanket. Leaning down, he placed his nose against her neck and breathed in her scent as he moved from her neck down past her breasts. "Mmm. So nice."

Pervert! Despite his creepiness, she kept her wits about her. She needed to get out of the handcuffs. Then, if she could somehow get either the handcuffs or the bandana around his neck, she thought she had a chance of strangling him or at least incapacitating him long enough to get the key to unlock her ankle shackles and make a break for it. It was a long shot, but she had few options. For now, she saw a chance to use what she saw as a possible weakness. *Gotta go for it, however distasteful it might be!*

"You like that, do you?" Melissa said in a sultry attempt to play to his libido.

"What's not to like?"

"Why don't you unlock these cuffs and I'll show you a good time like you've never had before."

"You think I'm stupid?"

"No, I think you've never had a really hot girl like me before, that's all."

"Oh, yeah?"

"Yeah. You see, I could just lay here and let you do whatever you want. You're going to do that anyway, right? Or I could join you and share in the fun. And I can tell you'd like it a lot better. What do you say?"

"You're fucking with me. And I don't like people fucking with me."

"Just imagine. Deep kisses, my hands softly caressing your body. Would you like that, Michael?"-

"Stop it!"

"Imagine my hands, my lips, my lips touching—"

He screamed, "FILTHY BITCH!" And a split second later she felt a hard blow to the side of her face that left her dazed.

Grabbing her hard around the throat, he muttered through gritted teeth, "Shut your filthy mouth." She heard his belt buckle, his pants slide down, and felt him pull the blanket off. And then he jumped on top of her, his smooth skin sliding against hers.

When he was finished with her, he angrily rolled off and pulled up his pants. He muttered to himself as he stomped out of the building and locked the door.

Something in her brain had shut down. She lay there, dazed and in pain, and it was like time stood still and she existed in another dimension. When she gathered her wits about her, she realized she had lost track of time. How long had it been since he left? Five minutes? An hour?

Her idea had been wrong, but how could she have known he would react that way? It was a gamble she was willing to take and she lost. Now she knew this wasn't only about sex, it was about something else. She would need to rethink what to do.

Chapter Thirty

A rea lamps created bizarre shadows as people moved in and out of the light. Midnight had come and gone, and the Kincaid's home was teeming with law enforcement. When Tom and Mary were informed of Melissa's abduction, they reacted in quite different ways. Mary collapsed into tears, and Tom became furious, not only with himself, but also with everyone involved in the investigation.

Mary was sitting on the couch, wiping away tears as she answered questions from Sheriff Pollock. Tom sat on the arm of an overstuffed chair nervously rubbing his fingers as Jeff and Destiny looked on.

"I told you, she said she was going to a jazz concert with a friend she was meeting in Storm Lake. That's all I know," trembled Mary.

"How could he have known where she was going?" Tom broke in.

"That's what we—" Before Pollock could answer, Tom got into his face.

"I thought you arrested the guy. We assumed it would be safe for her to go places again!"

"We arrested a person but upon further investigation, we found he had a solid alibi. He wasn't the perpetrator."

"Then why was he arrested in the first place?" exclaimed Tom.

"There were certain things that placed him under suspicion. Things that couldn't be explained until his alibi was confirmed," clarified Destiny. "It was a justifiable arrest at the time."

"So, you're back to square one!"

"We're doing everything we can," countered Pollock a little too firmly for the situation.

His response set Tom off. He abruptly stood, pointed a finger at Pollock and yelled, "Well 'everything' isn't good enough! My daughter has to be—"

""STOP IT!"" screamed Mary. ""STOP IT, BOTH OF YOU!""

She collapsed back into the sofa. Tom sat down next to her and comforted her as best he could. It wasn't something he was particularly good at doing, and it was clearly awkward for him.

Jeff looked at Pollock and motioned him over. "Can I speak with you for a moment? Outside?" he asked.

Jeff knew he needed to get him out of the room. His continued presence was going to make it harder to get information from the Kincaids. Ordinarily, Pollock would not have taken Tom's outburst personally, but all the stress he was under was beginning to take its toll on his ability to remain coolheaded.

Pollock rose from his chair, and he and Jeff stepped outside, leaving Destiny to cope with the distraught couple. She wasn't pleased Pollock had allowed the situation to escalate. She didn't know why he failed to sense things were intensifying and attempt to calm things down. Good for Jeff for intervening.

While all this was going on downstairs, Joe and Del were upstairs in Melissa's bedroom. Joe was looking over Del's shoulder as he worked the keyboard of Melissa's computer in an attempt to hack into her email.

A few more key strokes later he said "Yes!"

"You're in?" asked Joe.

"Yeah," replied Del. "Here we go…"

A list of her email messages appeared, and as Joe was scanning them, he saw a possibility.

"What about that one, the one from Michael."

Del clicked to open the email, which filled the screen along with previously exchanged messages.

"Let's see…uhhhh…yeah! It's our guy," said Del. "Same IP address."

"I knew it!" said Joe. "He set up a meeting with her in Storm Lake so he could intercept her."

"Freakin' clever, man," said Del.

"Open the one dated July twenty-first—that was the night of Wilson's accident."

Del clicked on the message.

"I knew it," snapped Joe. "He was going after her that night, too. Wilson must have screwed up his plans."

Downstairs, Sheriff Pollock walked into the living room.

"I have to go. There's been a two-car accident with personal injuries over by Alta." Looking at Tom and Mary, he said, "If you think of anything—anything at all—you can call the sheriff's office or talk to any of these folks. Joe, Jeff, or Destiny will keep me informed."

Tom nodded without looking at him while Mary seemed oblivious to the fact he was even there. Pollock looked at Destiny who acknowledged him with a nod. As he turned to go, Destiny rose and followed him out the door.

Joe came downstairs. Tom saw him out of the corner of his eye and looked up. He rose as Joe stepped toward him.

"Did you find anything on Melissa's laptop?"

"Yeah. Del's unhooking the computer so he can take it along with her cell phone down to Storm Lake."

Mary looked up at Joe. "What did you find?" she asked softly.

"Email correspondence with someone named Michael. It's the same M.O. the abductor used with the other two girls. He poses as an attractive young man, claims to have seen them somewhere, and sends a bogus photo of himself. He uses considerable charm to lure them into meeting him someplace—in Melissa's case, the jazz concert in Storm Lake. Then he intercepts them, posing as a county deputy conducting a traffic stop. That's how he abducts them."

"Oh my god," Mary said to herself.

Something struck a chord in Joe. It was something Tom had said some time ago. But he thought it would be better if he talked with him alone.

"Excuse me, but I'd like to borrow Tom for a minute. Do you mind?"

Glancing at Mary, Tom reacted, "Right now?"

"Right now," confirmed Joe.

"I'll be all right," said Mary. "Why don't you take a walk? Getting out of the house will do you good."

Tom hesitated a moment and then got up. "You're sure?"

"Go!"

Just as Tom and Joe turned to make their way to the front door, Destiny entered. She and Joe exchanged glances.

"We're taking a stroll," he informed her and gave her a look.

She nodded and walked over and sat next to Mary.

It would have been a nice night had the circumstances been different. The temperature had dipped into the high-seventies and cicadas were providing a background chorus to an otherwise peaceful evening. Jeff was busy talking with Deputy Mike Stevens, who had recently been reassigned to the Marathon area after Tucker's arrest. Joe and Tom walked down the sidewalk, and once out of earshot of the others, Joe stopped by one of the large silver maple trees that grew along the Agora Street.

"I know there's a link between these abductions, and we haven't found it yet. I need your help now more than ever," Joe pleaded.

"Anything," Tom replied.

"I remember you told me you know Jack Callaghan and Mike Olson."

"Yeah. I mean, I did."

"How do you know them?"

"We went to the same high school."

"Friends?"

"Yeah, at the time."

At that point, Joe's questioning took on an urgency that made Tom squirm.

"I need to know if there is anything, and I mean anything, the three of you did that may have upset someone."

"Nothing. We're not that close anymore."

"What about you personally? Any foreclosures, business failures, insurance issues...?"

"Nothing like that."

"Think, god damnit! Anything at all? Even way back? Many years ago? It's your daughter's life we're talking about here."

Tom was getting very uncomfortable and couldn't look Joe in the face. "Please, I..."

"If this holds true to form, we only have four days until she winds up a corpse on a river bank. Now think!"

As he struggled with his decision to say something, Joe sensed his reluctance and pressed him further. "What? What is it?"

Finally, Tom looked him square in the eye and said, "You have to keep this strictly confidential, okay?"

"This will not be made public, I promise. Whatever it is, I won't tell a soul. Now spit it out."

Tom paused a moment and took a big breath. "I haven't spoken about this to anyone. Not ever. I don't know if this has any relevance or not. It happened back in high school...we were going to be seniors that fall. We were pretty wild back then—used to party hard, drink a lot, you know."

"Yeah, go on."

"Anyway, one summer night we were in Mike's '57 Chevy, and we pulled into a gas station in Sioux Rapids to put in a few bucks. I went in to use the restroom, and Mike and Jack stayed in the car waiting for the attendant to fill the tank and wash the windshield. As I went into the station, there was this mousy girl named Rose Henderson standing inside drinking a bottle of Coke. She was looking through the window at Mike's car. She kind of ignored me, but when I came out of the restroom, she was sitting in the front seat with Mike, and Jack had moved to the back seat. So, I got in the back with Jack and the four of us took off driving around."

"How old was she?" Joe asked.

"About fifteen. She was going to start her freshman year."

Tom stopped for a moment, took a couple of breaths, and then went on relating the events as they took place. Joe could tell this was a confession he had probably suppressed for a long time, and it wasn't easy talking about it.

"This is hard for me to tell."

"Take your time."

"Well...Mike drove around town for a while, and then he took a country road for a few miles and turned into this lane leading to a pasture. Jack got out and opened the gate and we drove in. Mike shut off the lights and everybody got out. There was a full moon, so it wasn't all that dark. Anyway, Mike opened the trunk and Jack handed everybody a beer but Rose didn't want one. She acted kind of nervous about being there."

Again, Tom paused and took in a long breath and then continued. His forehead had broken out into a sweat.

"Mike pulled out this blanket from his trunk and spread it on the ground. And Rose, she said something like, 'What're we doing here. I thought we were going to ride around.' And Jack told her we were going to have a picnic. And she said, 'At night? There's nothing to eat.' And Jack said, 'Sure there is. We're gonna have a sheepherder special.' And she said, 'What's that?' And Mike grabbed her and said, 'A piece of ewe.' And he put her down on the blanket and he and Jack started pulling off her clothes. And she was screaming and kicking and crying and Mike..."

"He raped her."

"Yeah......"

"And?"

"We...all took a turn."

"Jesus," Joe muttered.

"I knew it wasn't right, and I wasn't going to do it, but when I said I didn't want to, they accused me of being queer, and maybe they should go get her brother for me, so I...God! I'm still ashamed...and I regret it to this very day."

Emotionally spent, Tom leaned against the tree and slid down its trunk to a sitting position on the grass.

"I assume she didn't report it," Joe queried.

"No, I don't think she told anybody."

"Whatever happened to her?"

Tom paused and tears welled up in his eyes and his voice quavered as he spoke. "Mid-way through the first semester of our senior year, she committed suicide. She swallowed a bottle of iron pills and...it destroyed her liver. They said she was pregnant. I don't know if what we did to her had anything to do with it or not, but if it did...if we were responsible...."

"And you've kept this inside all these years?"

Tom nodded, pulled a handkerchief from his pocket, and wiped his eyes. "Are you going to inform the authorities?"

"I told you I would not tell a soul, and I meant it. Besides, the statute of limitation on the rape ran out years ago so you and your buddies can no longer be prosecuted. Sued, yes. Prosecuted, no."

"You have no idea how this has been eating away at me."

"You said she had a brother?" Joe asked.

"Barry. He was in a class behind us."

"You think he could have known about it?"

"I don't know. He was such a weird kid, it would have been hard to tell."

"What do you mean he was weird?"

"He always kept to himself, a real loner. It may have been because he had this sort of condition…"

"What do you mean condition?"

"It was this thing he was born with, I guess. He didn't have any hair—I mean anywhere—head, arms, legs. His entire body was smooth as a cue ball. Didn't even have eyelashes. And because he looked so strange, he didn't have many friends. Always getting picked on, pushed around, you know how mean kids are."

"Yeah."

"They teased him all the time, his nickname was Greedo. They'd ask him things like, 'Where's your blaster?' or 'Have you seen Jabba the Hut lately?' Shit like that."

"Is he still around here?"

"No idea. Haven't seen him for…I don't know…since we graduated from high school, I guess. I think their mother might still live on the old farm place."

"Okay."

"I can't imagine him doing something like this, though. A skinny weakling like him? He couldn't even climb the rope in gym class. You don't think…?" Tom's question trailed off.

"I don't know. Given we've struck out so far, it can't hurt checking it out. If nothing else, we can eliminate him as a suspect and move on."

Chapter Thirty-One

When Joe and Destiny finally left the Kincaid's home, it was past two a.m., and they were both fatigued. As they walked down the sidewalk toward Joe's father's house, Destiny admitted, "I feel exhausted. How about you?"

"That makes two of us."

"Mind if I stay over at your place? I don't see any point in you driving me back to Storm Lake at this hour."

"So, does this mean I'm now fit for human companionship?" he quipped.

"I'd say it's a definite maybe," she said with a twinkle. And she reached down and took his hand. "A definite maybe."

"Well, I'll accept that as progress."

And progress it was. They didn't sleep much that night. Nevertheless, Joe was up and jogging alone. It was unsettling without his usual companion, especially given what had happened. While Joe was out, Destiny showered, dressed, and made breakfast. On the way to Storm Lake, Joe shared what he had learned from Tom the night before without going into any detail about the gang rape of Rose Henderson. He asked Destiny to find any Hendersons still living in the Sioux Rapids area while he chased down a possible lead there. He had a hunch and wanted to be sure about it before informing Sheriff Pollock.

After dropping off Destiny at her car in the motel parking lot, he drove to Sioux Rapids. As he reached the south edge of town, he pulled into the high school and parked near the front entrance. After finding his way to the office, the secretary, a friendly, rather robust woman in her mid-fifties, greeted him as he walked in. A red nametag with "Beverly" imprinted on it was attached to her blouse.

"Good morning," she said in a cheery manner. "May I help you today, sir?"

"I hope so," Joe said with a hint of a smile. He showed her his temporary deputy identification.

"Oh!" she responded, a little surprised. "Of course. Are you investigating those awful murders?"

"I am."

"I have to tell you that people around here are frightened out of their wits."

"I know."

"And this business just makes me sick to my stomach. I knew Jennifer Callaghan. Her parents, too. She went to school here, and I can tell you it broke my heart when I heard she'd been killed. And now a third girl has been kidnapped. How long can this go on?"

"Hopefully, not much longer," Joe reassured her.

"So, what brings you here, if you don't mind me asking?"

"Do you keep past high school yearbooks here?"

"Yes, we do. We have them archived in the library."

"Could I take a look?"

"Of course. What years would you like to see?"

Knowing that Tom and his buddies were about forty-five years old, he explained, "What I need is access to yearbooks going back about thirty years. Is that possible?"

"We have them. Come with me."

She reached into a cabinet on the wall and removed a key, and then walked around the counter. Joe followed her out the door and down the hall to the library. Beverly used the key to unlock the library door and flipped on the lights, and then strode to the office of the librarian. After she unlocked the librarian's door, she indicated the wall with shelves lined with yearbooks.

"Here you are, Mr. Erickson. As you see, we have them going all the way back to 1931 in case you're interested. Unfortunately, we have to keep them locked up so students won't deface them."

"I understand. Thank you," Joe said, "You've been very helpful, Beverly."

"You can call me Bev," she said, smiling coyly. "And if you need anything like photocopying, I'll be in the office. Just walk down and get me." She smiled, turned, and walked out into the hallway.

She was right. There were rows of yearbooks from 1931 up until last year, most of them in pristine condition. Joe pulled a yearbook from twenty-eight years ago, and leafed through it. Tom, Jack, and Mike had small photographs printed as members of the sophomore class. He returned it and pulled out one from two years later. Members of the senior class were featured in formal photographs. Tom, Jack, and Mike were there, good-looking young men ready to make their mark in the world. He thumbed through pages until he came to photos of the junior class, and there was Barry Henderson. Like Tom said, he was a strange-looking kid all right, complete with bald head and prominent nose and ears. He vaguely reminded Joe of Max Schreck in the silent film, *Nosferatu*. Poor kid. It wasn't hard to understand why he would have been the target of ridicule by mean spirited students.

Joe flipped through a few more pages to where the freshman class was featured. And there at the top of the page was an "In Memorium" window featuring a photograph of Rose Henderson along with a paragraph about her and how much she would be missed by her fellow class members. He studied her face for a while and imagined the hell she went through being raped by the three older boys that summer night in the pasture.

After closing the yearbook, he returned it to the shelf and pulled the next year, looking for Barry Henderson's senior picture. But after scanning the senior class photos, his was not among them. *Hm,* Joe wondered. So, he pulled the following year's book, and he wasn't among those seniors either. *Why is his picture missing? Did he move away? Drop out? Or what? Maybe Barry's mother could shed some light on what could have happened.* He returned the yearbook to the shelf and walked down to the office to speak with Bev.

"Did you find what you were looking for?" she asked as he walked into the office.

"Yes, I did. Thank you. I was wondering, did you graduate from this high school by chance?"

"Oh, no," she said, "My husband and I moved here when he began managing some hog confinements about ten year ago. We're both from Nebraska. Why do you ask?"

"Just curious, that's all."

"Is there anything else I can do for you?"

"No, thanks. I need to be going. It was nice meeting you."

"It was nice meeting you, too," she smiled.

He left the school building, and as he was walking to his car, his cell phone rang. It was Destiny.

"I found two Hendersons with Sioux Rapids addresses. One is Aaron Henderson. He lives on the edge of town. He works as a supervisor at a manufacturing plant in Spencer. Then there is a Louise Henderson, recently deceased, age seventy-four. She lived on a farm about five miles outside of town."

"What was the address for Louise Henderson?" asked Joe.

She gave him the address. "You think you can figure out where that is?"

"Yeah, I can find it. Thanks."

"Talk to you later."

Joe had no idea where the Henderson farm was located so he drove to the city hall, and asked if they had maps for the surrounding area. They did, and he was able to determine the location of the farm based on their name. Tracing the convoluted way of getting there from town, he discovered it was one of several farms that bordered the Little Sioux River.

Taking gravel roads to the Henderson farm proved to be a dusty venture, and his black Camaro was covered with road dust. He parked about a half mile down the road from the lane leading to the farmyard. Trees grew on three sides of the farmyard forming a windbreak that shielded it from winter winds. He walked up the road to a vantage point where he could use his binoculars to check out the place. Old buildings were remnants of a once thriving farm, weathered gray by years of neglect. An aluminum fishing boat sat on a trailer next to an old red pickup, an early fifties GMC or Chevy model, he wasn't able to determine which. Joe was thinking the pickup looked somewhat familiar but had no specific memory of where he might have seen it. Maybe it was something he saw parked somewhere around town. He was scanning the farmyard for activity when a middle-aged man exited what looked to be an old hog house. He was wearing a baseball cap, an olive-green T-shirt, and camouflage pants tucked into military-style boots. This was no farmer. But what got Joe's attention was when he turned and placed a padlock on a hasp attached to the door. That looked pretty damned fishy. Why would someone place a hasp and padlock on the door of an old farm building? Unless of course there was something quite valuable inside...or perhaps, something he wanted no one else to see.

After locking up, the guy walked to the house and went inside. Could this be Barry Henderson? Or someone else entirely? Joe had to know. He walked back to his car, got in, and pondered how to approach the situation without having the guy suspect something. After a moment, he drove into the farmyard, parking next to the old pickup.

As he got out of his car, the man came out the door. Despite the passing years, there was no mistaking the fact that this was the Barry Henderson he saw in the yearbook. He was no longer the skinny kid Tom described. Joe could see that this guy had bulked up.

"Whatever you're selling, I'm not interested," he said with a scowl as he pushed back the bill of his Houston Astros baseball cap.

Joe put on a benign front, acting as though he was a fish out of water in this neck of the woods. "Oh, I'm not a salesman. Actually, I'm just a guy from Chicago who's a little lost."

Barry walked over to Joe.

"You city dudes kill me," he said with an air of superiority.

"Well, what can I say?" said Joe, feigning embarrassment.

"Where you headed?"

"I'm a...trying to get back to Sioux Rapids."

"Sioux Rapids, huh?"

"Yeah."

"Okay, listen up. You leave here and turn left and follow this road for three miles, then you turn west for a mile and a half, and that will take you to the highway. From there you should be able to figure out how to get back to Sioux Rapids. Now that's assuming you know what north, south, east, and west are."

"Yeah. I, uh...think I do. Thanks." Joe looked around and asked innocently, "You—you—farm this land?"

Barry bristled at the question and gave a quick, "Nope."

"I see."

"Chicago, huh?" Barry asked in a menacing tone. Joe was almost expecting him to step into his personal space and try to intimidate him so he tried laughing it off to quell the tension.

"Yeah," he chuckled. You probably think I'm an idiot getting lost in the country like this."

"You have no idea what I think."

"Truth is, I don't get out of the city much. I'm here doing a little research on an article I was assigned to write."

"Yeah? On what?"

"Corn," replied Joe.

"Corn?" Barry snorted incredulously.

"Yeah. Corn and how its derivatives have become hidden ingredients in many of the foods we eat."

"Oh. Well, good luck with that," sneered Barry, and he turned and swaggered back toward the house.

"Thanks again for the directions," said Joe. "Much appreciated."

Barry chose not to acknowledge him, just shook his head. As Joe walked to his car, he glanced at the hog house and saw that the hasp and padlock on the top Dutch door looked shiny and new. He fired up his car and noticed that Barry was watching him as he pulled out of the yard. *There's something hinky about this guy*, Joe thought. *Something very hinky.*

Chapter Thirty-Two

As Joe drove back to the sheriff's office, Jeff and Destiny worked on information they had collected about the sale of used police vehicles. Destiny's office table was covered with an array of printouts they'd received, and she was busy entering data into a spreadsheet on her computer.

"There were sixty-four police cruisers sold this year and fifty-nine last year. Slightly over a third were Chevy Impalas. None were purchased by anyone from this area," Jeff stated.

"It's possible someone re-sold a unit to a second party," Destiny suggested.

"I wonder how many used car dealers were buying them up for resale. We could trace current ownership through the VIN numbers. Any way you look at it, it's going to take some time."

"Yeah, and that's what we don't have. Can you get that information, Jeff?"

"Uh-huh. I'll get right on it."

The office door opened and Joe entered.

"I got the list of buyers," said Jeff.

"Any luck?" Joe asked.

"No," replied Destiny.

"Is the name Barry Henderson on the list?"

Jeff looked through the two lists.

"Barry Henderson," he mumbled to himself as he looked through the lists. "Barry Henderson...no. He looked up, "No Barry Henderson on the list. Why?"

"Try contacting authorities in Texas. Check with the DMV to see if he has a driver's license, and what cars he may own."

"Texas?" questioned Jeff.

"Yeah, I think I may be on to something."

"What is it?" queried Destiny. "She was familiar interpreting Joe's terminology, and when he said he was "on to something," it meant he had discovered something major.

"I need a cup of coffee but I'd rather not try to drink that five-hour energy sludge they have in the pot here. Want to discuss it at the coffee shop up town?"

"Sure. It would feel good to stretch my legs," said Jeff.

"You mean, smoke a cigarette," kidded Joe.

"That, too."

"Who's Barry Henderson? He wasn't on the list I gave you," asked Destiny.

"I'll explain later. Let's go."

Jeff and Destiny accompanied Joe out to his dust-covered car. Destiny noticed how dirty it was.

"This thing is filthy," she commented. "What in the world...?"

"Ten miles of gravel roads does wonders for a black car."

"I'll follow you," said Jeff. "I'm not going to try squeezing into the back seat of a Camaro."

They arrived at the coffee shop and placed their orders. Joe and Jeff each opted for a double shot cappuccino while Destiny ordered a low-cal caramel latte. They found a corner booth and sat down. There weren't many people in the shop so Joe felt comfortable talking about Barry Henderson and the location of the Henderson farm.

"He's got what?" asked Jeff.

"Alopecia universalis," repeated Joe.

"What the hell is that?"

"It's a rare genetic mutation. It's when no hair grows on the entire body."

"None?"

"None. Not even eyelashes."

"Huh. Never heard of it."

"That could explain why no evidence of foreign hairs have been found," concluded Destiny.

"Okay," agreed Jeff, "That makes sense. But what makes you think he's from Texas?"

"He was wearing a Houston Astros baseball cap."

"And that proves he's from Texas? I'm a Yankees fan but I don't live in New York."

"Nobody's a freakin' Astros fan outside of Texas," said Joe.

"Jesus," Jeff laughed incredulously.

"It sounds like it's worth a shot," said Destiny. "We've struck out with Iowa so far."

Jeff stood up and slid out to the booth saying, "If I'm going to check this out, I'd better start now. Why is it I'm always the one that has to leave early?"

At that moment the waitress called out their orders. Jeff grabbed his coffee and said, "I'll request those VIN numbers you mentioned, too."

"VIN numbers?" asked Joe.

Jeff was the out the door, moving like a man on a mission. Destiny explained the VIN numbers to Joe as they picked up their coffees. They spoke as they walked down the sidewalk.

"I have some confidential information. I promised the person I would keep it confidential, but I'm going to share it with you because you need to know about it. So, I have to trust you not to disclose it to anyone, okay?"

"You can trust me with it," assured Destiny. "You know that."

Joe repeated the story Tom had told him about the gang rape and subsequent suicide of Rose Henderson. Destiny took it all in and paused to consider it.

"So, if the rape of this young girl caused her to get pregnant and led to her suicide, it could have produced a powerful rage in her brother," Destiny pointed out.

"That's assuming he knew about it."

"But a scrawny kid like him couldn't do anything against three football players so he was forced to suppress it."

"Right," agreed Joe. "And the anger at being a ninety-eight-pound weakling motivated him to start body building so he wouldn't have to endure the kind of harassment and intimidation he had to put up with in high school."

"Coming back for his mother's funeral twenty-three years later may have rekindled the grief he felt at the loss of his sister. And it may have been especially galling if he found out how successful these three guys had become. That could've fueled his rage and led to a desire for vengeance against those he held responsible. Twenty-seven years of pent up anger. So he decides to inflict pain on his sister's attackers by raping and murdering their daughters."

"I don't know," questioned Joe. "I think he may have been planning this for some time. The preparation of the police cruiser, acquiring the cop's uniform, the research into the three families and finding out about the three daughters, all that would have taken some time. He could have been planning this for more than a year. His mother's death simply gave him opportunity."

Then Destiny realized something, and she found it upsetting. She stopped walking. "Oh, my god."

"What is it?" asked Joe turning back to her.

"This would mean my profile is all wrong. These are revenge killings! Revenge killings made to look like the work of a serial killer. You were right when you questioned if it was the work a serial killer."

"Yeah, but you—"

"Everything I stated was inaccurate."

"Hey. There's no way you could have known that."

"Tucker was arrested and then suspended because of my profile."

"They handed you a false assumption. It's not your fault. Hell, we all based our investigation on that same false assumption."

"I have to rework this entire thing." She'd now lost a taste for coffee and dropped the half-finished cup in a nearby trash receptacle. She looked at Joe who had stopped and was staring out into the street. "What are you thinking?"

"If this guy's the one, he's pretty damned smart to throw us off like this."

"Smart. And very sick."

After their ten-minute stroll, they drove back to the sheriff's office. As they made their way to Destiny's office, Jeff stepped into the hall holding several sheets of paper from the fax machine.

"You must have a god damned sixth sense, Joe!" he said, handing him the papers. "He does live in Texas. Houston. Just got this from the Texas DMV."

Joe looked at an enlarged printout of Barry Henderson's Texas driver's license. "That's him," he acknowledged, handing the paper to Destiny. "Cute, isn't he?"

"Yes, he is."

"You should have the pleasure of meeting him in person. He's about as pleasant as he looks."

"Something else—he works as a website designer," added Jeff.

"Computer geek," blurted Destiny. "He would know all about hiding his identity on the web."

"He also belongs to a paramilitary group down there, so it's safe to assume he has weapons. His mother died two months ago. That's why he came back here. He's been living at the family farm since. He's been an only child since his sister died, so he would be the sole beneficiary of his mother's estate."

"How much would that be?" asked Joe.

"She owned 220 acres outright. She had been cash renting the land for years. You figure land is selling for over nine thousand an acre. That's what—around two million in land he's set to inherit, not to mention any other assets she might have had."

"That enough to disappear and never be found," warned Destiny. "That makes him a serious flight risk."

"We need to conduct a search of that farm," urged Joe.

"We don't have enough evidence to establish probable cause. He's a computer geek, lives by a river, and his outbuilding has a new lock. No judge is going to issue a search warrant based on that."

Joe knew there was more he could say, but he was bound by his promise to Tom. "Does he own a car?"

"The Texas DMV reported a SUV registered in his name. The list of owners of the VIN numbers may take a day or so."

Joe threw the papers down on the table. "We don't have a day or so!"

"Are we assuming she's there, at the farm?" asked Destiny.

"He's clever," said Jeff. "He may have her hidden away elsewhere.

"I'll go in and scout the place tonight," said Joe.

"That constitutes an illegal search," objected Jeff. "You're a deputy. If he's the one and it goes to court, any evidence would be inadmissible, fruit of the poisonous tree. You know that."

"Not anymore. I quit."

"What?" exclaimed Destiny.

"I quit as of this minute. I'm a temporary deputy, and I consider my job is done. I'm going back to being a civilian."

"I don't know about this," said Jeff.

Joe pulled out his special deputy identification and placed it on the table. "Here. I'm turning in my ID. I'm terminating my tenure as a special deputy."

Destiny looked him in the eye and with a glint said, "You have a plan, don't you?"

"Uh-huh," Joe said, giving her a quick wink.

"What do you have in mind?" asked Jeff, not sure he was liking any of this.

"For this to work, we need the cooperation of Sheriff Pollock and his deputies. I don't know if he'll go for it if he knows it came from me. We've made amends, but that doesn't mean I'm on solid ground with him yet so I'd rather not push it. Do you think you can convince him this is all your idea?"

"I think so. What's the plan?"

Chapter Thirty-Three

After laying out his strategy with Jeff and Destiny, Joe was confident it would work as long as Sheriff Pollock would agree to his part in it. He was pleased that both Jeff and Destiny approved of it. Jeff agreed to inform Pollock of his discovery, show him the evidence, and then present him "his" plan. Jeff could be persuasive, and Joe felt he would be able to lay out their strategy in such a way that Pollock would buy into it. Desperate times require desperate measures, so to speak.

But Joe didn't feel as though he could accomplish his part in it alone. He needed a partner, and it couldn't be anyone associated with law enforcement. The perfect person came to mind, and it was someone in need of redemption. He drove out into the country and pulled into the lane of a small acreage with a farmhouse and an unattached garage. It was an older house, nothing fancy. But the mowed lawn, the trimmed spirea bushes, and some recent repairs made to the porch railing and roof fascia showed a caring owner. It was the home of Will Tucker.

Joe parked his car next to Tucker's pickup and walked up to the porch. The inside door was open, and as soon as Joe rang the bell, he heard little steps running toward the door. Jimmy appeared and was looking at him through the screen.

"Hi, Jimmy. Is your dad here?"

Jimmy ran back into the house, and a moment later, Joe heard heavier footsteps. A moment later Will Tucker stepped into view. He was barefoot, wearing cutoff jeans and a faded tank top. When they made eye contact, Joe spoke up before Tucker could say anything.

"Before you slam the door in my face, hear me out."

Pause.

"All right," said Tucker, pushing open the screen door and stepping out onto the porch.

"First, let me say I'm sorry you got suspended. Regulations can be a bitch sometimes."

"Yeah."

"Given the fact they arrested you, ruined your vacation, and forced you to spend time in lockup, I think it would've been fair to have made an exception about the suspension. But I'm not the sheriff."

"Thanks. You're not a by-the-book kind of guy."

"That's right. It tends to get me into trouble sometimes. I need to talk to you about something. Something important."

"Okay. You want a beer?"

"Sure."

The house was neat and well cared for but lacked a woman's touch. A leather couch and matching love seat faced a large screen television that sat on what used to be an oak bedroom dresser. There were two end tables with matching lamps and an area rug on the floor. But the walls were bare and the room was devoid of any knickknacks or mementos. A few toys lay on the floor and some magazines sat in a magazine rack next to a recliner.

Tucker grabbed a couple of beers from the refrigerator, and then led Joe into the backyard to a large picnic table. Joe told him about the situation while Tucker intently listened. Then Joe began detailing his plan of action.

"You want me to do what?" Tucker asked in amazement.

"As a citizen, not a law enforcement officer, I want you to help me conduct a search of a suspect's place of residence."

"Why should I go out on a limb to help you with this scheme?"

"Because Melissa Kincaid needs our help. Tomorrow's the fourth day. He kills his victims on the fourth day!" Joe stated emphatically.

"Then why doesn't the sheriff search the place?"

"Not enough evidence for probable cause."

"Oh, I get it," responded Tucker. "Because we're both citizens, we can illegally trespass on someone's property and conduct a search."

"Right. And law enforcement officers can then come on the property to apprehend us if we find Melissa. If she's not on the premises, no one will know we were ever there."

"How will the police find out about the so-called trespassers?"

"Anonymous call from a concerned citizen who just happens to have a burner phone."

"Uh-huh. And the concerned citizen?"

Joe pointed to himself. "That would be me."

"So, you think this guy is the perp?"

"Oh, yeah. Based on what I've seen and heard...yeah. There's a very good chance it's him." Joe took a drink from his beer and then looked at Tucker. "So, you with me?"

Tucker nodded, "Yeah. I trust your gut. I'll do it for Melissa."

"You have a rifle?"

"Several."

"What've you got?"

"How about a .308 Ruger with a scope?"

"Perfect," said Joe. "Bring it. We have to do this tonight. Tomorrow may be too late.

"Tonight's good. I'll drop Jimmy off at my mom's."

I'll pick you up at nine. I'll coordinate with the sheriff and we'll plan on going in at ten. It should be dark enough by then."

"I'll be ready. You want me in black or camo? I have both."

Chapter Thirty-Four

T he new moon worked in their favor, and at ten o'clock, it was dark enough to conceal Joe and Tucker as they reconnoitered the farm. Joe had parked his Camaro at the edge of a cornfield half a mile down the road from the Henderson farm. Both he and Tucker wore black as well as Kevlar vests that Joe had borrowed from the sheriff's office. The terrain was hilly, and they moved toward the farmyard, walking between rows of corn to conceal their presence.

They arrived at the edge of the field that bordered on the Henderson's grove. An old, rusty fence with two strands of barbed wire separated the grove from the field, and Joe held the wires down so Tucker could climb over it. Then Tucker did the same for him. They walked slowly through the trees to a rise overlooking the farm buildings. A mercury vapor yard light illuminated the center of the farmyard near the house and garage. The barn, chicken house, corncrib, hog house, and machine shed were much more dimly lit. Several windows of the house gave off the faint glow from a light inside. Situated in the backyard was a large white propane tank that provided fuel for the furnace during the winter.

Joe looked through his binoculars scanning the yard. Tucker's hands firmly gripped his rifle and he raised it and began looking around through the scope.

"I'd sure like to know what's in some of those buildings," said Tucker.

"You probably can't see it in this light, but there's a shiny new hasp and padlock on that old hog house door," Joe replied.

"You're kidding! What for?"

"That's what I'm about to find out. I'm going in," said Joe, and he began making his way toward the farm buildings. Crouching down and staying away from the light as much as possible, he used old discarded farm machinery as cover.

***

Meanwhile, three miles up the road, Jeff, Sheriff Pollock, and two of his deputies, Barnes and Taylor, were waiting for Joe's call. Jeff nervously puffed on his third cigarette.

"I'd better not get my ass in a sling over this," Pollock grumbled as he chewed on a toothpick.

"Hey, if they don't find anything, we can go home and no one will ever know we were here," Jeff assured him.

"What do you mean they?"

"Joe and Tucker."

"Tucker? Jesus H. Christ, what's he doing here?"

"Joe insisted. He said he needed a second man, someone not associated with law enforcement."

"Ah, shit!"

***

Joe moved to the backside of the corncrib. Two large wooden doors covered the entrance, both front and rear, doors originally built to allow tractors pulling wagons to pass through. He tried moving one of the doors to the side and let out a sigh of relief. It wasn't locked from the inside. He pulled the door open enough to squeeze through. His flashlight revealed the grill of a Chevy Impala. He moved his flashlight over the car. It was black with spotlights on each side of the windshield and emergency lights on the roof. Just like a police cruiser. He knelt to examine the license plate. What the hell? It was a Buena Vista County sheriff's office plate with the county number eleven followed by a dash and the numeral "11." But the second numeral "1" was skillfully painted in to form the number "11." Evidently, Barry was the one who had stolen Pollock's license plates. The county sheriff's cruiser always had the plate with the numeral "1" following the county number while deputies each had ascending numbers corresponding to their call signs. *Gotcha, you motherfucker!* Joe thought. He slipped back out the door and cautiously pulled it shut.

His eyes were now drawn to the hog house, and he moved to the various entrances trying to find a way to enter. The rear door had been secured from the inside and would not budge. The two small side doors used by hogs to go in and out were also fastened shut, and all the windows were covered over with plywood from the inside. *How the hell am I going to get in?* In a different scenario he would have broken a window and tried forcing back the plywood. But stealth was the name of the game tonight, and he had to find another way.

Looking up at the roof, Joe discovered several vents used to expel hot air in the summer to help keep the hogs cool. He wondered if these had been secured from the inside, too. Grabbing a corner of the roof, he pulled himself up onto the old wooden shingles and slid along on his belly up to the first vent. It was made of wood, and with some difficulty, he carefully pried it up with his fingers, trying not to make any more noise than was absolutely necessary. The old wood began to splinter as he pulled. *Yes!* It had not been secured like the other openings. *Forgot something, didn't you Barry? Thank you!* Once he had removed the vent cover and moved it aside, he pulled out his flashlight and shined it between the rafters. As the beam illuminated parts of the interior, it caught the edge of the metal bed, and then Melissa. Seeing her blindfolded and her ankles and wrists handcuffed to the bed frame momentarily sent shock waves through him. Her bare arms and legs protruded from under an army blanket covering her mid-section. Hearing some activity on the roof, she wasn't sure what to make of it, and Melissa listened, trying to determine what was happening. Joe saw her move and thanked God she was still alive.

Time to call this in, he thought, and he pulled the burner phone from his pocket and called nine-one-one. The Buena Vista County Sheriff's Office dispatcher answered and he reported seeing a prowler and gave the address.

***

Barry was sitting at his computer watching porn at the dining room table when his police scanner squawked a call between the dispatcher and Deputy

204

Barnes.

"Buena Vista County eleven-four. Buena Vista County eleven-four."

"Buena Vista County eleven-four, go ahead."

"We have a ten-thirty-nine, report of a prowler, five miles east of Sioux Rapids at 2440 East 1300. Use North 900 from County Road C-13 and turn on East 1300 to 2440. It's the Henderson farm."

Upon hearing this, Barry leaped from his chair and then froze, listening intently to the voices on the scanner.

"Roger. 900 North to 1300 East to the Henderson farm. ETA approximately ten minutes."

"Roger, eleven-four."

"Ten-four."

Barry ran from the room in a panic, entered the kitchen, and flipped a light switch that turned off the yard light. Then he turned off all the lights in the house.

Deputy Barnes walked up to where Jeff and Sheriff Pollock were discussing Tucker's participation in this venture.

"You heard the prowler call?"

"Yeah," said Pollock, tossing his toothpick onto the ground.

Jeff dropped his cigarette and pushed it into the gravel with his shoe. "That means he found her. I hope to hell she's alive!"

Joe slid through the roof vent and down onto a joist. Melissa responded with, "Who's there?" and Joe responded with "It's Joe! You have to keep quiet!"

Joe moved to a small area where the joist met the rafter. As he did, tiny dust particles fell from the joist and were illuminated by his flashlight.

At that moment the padlock rattled on the door. *Oh, shit!* he thought. He clicked off his flashlight and hunched down making himself as small as possible, hoping the dust particles would not give him away.

The padlock slid against the hasp, and the top half of the Dutch doors swung open. There stood Barry. He looked around the interior of darkened hog house checking for anything out of the ordinary. But he shined no flashlight. No need for one. He was wearing night vision goggles. Joe was

205

not in a position to see very well but his eyes had adjusted enough to see Barry was carrying something but he was unable tell exactly what it was. Satisfied everything was copacetic, Barry shut the door, closed the hasp and replaced the padlock, clicking it shut before leaving.

Joe let out a huge breath, thankful that Barry never saw the dust or thought of looking up as he probably would have noticed him crouched on the rafter. He turned on his flashlight once again and silently crawled along the joist and let himself down, hanging from it and then dropping to the floor. He moved to Melissa, untying the bandana and used his handcuff key to unlock her cuffs.

Melissa embraced him. "Oh, god!

Joe clamped his hand over her mouth and pressed his mouth close to her ear. "Shhhh! We have to be quiet," he whispered. "For all we know, he could be standing outside the door listening." Removing his hand, he pulled out his cell phone and pushed a button and walked to the center of the building, away from the door.

Out on the road, Jeff's cell phone rang. "Yeah," answered Jeff.

"I found her. She's alive," said Joe in a hushed voice.

"Thank god."

"Send in the troops!" and he ended the call.

"She's alive! Let's go!" exclaimed Jeff. Sheriff Pollock and his deputies ran to their cars, and they proceeded down the gravel road toward the Henderson farm.

***

Back inside the hog house, Melissa was fumbling with the blanket trying to cover her unclad body.

"You have any clothes here?" he asked.

"No. He cut them off."

"Well, you can't run that way." He pulled out a pocket knife and said, "Give me the blanket."

"What?" she whispered.

"Give me the damned blanket! Now is not the time to be modest." She gave him a horrified look and he rolled his eyes. "Don't worry, I'm not going

206

to look at you." He turned away from her and held out his hand. Melissa handed him the blanket. Holding the flashlight in his mouth, he folded the blanket to find center, cut a slit large enough for her head and handed it back to her.

"Here. Put your head through the slit so it functions like a poncho. That way you won't have to hold onto it. Think you can run in that?"

"Uh-huh."

"Good. Put it on."

Returning the knife to his pocket, he examined the entrance door. Dutch doors were common to old farm buildings, and he knew that only the top door was padlocked. A large hook and eye held the bottom door closed. He released the hook, but he had no way of releasing the top door. He would have to kick out the bottom door, and they would have to duck through it. He hoped it wouldn't take multiple kicks to break it open. He looked at Melissa.

"Get ready," he warned. "We'll have to move fast."

With the most powerful kick he could muster, he put his foot into the door, and with a loud crunching sound it broke open halfway, giving them enough room to escape.

"Let's go!" he exclaimed as he grabbed Melissa's hand. They each ducked under the top Dutch door and into the night air. Just as they were turning to run, a bolt from a crossbow slammed into the exterior wall of the building, missing Joe by inches. Joe saw it but had no time to react. With Melissa in tow, he ran to the tall weeds at the edge of the grove to give them some cover. They reached the weeds without incident and lay on their bellies to avoid being detected. But Barry would still be able to see them by scanning the area. Joe needed to get her to Tucker so she could escape from Barry's sight until backup arrived.

"We're going to run to that large tree behind us, okay?" he said to Melissa.

As they were about run, Joe could see the red and blue flashing lights of three police cruisers as they came over a hill a quarter of a mile in the distance. Figuring that was enough of a distraction, they ran to the tree for cover.

"Do you see that rise over to your left?" Joe asked Melissa.

"Rise?"

"Watch." Joe pulled his flashlight and pointed it toward Tucker. He flashed it once. Tucker flashed back. "Did you see that?"

"Yeah," Melissa answered.

"We need to get to that spot so Deputy Tucker can protect you."

Joe and Melissa got to their feet to make the run toward Tucker's position when the sound of a bolt whizzed near them. Melissa cried out in pain as one of her knees buckled. She reached for her shoulder.

"What is it?" Joe asked.

"My shoulder," she said through gritted teeth. Joe reached over and felt blood.

"You've been hit. We can't stay here any longer. Think you can you run?"

"I think so."

"Come on!"

Joe took her hand and they ran to Tucker's position forty yards away, zigzagging behind trees. He placed her in an area below the sightlines where she would be safe.

"She's been hit in the shoulder," said Joe, pulling a bandana from his pocket and handing it to Tucker. "You may need to put pressure on it."

The three cruisers pulled into the yard, and Taylor, Barnes, Jeff, and Pollock left their vehicles with guns drawn.

"Take the backside of the house," Pollock ordered Barnes. "We'll take—" The Sheriff's instructions were interrupted when a bolt from Barry's crossbow slammed into his neck. Pollock toppled back, his neck spurting blood like a geyser.

Seeing Sheriff Pollock go down, Barnes yelled, "Take cover!" Taylor crawled to where Pollock lay on the ground and dragged him behind his cruiser. His flashlight revealed Pollock's face. He was alive but not for long. Taylor did his best to try to stop the bleeding, but there was no saving him. He gurgled a last breath, and then his body went limp.

"God damnit!" swore Taylor. He paused a moment and then wiped Pollock's blood from his hands. He reached for his gun as Jeff ducked in from his place behind the third cruiser. He saw Pollock's lifeless face.

"Holy shit!" he reacted.

"He's gone," said Taylor.

"Did you see where that came from?" asked Jeff.

"No."

"Son-of-a-bitch could be anywhere!"

"I'm calling for back up," said Taylor, and he crawled inside Pollock's cruiser. As he reached for the radio, a bolt shattered the driver's side window not far from Taylor's head. The window exploded sending tiny fragments of glass all over Taylor, cutting his face.

He grabbed the microphone and made the call to dispatch.

Jeff yelled, "Turn off your headlights. We're sitting ducks out here!"

Taylor and Barnes moved to their cruisers and turned off their headlights while Jeff reached inside Pollock's cruiser and did the same. The yard was now a bizarre light show, only lit by the red and blue flashing emergency lights.

"Take cover away from the vehicles," yelled Barnes.

Taylor ran to the old red pickup and kneeled behind it while Jeff and Destiny ducked behind a large barrel used to store gasoline. Barnes ran for the aluminum boat trailered not far from the pickup. Just as he was about to duck behind it, a bolt hit him square in the chest, penetrating his Kevlar vest and lodging in his heart. In a surreal moment, he stopped, looked curiously down at the bolt sticking out of his chest. Then he looked up as blood dribbled out of his mouth, and collapsed onto the ground. Taylor saw Barnes go down.

"Barnes!" Taylor called out. "BARNES!" There was no response. Taylor crawled to Barnes to lend aid, but when he got there, he could see that Barnes was already dead.

"Damnit!" he growled and crawled back behind the pickup. "Jeff!"

"Yeah," Jeff replied.

"Barnes is dead! These Kevlar vests are worthless against a crossbow!"

"How can he see us?" asked Destiny.

Jeff's cell phone rang. "Yeah," he answered.

"What's your situation?" Joe asked.

"He has us pinned down. Pollock and Barnes are both dead."

"Shit! He's using night vision goggles! Get outta there!"

"Keep this line open," Jeff insisted.

"Roger that," replied Joe.

"Taylor!" yelled Jeff. "He's using night vision. We have to get outta here."

"I'll go first and get his attention. Then you two go!" ordered Taylor. Then he jumped up and ran across the yard to an old metal pig feeder while Jeff and Destiny ran in different directions. Destiny ran for the tree line while Jeff ran behind a rickety old garage not far from the house.

Back at Tucker's position, Melissa trembled. "Is he going to kill us?"

"No," was Joe's immediate, firm reply. "Not if I can help it." He looked at Tucker. "How's her shoulder?"

"It's not deep, but she'll need stitches."

Melissa sat up. "I can do this," she said. And she began holding the bandana against her shoulder.

"What's the best way to defeat night vision technology?" asked Joe.

"Bright light," replied Tucker, "but we don't have any."

"Maybe we can make some. That white tank there by the house…"

"The propane tank, you mean?"

"Yeah," said Joe. "Can you hit the brass valve at this distance?"

Tucker picked up the rifle and looked through the scope. "I could if I could see it. It's too dark to line up a good shot."

Joe reached for his cell phone. "Jeff, do you copy?"

"Yeah."

"Where are you?"

"Behind the old garage by the house."

"The sheriff's cruiser…I need you to turn on the headlights."

"What?"

"I need you to turn on the headlights of the sheriff's cruiser. Can you do that?"

"Run back there? Are you crazy?" came Jeff's response.

"You have to!" Joe demanded. "Right now!"

Jeff made a B-line for Pollock's cruiser. Huffing and puffing, he opened the driver's door and switched on the headlights.

"Anything else?" he spoke into the phone.

"Yeah," said Joe, "Get the hell away from there!"

As Jeff was getting up on one knee preparing to run, a bolt slammed through the driver's door, its tip stopping an inch from his face. Before Barry could get off another shot, Jeff jumped up and hauled ass down the lane and took cover in the ditch.

Joe heard a rustling in the grass, and he turned holding his Glock, ready to fire.

"Don't shoot," said Destiny, "it's me."

Joe let out a breath.

"Is there anything I can do?" she asked.

"Keep an eye on Melissa's shoulder," Joe said. "She's been hurt. And watch our back. He could try to flank us."

"Got it."

"Where's Taylor?" asked Joe.

"Right here," Taylor said as he came into view.

Joe looked at Tucker who had his rifle raised and was looking through the scope.

"What do you think?" he asked.

"I should be able to hit it now," Tucker replied.

"Good. Wait for me to get into place first."

At that moment, Jeff arrived, coughing and out of breath. "Way to go, man!" said Joe, giving him a slap on the shoulder. Then, with his Glock in hand, he took off running toward the tall weeds at the edge of the grove.

"Where's he going?" asked Jeff.

"I don't know but he seems to know what he's doing," replied Tucker, looking through the scope of his rifle.

Joe situated himself in tall weeds near a tree that would not only give him some cover but also a view of the grove and Barry's location. He figured Barry was in a place that provided him the best view of the farmyard. But he didn't know if he was mobile or stationery. Joe pulled out his phone and spoke into it.

"Jeff."

"Yeah."

"Tell Tucker to take the shot."

Jeff turned to Tucker. "Joe said to take the shot."

"The rest of you had better get back. There's going to be a muzzle flash, and it's going to give away our position."

"All right, everybody get down!" ordered Jeff, and everyone but Tucker got down around Melissa where they would be out of sight. Tucker lined up the shot using a tree branch for support. Then he fired. He saw it hit and…nothing happened.

"Ah, hell! Don't tell me the tank is empty. Come on!"

Barry was perched in a deer stand twelve feet off the ground. He was looking through the scope he had attached to his crossbow. As he was panning an area of the grove for movement, he spotted Joe kneeling behind tall weeds, speaking into his cell phone. He lined up the crosshairs on Joe's chest and was about to pull the trigger.

Simultaneously, Tucker aimed at the propane tank valve again and fired a second time. The second shot hit its mark, and the propane tank exploded in a ball of flames that engulfed the house, most of the farmyard and the surrounding trees. The sound was deafening and everyone felt the powerful concussion from the blast.

In the aftermath of the explosion, Joe picked himself up and ran toward the burning grove, searching for Barry. As he felt the heat from the flames, he looked up and saw a deer stand on fire. *So that's where your vantage point was.* Then, from the top of an old combine, Barry leaped. Blistered and burned, he screamed like a wild animal as he pounced on Joe, sending them both to the ground. Joe's Glock flew out of his hand, landing several feet away. With a bolt in his hand, Barry drove the razor-sharp point into Joe's unprotected left shoulder, breaking off the shaft and leaving the point buried in his flesh. He was growling like a wounded beast, his teeth bared and eyes wild. Very strong from all his bodybuilding, Barry was out-muscling Joe. Knowing he had to do something, Joe pulled his handcuffs free from his belt, he swung them hard against Barry's face sending him reeling backwards. It was enough to momentarily disorient him.

As Joe struggled to get to his knees, he dove for his gun but Barry jumped him again. Barry was even closer to where Joe's Glock lay. As Barry reached for the gun, Joe tried grabbing his arm, but lost his grip. Barry now had his hand on the Glock, but Joe got hold of his wrist, and with his other hand, punched him hard in the face. It did little to deter him. They each were trying to gain control of the gun, and it was moving back and forth between their two bodies. With all his might, Joe gave a huge push against Barry's wrist and the Glock fired. Barry screamed out in anguish as a round went through his side just above his pelvis. Barry's grip weakened, allowing Joe to wrestle the gun away and scramble to his feet.

Barry struggled and got to one knee, holding his wounded right side. He looked up at Joe and his expression changed as he recognized Joe as the man from Chicago he'd encountered at the farm days ago. "You said you were a writer," Barry sneered.

"I lied."

"You've ruined everything!"

"Yeah."

Then Barry's free hand swung up, holding a small canister of pepper spray and fired a stream into Joe's face. Joe cried out and fell backwards onto the ground. Blinded by the chemical, he knew not to breathe in the vapors. He held his breath, raised the Glock, pointed it at what he believed to be Barry's last known position and emptied the seventeen-round clip. Then he let out a breath and took in some air. He managed to get to his knees but was blind, coughing, and short of breath. He didn't know if he had killed the guy or if he had just wounded him. Was he in danger of being attacked again? He had never felt desperation like this before.

Instinctively, he managed to drop the empty clip from his Glock, reach in his pocket, pop in a full clip, and chamber another round, ready to fire again. He tried to listen for any sounds around him. He only heard the crackling of burning branches and sirens in the distance.

The next few minutes seemed like an eternity as Joe tried to overcome the effects of the pepper spray. He didn't know if Barry was alive or dead, if he was safe or if he was being set up for another shot from that deadly crossbow. In an effort to regain his vision, he pulled off his Kevlar vest and used the front of his T-shirt to wipe the pepper spray from his face.

Then he heard Tucker's voice yelling in the distance. "OVER HERE! HE'S OVER HERE!" Then he called out, "JOE!" He had heard the multiple gunshots Joe had fired, and he came running in their direction.

"YEAH!" Joe yelled back as best he could.

As Joe heard the footsteps coming closer, he pointed his Glock in their direction and through his coughs yelled, "TUCKER?"

"PUT THE GUN DOWN, IT'S ME! TUCKER!"

Joe lowered his Glock and a moment later he felt Tucker's reassuring hand on his good shoulder as he knelt next to him. He saw the remains of the bolt sticking out of Joe's shoulder. "How bad you hurt?"

"I can't see. I can't see anything. He got me in the face with pepper spray," said Joe. "Where is he?"

Tucker saw Barry lying on the ground motionless and said, "Over there." And then he saw the wounds. "You'd better let me have your gun. You're not going to need it."

"Why? Did I kill him?" he coughed.

"It looks like you killed the hell out of him," Tucker said as he pulled a handkerchief out of his pocket and placed it in his hand.

"You're sure? He's dead?"

"Oh, yeah. Not much question about that."

Joe handed Tucker his Glock and concentrated on clearing his eyes.

When Joe emptied his seventeen-round clip in Barry's direction, half of them hit their mark, three of which would have been fatal. Barry was dead before he hit the ground.

A few moments later, Destiny, Jeff, and Taylor came running up to where Tucker was attending Joe.

"The perp's over there. He's dead," Tucker informed Taylor. "Joe needs medical attention—he got pepper sprayed in the face and a shoulder wound."

"I'll get the EMT's over here," said Taylor, and he ran to alert the ambulance personnel who had just arrived.

Destiny knelt next to Joe and grabbed his hand. Then she noticed remains of the bolt sticking out of his black T-shirt and the wet spot on his shoulder getting bigger. "Your shoulder. What the hell happened?"

"He stabbed me with a bolt from his crossbow. I don't think it's too bad. Maybe I can pull it out." He started to reach for it but Destiny grabbed his arm.

"No way! Not until the EMT's look at it first. Stay put!"

"You'd better do what she says," agreed Tucker. "Let them check you out first."

Jeff, who had been looking at the body of Barry Henderson, stepped over. "So, he sprayed you and then you shot him? Is that how it happened?"

"Yeah," replied Joe.

"Looks like you hit him a bunch of times. Pretty good shooting for a blind man."

An EMT arrived and began washing the pepper spray from Joe's face. Another began treating his shoulder wound. He left the bolt in place thinking it was better to have a doctor remove it. Then Joe was placed on a stretcher and carried to the waiting ambulance. Melissa, who had received attention for her shoulder laceration, was also loaded aboard the ambulance and they were transported to the hospital in Storm Lake. Destiny followed in Joe's Camaro while Tucker remained at the scene, assisting deputies.

Iowa State Patrol officers sealed off the road leading to the Henderson farm. Fire fighters from Sioux Rapids, Linn Grove, and Peterson were called in. The house and garage were completely destroyed but most of the out buildings were saved. The Iowa Department of Criminal Investigation was immediately called in to process the crime scene, and within two hours technicians were on the scene aiding Jeff and the Buena Vista County Sheriff's Deputies. Deputy Taylor, now the acting sheriff, had the grim duty of informing Georgia Pollock and Shirley Barnes that their husbands had been killed. It was a long night that would extend well into the next morning. Evidence had been collected and the scene had been thoroughly documented with sketches and photographs, and interviews. And the body of Barry Henderson, along with those of Sheriff Vincent Pollock and Deputy Philip Barnes, were being transported to Des Moines where autopsies would be performed.

Chapter Thirty-Five

The Emergency Room of the Buena Vista County Hospital was a busy place that evening. An ER doctor removed the head of the bolt, cleaned and sutured the wound, and wrote Joe a prescription for an antibiotic. He refused pain medication that was offered, preferring something over-the-counter if he needed it.

His eyes would still be irritated for another couple of hours. With his arm in a sling, he walked out into the waiting room where Destiny was waiting.

"Just a flesh wound, right?" she quipped, knowing he might appreciate some levity.

"That's what it is. And I want to tell you, flesh wounds hurt like hell!"

Over Destiny's shoulder he caught sight of Tom and Mary Kincaid walking into the waiting room. When they saw Joe, they stepped toward him.

"You're hurt," Tom observed.

"It's not too serious," Joe replied. "I'll be all right."

"Have either of you seen Melissa?" Mary asked Destiny.

"No, we haven't. Not since she and Joe arrived at the hospital."

Mary stepped to Joe and put her arms around him. "Thank you."

Joe winced when her arm went around his injured shoulder but he managed a smile.

"Easy, Mary. The man's got his arm in a sling."

Mary released him and backed off. "I'm sorry. Did I hurt you?"

"It's okay."

"The guy who...is he...?" asked Tom.

"Dead? Yeah. He's dead."

"I heard them saying Sheriff Pollock and Deputy Barnes were both killed. Is that right?" asked Mary.

"They were," confirmed Destiny.

"Dear god. Why would someone do such horrible things?"

Joe looked at Tom. "We may never know. It's hard to understand the inner workings of a deranged mind."

The ER nurse entered. "Is there a Mr. and Mrs. Kincaid here?"

"Yes," answered Tom.

"You can see your daughter now. And she's been asking for someone named Joe Erickson."

"That would be me," replied Joe.

"If you'd follow me, please."

Joe looked at Destiny. "Go on, I'll wait here," she said.

Tom, Mary, and Joe followed the nurse to Melissa's room.

"You two go in. She'll need to see you first," advised Joe. "I'll wait out here."

He paced the hall as he waited for Tom and Mary to come out of Melissa's room. He looked out a window and thought about what the ordeal may have done to her, hoping that it had not permanently damaged her psychologically. He had seen how rape had affected its victims, and he knew that good parents and counseling could be a positive step toward her recovery. But so much of it depended on her resiliency to deal with the trauma and the strength to move on from it.

The door opened, and Tom and Mary stepped into the hall. They were both visibly shaken. "She's asking for you, Joe," said Mary.

"Thanks." Joe opened the door not quite knowing what he'd find on the other side. He saw Melissa sitting on the side of the bed, her arm in a sling as well. Upon seeing Joe, she ran to him, teary-eyed, and hugged him with her good arm. Had the circumstances been different, it might have been comical to see two people with arms in slings awkwardly trying to hug one another. But as Joe held her, the tears flowing from his eyes weren't only from the irritation from the pepper spray. For the longest time they just stood there holding each other and saying nothing.

Finally, Joe broke the silence. "You'd better let go. We might end up tearing our stitches."

Melissa managed a smile and let go of him. "How many stitches did you get?"

"I don't know. They didn't tell me. He knew it took twenty-three to close up three gashes to his shoulder but he didn't want to alarm her. How about you?"

"Seven. My lucky number."

"Don't worry. They can Photoshop scars out now, you know," he joked. She managed a smile. "Say, shouldn't you be in bed? Come on." He put his good arm around her and led her back to the bed. She got in and he helped pull her covers up, the bruises showed around the bandages covering the abrasions on her wrists and ankles. He dabbed his eyes.

"You're crying," she observed.

"Well...I got hit in the eyes with pepper spray, remember?" he said.

"Oh...I thought..." And she quickly changed the subject. "Dad said you killed him."

"Yeah."

"Good. If anyone deserved..." She started to break down again but paused and choked it back. "He was evil. Evil. Oh, god! He...he raped me, Joe. He raped me...over and over. Omigod, it was...horrible."

Joe took her hand. "I know."

"How can I tell my parents what...?" And she broke down, unable to hold it in any longer. She cried and he held her as she sobbed, comforting her as best he could.

"He baited me and I fell for it. I thought I was meeting this cool guy and...

"He fooled all three of you using the same tactics. He was clever."

"He was going to kill me, wasn't he? Like those other girls?"

"If he stuck to his pattern, he would have killed you the next day. That's why it was so important to find you when we did. Time was running out."

"Then you saved me just in time, didn't you?"

"Well, I—"

"You saved my life, Joe. How can I ever thank you?"

"It wasn't only me. There were a lot of other people involved in your rescue, too."

"I...I can never thank everyone enough."

"You can thank us all by living a good life," he said. "And now that this ordeal is over, you need to concentrate on healing. Time will be your best friend."

"I will."

After a pause, she said, "Why did he choose me? And Tina and Jenny? Why did he choose us?"

"Like I told your dad, we may never know why a deranged mind works the way it does. I'll tell you some things about it when you're out of the hospital and you're home and feeling better. But for now, your parents are waiting outside, and I have someone waiting for me so..."

"Destiny?"

"Yeah."

"I hope she knows how lucky she is."

"You'll have to ask her." Joe smiled and let go of her hand. Melissa winced as she sat up.

"Am I ever going to meet her?"

"Whenever you're ready," he smiled, "I'll tell you what. We'll stop by the house and see you once you're released. How's that?"

"I'd love that."

"I have to go." He leaned down and kissed her on the forehead. "I'll see you soon." Then he walked to the door. Before he pulled it open, he turned to look at her and gave a little nod and a wink. She smiled. Tom and Mary were waiting outside her room. Joe stepped to them and said, "She's going to need your understanding and support now more than ever. And she's going to need counseling to cope with what's happened to her. But she's a strong girl. I think she'll eventually work her way through this. But it'll take some time."

"Thank you, Joe. For all you've done," said Mary.

"Joe," acknowledged Tom, offering him his hand. Joe shook it, and looking each other in the eye, they both sensed a lifelong bond had been made. Tom and Mary entered Melissa's room and Joe went back to the waiting room.

"Come on, I'm taking you home," said Destiny. "You need tending."

"I do, I could use some tending," Joe replied with a hint of a smile. They walked down the corridor toward the exit.

"I've been thinking..." said Destiny.

"So have I. I don't know if I can do this anymore."

"I don't understand. You were amazing."

"No, it's not—"

Cutting him off, Destiny argued, "You broke this case, you saved Melissa's life. You were at the top of your game again."

"I know. But I keep thinking about what my first partner told me. You'll know when it's time to hang it up. I'm wondering if it may be time."

As they walked through the exit, Joe stopped. There was Tucker standing next to a police cruiser, its paint badly scorched.

"What are you doing here?" asked Joe.

"Jeff wants you back at the scene...if you feel up to it," said Tucker.

Destiny piped up, "He's been stabbed and blinded by pepper spray. He's not available tonight. Doctor's orders."

"Okay, Doc. I'll let him know," Tucker grinned.

"Why are you driving a cruiser?" asked Joe.

"Acting Sheriff Taylor lifted my suspension and put me back on the job. We're kind of short on staff given what's happened tonight."

Joe gave Tucker a nod. Tucker gave him a salute and climbed into his cruiser and drove away.

"There's a teaching position that opened up at the Police Academy in Springfield. I was thinking..."

"Is that what you want?"

"I don't know. Maybe."

"Well, I guess I could work out of Springfield just as easily as Chicago."

Joe stopped walking and faced Destiny. "Is that what you want?"

"I don't know," she smiled. "Maybe."

221

Chapter Thirty-Six

I n the words of the late Sheriff Vince Pollock, it was "a media wet dream." All the local television stations in Iowa covered the story, and it was picked up nationwide by the major news networks. The story of the "daring rescue" of Melissa Kincaid, the deaths of Sheriff Pollock, Deputy Philip Barnes, and the "budding serial killer Barry Michael Henderson," appeared in all the major Midwest newspapers. As a result, reporters flocked to Storm Lake, Sioux Rapids, and Marathon looking for interviews and follow-up stories.

Joe's name figured prominently in the stories. That brought a group of reporters to his father's home in Marathon. They had congregated on the front lawn, and he knew he couldn't avoid them forever so he chose to address them in the same way he addressed reporters who approached him for a statement in the David Eugene Burton case.

"Look, I know you want an interview given what you've heard about my participation in the case. So, I've decided to provide you a statement, and one statement only. And I will not be taking any questions or conducting further interviews. This will be it. As some of you already know, I'm a Chicago detective, and as fate would have it, I happened to be in Marathon because of the death of my father who lived in this house. I was available and agreed to consult on this case because I had previous experience tracking a serial killer in Chicago. For that reason, Sheriff Pollock brought me in as a special deputy to assist with the investigation. The details about the rescue of Melissa Kincaid you already know from the briefing you received from representatives of the Department of Criminal Investigation and the Buena Vista County Sheriff's Department so I'm not going to repeat what they've already told you. I would like to emphasize this was a team effort, and I'm grateful to have worked with some very dedicated, hard-working professionals on solving this case. In addition, I want to express my condolences to the families of Sheriff Vince Pollock and Deputy Phil Barnes. I deeply regret they lost their lives during the course of the rescue operation. I knew them both, and I had upmost respect for each of them, both as men and as law enforcement officers. Working with them was an honor. Thank you very much."

Despite an avalanche of questions and microphones shoved in his direction, he turned away and walked toward the house. They followed, pressing in around him and continuing to pepper him with questions, but he wasn't going to answer any. Standing at the door, he turned and reaffirmed, "I have no further comments. Thank you for respecting my privacy." Then he entered the house and closed the door. Eventually, they went away realizing that was all they were going to get.

Joe spent much of the day was preparing to leave his parents' house for the last time. He packed items he wanted to take back to Chicago: a few tools from the garage, some framed photographs, photo albums, his parents' jewelry, and three cases of wine. He donated clothing to the Salvation Army. The rest of the wine was boxed up and taken to the Community Center. It would be served after a celebration of life ceremony for his father prior to Joe's departure for Chicago. An auction house would come in later and collect the remaining household items to sell.

When Joe's lieutenant, Sal Vincenzo, read about his exploits in the newspaper. He called.

"Hey, Erickson! I thought you were supposed to be on medical leave. What the hell ya doin' solvin' crimes in Podunk, Iowa, for crissakes?"

"Got dragged into it."

"And ya just couldn't say 'no', I suppose?"

"You know me."

"Yeah, well, get your ass back here. Your desk is gatherin' dust."

"I have to be declared fit for duty first."

"Ah, fuck that. I talked to your Acting Sheriff Taylor. He told me what ya did. If that isn't fit for duty, I don't know what is."

"Give me another week, okay?"

"All right. Talk with ya then."

Destiny overheard the call and knew who it was. "So, that was Vincenzo?"

"Yeah."

"What are you going to tell him?"

"I don't know. I guess I have a week to make up my mind, huh?"

The funerals for Vince Pollock and Phil Barnes were huge. Mourned by many, Pollock was survived by his wife, Georgia, along with three grown sons, a daughter, and six grandchildren. While he was gruff and hardnosed on the outside, he was praised as a good-hearted, loving husband and father, and a real soft touch with his grandchildren. A popular figure in Buena Vista County, his tragic death at the hands of Barry Henderson was especially poignant given his pending retirement and his wife's recent diagnosis with terminal cancer. Law enforcement personnel from across the state attended his funeral as well as representatives from the governor's office, state senators and state representatives.

Phil Barnes' funeral didn't have all the fanfare of Vince Pollock's, but there was an outpouring of support for his family. A fifteen-year member of the Buena Vista County Sheriff's Department, he was survived by his wife, Shirley, an early childhood teacher, and two teenage sons. Known as a kind and decent family man, Deputy Barnes was the one Sheriff Pollock could always count on when things got difficult and next of kin had to be notified. People from across the state and around the nation were quick to show their generosity by donating to a fund set up online by a local bank to take care of his family and fund his boys' college educations. Praised as a selfless hero who placed himself in harm's way to save the life of another, it was announced that his name, along with Vince Pollock's, would be placed on a special monument to be constructed on the grounds of the Buena Vista County Courthouse honoring county law enforcement officers who gave their lives in the performance of their duties.

Joe and Destiny attended both funerals and paid their respects to the families of the two men they had come to know during the course of the investigation. After they conferred with Jeff, they decided to conclude that Barry Henderson's motive was to seek revenge against his former high school tormentors by murdering their daughters and disguising his acts to look like the work of a serial killer. Nothing in the final report cited his true motive: vengeance for the gang rape of his sister by Mike Olson, Jack Callaghan, and Tom Kincaid that may have contributed to her suicide twenty-seven years earlier. Because the statute of limitations had run out years ago, they felt that revealing the rape details now would only cause additional pain and suffering for them and their families.

The parents of Tina Olson, Jennifer Callaghan, and Melissa Kincaid filed suit against the estate of Barry Henderson for wrongful death, kidnapping, false imprisonment, and a string of other offenses that would keep attorneys busy for years. Money could never undo Barry Henderson's crimes. But unspeakable damage had been done, and the only possible recourse left to them was financial in nature.

Melissa put off going to the University of Northern Iowa for a year while she received counseling and tried to heal from the physical and psychological trauma inflicted upon her. Eventually she moved out of her parents' home and rented an apartment in Storm Lake where she enrolled at the college and took several general education classes she could transfer to UNI the next fall. She also joined a fitness center where she continued to jog and work out, but she chose not to run on the streets early in the morning anymore. The horrific experience caused her to withdraw, and she was no longer so flippant about using the sexual innuendo she had so frequently employed in the past. It didn't seem so clever and amusing anymore.

Amy Greene moved out of Dwayne's mobile home, hired an attorney, filed a restraining order, and sued for divorce. A local pastor and his family took her in and she lived with them until the divorce became final. When Dwayne got belligerent about the fifty-fifty split of their assets, she reminded him she had Joe's phone number and that Joe had agreed to make a return visit if she made a call. The threat was sufficient and the recollection of the pain Joe had inflicted on him was enough to make him reconsider and sign the divorce papers. Oddly enough, he never chose to bother her again. A day after the divorce was finalized Amy and Tucker got married.

Jeff returned to Des Moines and continued to work for the Iowa Department of Criminal Investigation before retiring as a field agent. He still remained in touch with Joe when he traveled to Chicago once a year to see his New York Yankees play the Chicago White Sox. The two of them would meet and take in a game together. He tried to quit smoking numerous times, but finally succeeded after surgeons implanted stents in two blocked arteries after he complained of chest pains. Despite making a complete recovery, he still eats junk food.

Joe and Destiny traveled back to the Windy City where Joe was reinstated as a homicide detective with the Chicago PD. Destiny continued her career as an independent criminal profiler and worked as an adjunct professor at the University of Illinois at Chicago. They found a condo to share in the Lincoln Park area of the city, and they settled in to enjoy a cozy life together.

Teaching at the academy was still in the back of Joe's mind, and maybe one day he would pursue it when he was really ready to turn in his detective's shield. For a while, he thought the time had come after closing the Henderson case. But he often felt that way after closing a tough one, when he had pushed himself to the limit and his body was abused and his mind was fatigued. He finally came to realize that pushing himself to the nth degree was a self-destructive approach to his work, and continuing down that path would only serve to exacerbate his problems and shorten his usefulness as a detective. But there was one thing that didn't change. Every morning he followed the same regimen: he rose early and jogged at least three miles to clear his mind, to get those creative juices flowing, to focus on the current homicide he needed to solve, and to hope for another eureka moment.

Barry Henderson's body was cremated and the ashes returned to Texas at the request of an individual who wished to remain anonymous.

Acknowledgements

Joyce Johanson, my trusted first reader and editor; Harriet Sackler, for her faith in a new writer; Shawn Reilly Simmons for her keen editing; former Buena Vista County Sheriff Chuck Eddy and former McDonough County Deputy Sheriff John Carson for their technical expertise; Verena Rose and the staff at Level Best Books.

About the Author

Lynn-Steven Johanson is an award-winning playwright whose plays have been produced on four continents. He first decided to pursue mystery-writing when his wife suggested expanding one of his screenplays into a novel. The result was *Rose's Thorn,* which introduces Chicago detective Joe Erickson.

Born and raised in northwest Iowa, Lynn holds a Master of Fine Arts degree from the University of Nebraska-Lincoln. A member of the Dramatists Guild of America and Sisters in Crime, he squeezes writing into his busy schedule. He and his wife live in Illinois and have three adult children.

CPSIA information can be obtained
at www.ICGtesting.com
Printed in the USA
LVHW041904300320
651613LV00005B/289